YANKEE HEIR

YANKEE HEIR

PATRICK A.
NIELSEN

Printed in the United States of America by Canopy Press.

FIRST EDITION

Edited by Erica Ford
Cover design and illustration by Catherine Ellis

ISBN 978-0-9993937-0-3
Library of Congress Control Number: 2017916113

For my eldest son, Stephen. Had you not written, "A Tale of the Frozen North," then there never would have been a Bran Gruffudd.

Also, a special thank you to my patient wife, Lori, who endures many an hour with my mind lost in far-off lands.

PATRICK A. NIELSEN

1

Pyrric Victory

The twenty-five-year-old light infantry captain approached the small crowd of soldiers from the rear of the assemblage. He paused to extract a wet, worn handkerchief from deep within his wool uniform. The intense heat conspired with an earlier rain to elevate the humidity to almost unbearable levels. Not that July in Eastern Ohio was ever a treat, but the dense woods and closed forest canopy seemed to fix the air in place, and the pungent smell of decaying wood and pine needles was everywhere. Bran Gruffudd would have traded a week's pay for a cool breeze across his face, but he also knew he did not suffer alone. He watched the nearest man slap a mosquito on the side of his neck, while another scratched at the inside of his leg with dirty fingernails. Bran barely had time to stow his handkerchief before a sergeant at the back of the group sited his commander.

"Comp'ny, 'tention!" The command was firm, but subdued.

One hundred men rose as one, and the rattle of wood and steel echoed though the surrounding trees.

"As you were, men."

The group relaxed, but no one spoke as Bran made his way

to the front of the ad-hoc formation. The relentless hum of the cicadas filled their ears and each man's eyes followed his commander.

Bran took a moment to survey his soldiers. Every face was covered by several days' worth of stubble, and when combined with the sweat and dirt of the trail, it made it difficult for Bran to distinguish their faces: Cole Smith, son of a farmer, John Morrison, son of a cobbler, and Benjamin Jay, son of a clerk, to name a few. He knew where each man was from and what they sought in life. Some would have called them boys, but Bran knew better. The youngest was seventeen, but even he had had his last remnants of boyhood driven out months ago. As the setting sun began sending flickering shadows through the forest canopy, all that mattered was they were his.

"Men, I know you are tired. We have been on the move for almost four days straight and as always, I could not be prouder of you. But now, I am asking for a little more. If Providence smiles on us, any time now our scouts will discover where the enemy is holed up. When that happens, we should get the chance to bring this chase to an end. I am expecting each man to do his duty. It will likely be an up-close and ugly fight. It is one thing to kill a man with a musket or pistol at two hundred yards; it is another to shove a bayonet through muscle, cartilage, and bone. Remember, just one volley and then it is bayonet only. I cannot afford for any of you to shoot each other in these dark woods. Also, make sure you twist the bayonet before you pull it out of your enemy. Your bayonet will release faster, and your opponent will stay down. You do not want to die because your blade gets stuck in a corpse." The corner of the captain's mouth curled up ever so slightly. A few of the younger soldiers laughed nervously. "I know some of you are scared. Just remember, we are now the hunters, not them. Imagine what it will be like for the enemy to be attacked in the dark by a hundred screaming fiends with steel claws. They attacked our homes and families; let us make sure they never see theirs again. Sergeants, prepare your squads. We head out as soon as our scouts return."

Some soldiers feared the forest, especially those fighting Indians, but not the light infantry companies of the Legion of the United States. This is what General Anthony Wayne bred them to do. Their general knew the enemy was smart and tough so he trained his men to be smarter and tougher. Each man was clad in a well-worn, navy blue, single-breasted coatee trimmed with scarlet facings, and held together by a single row of pewter buttons. But after days of marching and hardship, each uniform might as well have been gray. On each button was emblazoned the federal, or what the men called "frog-legged", eagle. Long-legged overalls went from the top of the shoes to well above the natural waist. Under one arm they held rounded bearskin hats. Each man's hat was ringed by an identical crown of salt stains. With the other hand, they leaned against their Pennsylvania rifles. Grimy rags encased the hammer and powder pan of each soldier's rifle; the dirty cloths kept the incessant moisture from wetting the powder. When it takes the average man twenty seconds to reload a musket, a misfire at close range often means death. On their backs, they carried blue waterproof knapsacks, at their sides blue cartridge boxes, and in their hands blue wooden canteens. To a contemporary observer these uniforms may have looked hot and restrictive, but each man had come to appreciate the numerous layers between them and the ticks, mosquitos, leaches, and other parasites the forest was so willing to offer up. Like their predecessors in the Roman legions, these warriors knew how to operate as a small unit, alone, and separate from the whole. Instead of a Roman gladius, each man carried a bayonet affixed to the end of his rifle, but unlike their European counterparts of the day, these men never removed their bayonets. General Wayne and Bran both believed battles were won with cold steel, and each man had thrown away his scabbard months ago. Even the officers carried rifles, since it was useless to try and swing a sword in the dense woods.

Bran was unique because he also carried an eighteen-inch hickory handled tomahawk strapped to his back. One time a new recruit laughed when he saw the unorthodox weapon. The man made a passing comment that he hoped no one would confuse the captain with an Indian.

A grizzled veteran quickly took him aside. "Son, that weapon has notched as many enemies as any rifle in this company. They say the captain learned it from some old Indian friend back when he was a surveyor, but wherever he learned it, it don' matter. Like all of us, it may not look like much, but she gets the job done. At less than thirty yards he don' miss. After all, if you want to defeat an Indian you must first learn to fight like an Indian."

And that is just what they were doing; hunting Indians. Five days earlier a notorious group of renegade Indians plundered and burned out three settler homesteads on the Western Pennsylvania border. Word quickly made its way back to the commanding general and he lost little time sending his most experienced light infantry company in pursuit of the retreating enemy. That was four days ago, and the captain had signaled a pause in the chase as they awaited the return of their own Chickasaw scouts. Most of Bran's men were experienced enough to know the enemy was close.

As Bran headed towards the shadows of the forest he

suddenly wondered if he ought to exchange his wool coatee for his cotton summer roundabout. Little more than a nine-button, cotton shirt, the roundabout was far preferable in close combat. Not only did it provide for excellent freedom of movement, a must when fighting with a blade, but the white cotton meant a much better chance for a clean wound if, God forbid, you were stabbed. There is nothing worse than losing a limb to gangrene brought on by bits of dirty, colored wool pushed deep inside the body by a blade.

Bran's thoughts quickly left his wardrobe when his eyes settled on a massive man perched on a stump. With a big grin he asked, "Well, first sergeant, what did you think of my speech?"

"Think, sir? Were you making speeches again?" The older man's unnaturally large hand covered his mouth to simulate warding off a yawn while he used his other to cradle an old, worn, tin cup.

Bran gave the man a chiding frown. He had no idea how the man could constantly drink lukewarm tea.

"My apologizes, Captn', musta dozed off. Were you reciting some of your fine poetry? I'm not book learned, you know."

Bran gave the large man a big shove with the bottom of his boot. The first sergeant toppled over, tea went one way, and invectives the other.

"Hell, sir, what did you have to do that for? You could have hurt me right before this important fight, not to mention you is wastin' some good tea. Wastin' tea is a crime, you know."

Bran raised an eyebrow and snorted, "Fitting, coming from you. How many times have you told me how your father stormed that ship in Boston harbor and threw all that tea overboard? Besides, you know I prefer coffee."

"Now sir, hold it right there. First off, that was King Georgie's tea and not mine. Second, did I ever say it was not a crime?" A smile quickly stretched across the unusually broad face of the former Boston fishmonger. James Abbot was 6' 5" and 240-pounds, a remarkable size in a time when the average man stood 5' 8". At six-feet Bran was not a small man, but he paled in comparison to the sergeant.

"Honestly, first sergeant, what did you think of my speech?"

The older man's face took on a more serious aspect. "I think your words might have helped some of the younger ones. The veterans know rousing speeches will not get them through the next few hours. They will each employ their own method to deal with this insanity we call war. But what about you, sir? How are you doing?"

"I—"

The sound of snapping twigs rose above the usual sounds of the forest. It was coming closer. The first sergeant's large hand reflexively grasped the stock of his rifle.

"Captain Gruffudd!" a young soldier called, emerging from a nearby deer trail.

"Corporal Rogers, noise discipline!" hissed the commander, in a quiet, but firm voice. Then in a slightly friendlier tone inquired, "Now what is so important you would risk telling all of Eastern Ohio where we are?"

The slightly red-faced young corporal did not hesitate, "Sir, one of our scouts is back."

Bran and Abbot locked eyes momentarily, then Abbott quickly brushed the remnants of his drink from his coat, and they followed the young corporal another hundred paces into the woods. They soon came upon a small man leaning against a tree. He was gnawing on hardtack and chasing it down with something from a wooden canteen which, Bran was pretty sure, was not water. The scout was shorter than most of Bran's soldiers. He was clad in dirty, sweat-stained buckskins and a braid of dark gray hair ran down his back. Bran recognized the oldest of his three Chickasaw scouts.

"Chula, I am glad you made it back safely. I hear you have news for us."

The old scout gave the captain a toothless smile. "Miko," the man greeted his commander with the Chickasaw word for chief, "me find them. They in camp two miles southwest. Not know we chase. They are feasting, enjoying spoils." The old scout spit into the dirt in disgust.

Bran contemplated the news. "Is it Maneto's band?"

"No tell, Miko. It too dark."

"How many would you estimate?"

The old man thought for a second. "Not very sure, maybe fifty. Hard to tell. Could not get too close. Must get back before you run into them."

"Hmm—, yes, you were right. The time, distance, and element of surprise are more important. You did well. Get some rest. First sergeant, get the men ready to move and then come see me with Private Steelman."

"Yes, sir," said Abbot, but he hesitated in his departure.

"Something on your mind, first sergeant?"

"Sir, I think I know what you have in mind, and I would ask you to reconsider. There are other men that can go besides you."

"I know what I am doing, first sergeant. I must see the situation with my own eyes before I commit these men to a night attack. Please do what I asked."

The big sergeant gave a slight nod and disappeared into the

thick foliage. A few minutes later he returned with a blond-haired boy that could not have been a day over seventeen.

Tom Steelman was the son of a Pennsylvania fur trapper, but that is not what made him special. Private Steelman had two unusual gifts. The first was the ability to move through the woods like a wraith. The other soldiers would joke that when Private Steelman walked his feet did not touch the ground. His second gift was he never, ever, got lost in the woods. He could walk fifty miles and come within twenty feet of his intended destination ninety-nine times out of a hundred. Bran quietly told Steelman what he needed and the man-child immediately went over and began conversing with Chula.

Bran squatted down and poured a little of his valuable water into the dirt. Using his fingers, he worked the dark clay into a paste. Once the consistency was right, he scooped a glob into his hand and began to smear the dark mud around his face and neck as he gave First Sergeant Abbot his final instructions.

"Steelman and I will head out in a few minutes. As I said, I need to put eyes on this group first hand. I assume this is Maneto's group of renegades, and if so, we have been hunting them for a lot longer than four days. As you know, I am not willing to commit the men based on incomplete intelligence. Chula's estimates match up with our previous report, but the tracks around those burnt-out settlements indicated a much larger force, maybe even 150 strong. Steelman and I will take a peak. Give us a thirty-minute head start. Take it slow. You know the drill. If all goes well, we will meet up with you long before you engage. If things do not go so well, then take care of them on your own. I will leave it up to you to determine whether you wait until daylight. Lieutenant Rogers would technically be in command but he is still nursing that bad knee, and he is not going to be able to keep up during a night movement."

The first sergeant snapped off a quick salute and slapped his captain on the back, "Good luck, sir," then playfully added, "do not step on a snake this time."

Bran frowned, "Listen, he got in the way of my boot. Besides, if all goes well then Maneto is the only snake I will be stepping on." Bran turned his attention to Steelman who understood it was time to head out, and by the time Abbot had slapped a mosquito off the back of his neck, the two men had disappeared into the night.

Even though he was considered one of the best woodsmen in Wayne's Legion, Bran could barely keep up with Steelman. More than once the captain was forced to tug on the younger man's coat just to make sure he was there. Each man carried his rifle in his left hand while probing for branches and underbrush with his right. Once in a while Bran would check the tomahawk on his back out of habit. Eventually Steelman raised his fist to signal a halt, but in the dark it was all Bran could do to keep from smashing into him.

Steelman gestured his captain closer until each could smell the other's breath. In a barely audible voice Steelman whispered, "Sir, they are right in front of us. I see the glow of the fire."

Bran stared into the gloom. The moon was in its waning gibbous, and only a handful of rays filtered through the branches. To Bran, every tree looked like a man and every log might as well have been a hundred-foot ledge. Fully dependent on his young guide, he nodded, and the two men began to move forward inch by inch. After another ten minutes they were able to make out a group of braves sitting around a fire, some eating, others talking and laughing. Bran knew if they were this relaxed they must be unaware of his company's presence; however,

Bran could see at least eighty men in the glow of the fire, which meant the actual size of the group must be on the larger side of their estimates. A successful infantry attack typically required at least three to one odds. Bran was not going to have that luxury. Just then, startled by their presence, a deer bolted through the darkness. Bran and Steelman froze, fearing detection. They did not dare move a muscle. Finally, they continued their ponderous advance. They had taken no more than three steps when Bran felt something sharp press into his back and a heavily accented voice muttered, "Move, you die."

Bran slowly turned his head to share a look with Steelman, but the boy was not there. He had simply melted into the darkness. Had his captors even seen the boy? As Bran was prodded forward he desperately prayed Steelman would be able to make it back to the company undetected. They broke through the woodline and additional braves immediately clustered around Bran. He was unceremoniously stripped of his weapons and gear and his hands were bound behind his back with fresh leather thongs. The straps around his wrists were so tight he could immediately feel the circulation in his hands begin to falter. As Bran quickly surveyed the campsite he saw there were, in fact, multiple fires. The glow of the smaller ones had been masked behind the flames of the large fire in the front. Fear immediately gripped his chest as he began to realize that the enemy force was much stronger than any of them had been led to believe. However, his fears did not have time to fester as strong shoves directed him towards the large fire. Unfortunately, one shove caught Bran at just the wrong moment. He was already off balance, and one of his toes found the protruding root of an oak tree. Bran pitched forward, and with his hands behind his back, his face and chest took the brunt of the fall.

The two braves walking behind him let out a chorus of laughter and effortlessly hoisted him back to his feet. Bran spit dirt and bits of leaves from his mouth, and he could feel several trickles of blood mingling with the mud previously caked on his face. A few steps later Bran was in front of the fire and heard the all too intelligible word, "Kneel." Bran refused, only to receive a sharp kick in the back of his knees sending him down yet again; only this time he was able to stay on his knees. Bran conceded and stayed put. Minutes passed and an eerie silence overtook the camp. Bran thought he could hear the beat of his own heart. Finally, a tall brave emerged from behind the glow of the fire. He was above-average height for an Indian and had a disfiguring scar marking the left side of his face. Due to the stretched nature of the scar Bran would have assumed it happened as a child, had he not already known this was the case. The man's immense biceps stretched his armbands to their breaking point. He delicately caressed the blade of Bran's tomahawk with his index finger and fixed the American with his dark, cruel eyes.

"Who are you? Are you alone?" The man's English was surprisingly intelligible.

Bran gave the man a smile that barely managed to mask his fear. "George Washington; who are you?"

The man's fist collided with Bran's face, sending him onto his side with a thud. Small clouds of dust rose from the ground, filling his lungs with dirt as he fought to maintain consciousness. The congealing blood on the side of his face disappeared under a thin coat of dirt.

Shaking off the effects of the blow, Bran worked his way back up to his knees. His face felt like it was in a pot of boiling water.

"Does not matter. I know who you are," the man said with a

sneer. "You are the one our people call Mhweewa."

Bran knew Mhweewa meant *wolf* in Shawnee.

"Only Mhweewa carry a Honniasont tomahawk." Maneto raised the weapon high overhead and then buried it deep in a short stump a mere twelve inches from Bran's left thigh. The handle vibrated and then was still. "Do you know who I am?"

"Let me guess, you are Chief Pain-in-the-Ass?"

The man's thick eyebrows knit together, betraying his momentary confusion. Then with a self-congratulatory look in his eyes he turned to his braves and proclaimed, "I am Maneto!" As the other braves gave their leader a rousing cheer, Bran's eyes caught what he thought was the faintest reflection just inside the wood line on the far side of the clearing. Was it his soldiers? If it was, he knew he was not making things easy for them by situating himself in the middle of the enemy force.

Bran knew he must remove himself from the line of fire. Therefore, as much as he hated the idea, it was time to eat a little more dirt.

"Oh yes, Maneto, I have heard of you. Maneto, that means snake does it not?" Bran did nothing to hide the derision in his voice.

The warrior turned, somewhat surprised by his prisoner's new-found talkativeness.

"But tell me, Maneto, why do they call you "snake"? Is it because all you are able to do is bite the ankles of un-weened squaws?"

The brave let out a roar. With eyes bulging, he loosed a vicious kick. Bran tightened his abdomen to receive the blow, but he had miscalculated. The blow struck home like a battering ram, and the ground found Bran's face for a fourth time. His abdomen felt like it had been trampled by a herd of horses.

This time he remained horizontal, but turning his head defiantly toward Maneto, blood trickling from the corner of his mouth, he summoned the strength to say, "You want to know something about wolves Maneto? We hunt in packs."

Like a lightning strike on a moonless night, the entire western side of the wood line illuminated with a blinding flash as over one hundred rifles discharged as one. Bran hugged the earth as a wall of lead swept over the top of him. Branches splintered and men screamed as they fell in the wake of the bone shattering hail storm. Seconds later he heard the familiar war cry of his men. The bayonet fight had begun.

Unfortunately, Bran knew his troubles were just beginning. He was trussed up like a chicken and in the middle of an all-out melee. Steel clashed and men screamed. Bran knew he was not going to last long if the status quo continued. He spotted the stump with his half-buried tomahawk. It might just be within reach. He worked his way backward towards the exposed edge of the blade.

Every inch felt like a mile as the pain in his abdomen coursed down his legs, but finally he was there. The numbness in his hands made it feel like he was controlling someone else's appendages. Fortunately, the tautness of the thongs aided his efforts. It only took a few passes across the sharp blade for his bindings to give way with a pop. With a grunt, he pushed up onto his hands and knees. Then out of the corner of his eye he saw Maneto. Knocked off his feet by the initial volley, the massive Indian warrior was coming for Bran. Still fighting numbness, Bran frantically grasped for the tomahawk. He gave the weapon a sharp tug, but to no avail. His internal organs gave a strong, collective protest. On the second tug the stump gave up its hold on the weapon, and with his last remaining strength he snapped his wrist and let it fly. At four feet, the weapon could not complete a single rotation, but its blade found Maneto's face nonetheless. The Indian let out a shallow grunt. For the briefest moment Bran thought he might just stand there, forehead cloven in two. But then, with a thunderous crash, the full weight of the brave landed squarely on the young soldier and both met the earth with a simultaneous thud.

Strangely, Bran's last thought before blacking out was how much Maneto's breath stank as the impact of the fall caused the renegade to exhale one last time.

2

The General

Major General Anthony Wayne sat in a sizable wooden chair that looked like it had been a gnarled tree only days earlier. The chair was precariously balanced on its hind legs as the somewhat corpulent occupant rested his two booted feet on an ill-matched footstool. His navy blue coatee trimmed in gold was partially unbuttoned, and sweat stains left their indelible mark below each arm pit. Since today's schedule was informal in nature, he chose to forgo his white powdered wig. Instead, his medium length gray hair hung in a small pony tail. An ornately decorated, black bicorn hat rested on the chair's left ear, and a smoldering cigar drooped from the corner of Wayne's mouth. An earlier day would have seen a pipe in his mouth, but his friend, Old Put—General Israel Putnam to most—got him started on cigars about ten years prior and he had smoked them ever since. His lap held a random assortment of partly read dispatches, but his attention was currently focused on the young captain lying in the bed in front of him.

Bran slowly drifted towards consciousness. His senses searched for stimuli, and the first thing his ears found was the distant echo of a soldier calling a marching cadence. He was also warm. Not hot, but the kind of warm you feel as you sit under a tree on a summer day with a warm breeze blowing against your face. Lastly, he smelled tobacco laden with the fragrance of earth and fresh grass. He knew the kind. It was a variety of Cuban tobacco only grown in Connecticut. General Putnam had brought the seeds to Connecticut years earlier, and a handful of planters still grew them. More important to Bran, he knew only one man, other than General Putnam, who smoked this particular brand of tobacco.

General Wayne saw Bran's blue eyes blink slightly and then slowly open as they adjusted to the light. Wayne smiled; the tension ever so subtly left his lined face.

"Good afternoon nephew, it is good to see you back among the land of the living. You have had us all worried for quite a while."

Bran fought to straighten himself in bed as a sign of respect to both his uncle and commanding officer, but his body would not cooperate.

"Easy now, probably better you did not try to move just yet," said a concerned General Wayne. "You have had a nasty few weeks."

"Few weeks!" Bran choked. "You are not telling me I have been out for a few weeks? What happened? How in the world did I even get here?"

The General paused, wondering how much information he ought to give the young officer. However, despite his weakened state his nephew looked alert enough, so he decided to fill him in.

"That group of renegade Indians I sent you after; well, apparently, your company had quite a scrap with them. Killed just about all of them. Also, according to First Sergeant Abbott it was just in time. From what he was able to see from the wood line, they were working you over pretty good."

Bran flinched, remembering the evening all too well.

"Apparently the battle lasted only twenty minutes. All of the enemy were killed with the exception of a few who managed to flee into the woods. Your men knew better than to pursue them in the dark. A good way to end up dead. It was only after they searched the battlefield for the wounded that they found you. Abbott said you were on your back making love to some big ugly Indian squaw. He said from all appearances, you killed her with your looks."

Bran started to laugh but quickly realized laughing hurt too much. "Sir, that ugly squaw was none other than Maneto."

"I know. From the report, it sounds like you did a job on him with that damn tomahawk of yours. I would have preferred if you had just shot him from a hundred yards away, but at least he will not be killing any more settlers. We are pretty sure that was the last group of renegades in a three-hundred-mile radius. Hopefully their timely end will serve as an example for any others who decide to make war on women and children."

"Sir, did you hear about the Crowley settlement? We went through there about two days before catching up with Maneto."

"Yes, damn shame. I liked Joseph Crowley a lot. He was a hell of a scout during the war. Neither he nor his family deserved to go out like that." The General proceeded to take a long draw from his cigar.

"I agree, sir."

The two men sat in silence for a moment. When Bran realized no further information was readily forthcoming, he asked, "Sir, if I may ask, what are the extent of my injuries?"

The general did not respond immediately. When he finally

removed the cigar from his mouth a shower of ash dusted the front of his coat. "Abbott may jest, but you were in rough shape when they found you. Unfortunately, you had significant internal injuries, but there was no way for your men to know that at the time. Unwittingly, they did the worst thing to you they could have done. They draped you over the back of a pack horse like a bag of flour. By the time you made it back to Fort Pitt, you were throwing up and your abdomen looked like hell. It was pretty touch and go for a while. You have been in a coma for most of that time. The doc is pretty sure you damaged your spleen, among other things. Sort of hard to know the full extent of your injuries without cutting you open. I personally was all for it. You have a lot of guts. I wanted to see what they looked like for myself." A small smile creased the older man's face.

"I am glad he did not," said a smiling Bran.

"Yes, Doc overruled me, which surprised me a little since Doc is all too willing to cut things off most of the time. He said to just wait, and if you woke up, then you would make it. A bit of a stupid statement now that I think about it. Most men who do not wake up do not fare too well in the end." Wayne laughed at his own joke and then took another draw at his cigar.

"Besides," said Bran, "I am guessing if you had let them kill me, my mother would have come back and haunted you the rest of your days."

"Hell, she scared me more than once when she was alive."

Bran let the General finish chortling before he continued. "Sir, when do they think I will be able to rejoin my company?"

Wayne hesitated, "Son, it is not going to be that simple. You may be out of the woods, no pun intended, but you have a good eight to twelve weeks of recovery in front of you. Even then, you will be far from the shape you were in prior to your injury."

Wayne paused again, knowing the thing he was about to say was going to be the least well received yet. "Bran—"

It was not lost on the young soldier that this was the first time his uncle was using his given name.

"—it pains me to say this, but I am sending you home. You are a hell of a leader, the toughest fighter I have, and not to mention my favorite nephew; but you have been through the mill and it is time for you to hang it up. In fact, I have already given your company to Porter. There is too much work still to be done and they cannot wait for you."

Bran felt his blood begin to boil, but then like a summer squall, the anger dissipated. He knew the general was right. The last thing his men needed was a damaged commander trying to keep up with them. They were too good for that and they deserved better. Besides, Robert Porter was a terrific officer. He would do them right. "Sir, what is going to happen to me?"

Wayne smiled, "The same thing that happens to all old soldiers who manage to outlive the army. You will get an honorable discharge and then you will go home to that lovely wife and baby girl of yours. If I am correct, you have only met the little one once?"

"Yes, sir. Rachael and I were married last summer, and most all my time since then has been spent here. Prudence was born just a couple months ago. I was able to take a five-day leave shortly following her birth. Rachael and the baby have been living with my father during my absence. I would be lying if I said I was not looking forward to seeing them."

"Then that settles it. You work on getting better the rest of the way and then we will get you home. I know you will miss the army but you have already done the work of ten men. The army is a jealous mistress, but eventually most smart men realize she asks too much. Only a handful of old idealists like myself hang on until she will someday leave us. I have no doubt there are other ways you can serve your country. I am proud of you and the army thanks you." With that General Wayne stood up and buttoned his coatee, all the while grinding his smoldering cigar under his boot. Grabbing his bicorn hat off the chair, he gave Bran a silent nod of finality, and was gone without another word.

Bran let his dapple-gray quarter horse ease into a gentle trot. Despite the warm November weather, what should have been a relatively short journey from Fort Pitt to Philadelphia took close to two weeks. He thought about pushing the pace, but what was the point? A lot of good it would do him if a random farmer found his unconscious body in an irrigation ditch. In many ways, the slow trip was a blessing. It gave his mind a chance to slowly make the transition from soldier to civilian. General Wayne made light of it, but it was not a flame you could just extinguish on a whim. He knew the preceding two years had been the best and hardest years of his life.

A few days earlier he had stopped over in Harrisburg just long enough to buy a necklace for Rachael and a small doll for Prudence, but he was now ready for the journey to be over. He was just approaching the outskirts of Philadelphia. A rain had swept through in the night and the morning tradesmen had done an adequate job turning the roads into a muddy pulp. He was now entering a somewhat developed area, not too far from where he grew up, and cobblestone was becoming more commonplace.

Bran's horse, Jackie, was also back in familiar country, so

Bran let his mind wander. He had given a little thought to what was next, but he had not yet settled on a plan. He was a surveyor by trade, having studied the occupation at the College of Philadelphia. Unfortunately, like the army, surveying meant little time at home, and Bran knew that was not what he wanted going forward. Besides, he had plenty of time to figure things out. All he knew at present were happiness and contentment, and he was going to make the most of living in the moment.

Bran emerged from his daydream and scanned the deserted street. What should have been a bustling hive of activity on a beautiful fall morning was instead eerily quiet.

The horse sensed Bran's tension and slowed her gait. Leaning forward, he gently patted her on the neck.

"Easy, girl, I feel it too. Something is not right." With each step of his horse, Bran's dread began to grow. He was familiar with death of all types and he smelled it now. It was not an actual smell inasmuch as it was a palpable gloom. Despite the early hour, Bran suddenly felt like the sun might slip away over the western horizon at any moment. A carnal, unnamed fear threatened to overtake him, and he briefly considered returning the way he had come.

Before his fear could fully metastasize, he heard the familiar sound of another horse's feet followed by the whining creek of wagon wheels.

An elderly man driving a buckboard emerged from a nearby ally. The large pile of cargo in the back was covered by a white linen sheet. The man saw Bran and gently pulled on his reigns, bringing his cart to a rickety stop. The grim-faced stranger clenched a pipe between his teeth. His manner was solemn but kind.

"Mornin' son, you from 'round here?"

Bran brought Jackie to a stop about ten feet from the man and he leaned forward on the pommel. The horse continued to gently shake her head from side to side as if to throw off the tension she felt from her master. "Used to be, but I have been away for a while. Been fighting Indians with General Wayne out West. But I am home now."

"Good for you, son." The man looked like someone who had experienced a lot of pain in a short period of time. "At the risk of sounding impertinent, may I ask you where exactly you are heading?"

Bran smiled weakly, "Talley Street, near Chester."

The man hesitated as if weighing his words. "Son, I am not sure who it is you are looking for, but you more than likely will not find them around here anymore. Over the past month yellow fever has ravaged this entire area. I have the unfortunate job of"—the man glanced back at his cargo—"well, of making sure these poor folks make it to their final resting place without taking anyone else with them. If I were you I would head somewhere else as soon as you are able."

Bran stiffened in the saddle, and his hands instinctively tightened on the reigns. He knew the one question he wanted answered, but a sickening dread overtook him, and the words never passed his lips.

Sensing the interview was over, the man snapped his reigns, "Good day, sir."

Bran mechanically tipped his hat to the man, more out of habit than courtesy, and gave Jackie a sharp kick in the side. A moment later he pulled up on the reigns in front of a modest brownstone. Hastily tossing the reigns over a nearby hitching post, he leapt up the steps, but before his hand could grab the door handle, he stopped. In the middle of the door a yellowing piece of paper carelessly flapped in the breeze. All that kept it from blowing away was a single iron nail. Bran read the crude printed type.

KEEP OUT - THIS PREMISE IS UNDER QUARANTINE FOR YELLOW FEVER.

Bran gave the door handle a sharp jerk, but the lock stood fast. He then threw his shoulder against the door, but the aged wood timbers remained intact.

Damn oak, he cursed to himself.

On the third exertion, the lock broke and he sprawled headlong into the room. His sliding body sent a billow of fine dust into the air. The room was cold and musty, and as he pulled his still ginger body to his feet, he glanced over at the table where the family typically shared its meals. Bowls were still laid out, as if the table had just been set for a meal.

Choking back fear Bran sprinted up the stairs. In the first bedroom he found his father's eyeglasses lying on a table next to an empty bed, the old man's clothes folded neatly in a walnut wardrobe. Bed sheets were rumpled and unmade.

Without pausing further he burst into the next room, almost knocking the door off the hinges. The otherwise silent room echoed with the smack of the door slamming against the opposing wall.

In his wife's room things were much the same. He saw a baby bassinet with clothes for an infant folded on a small adjacent table. In the nearby wardrobe all of Rachael's clothes hung neatly, including her favorite summer dress . . . but no Rachael, no Prudence, only silence. As he made his way to the bassinet, his tear-filled eyes fell on a small, yellow crocheted swaddling blanket. The blanket was the last thing he had given his pregnant wife before heading to the frontier seven months earlier.

Bile filled Bran's mouth. Grasping the blanket in his hand he fell to his knees in the middle of the room, unable to breathe. Like his experience kneeling before Maneto several months earlier, his insides were on fire, only this time for a completely different reason. He had lost soldiers, he had lost friends, but nothing in life had prepared him for this. Bran did the only thing he could do; he lay on a cold floor in a cold room and wept.

3

The Honorable Mr. Whitaker

To look at John Whitaker was to gaze upon a contradiction. Below the neck the man was as fashionably dressed as any gentleman in Philadelphia. This morning he sported a tan three-piece suit and perfectly tied cravat; however, once you moved above the cravat things changed dramatically. His face was framed by wild, gray, mutton chops. Combined with shoulder-length gray hair, which looked like it had not seen a comb or brush in ten years, the man's appearance was somewhat alarming to those who did not know him. Behind his back people would comment that John Whitaker's head looked like it should have belonged to the captain of a whaler off the coast of Newfoundland or Labrador. John used to chuckle when he would hear of these stories, mainly because he knew many of his real-life adventures probably were not far from the fanciful stories children told about him. Despite his flamboyant past, in recent years John Whitaker had become known as one of the finest legal minds in Philadelphia. He had benefited from a thriving legal practice for the past twenty-five years, and now he was at the point in his career where a man in his profession could be very selective about his clients. He could also afford to saunter into work at nine o'clock, that is, after he had enjoyed a nice breakfast and the papers.

This particularly cold, early April morning John was catching up on his correspondence. After finishing a rather boring letter about a tax dispute concerning a piece of land, he gestured for one of his clerks to get him another cup of tea. Turning back to his papers, his eyes fell on the postmark stamped on the next letter in the stack. He grabbed his silver-handled letter opener, and a minute later had forgotten about the tea. Five minutes more and he was thrusting on his greatcoat and telling his secretary he would be out for the remainder of the morning.

After making several inquiries as to the whereabouts of a certain young, ex-army captain, John made his way to the Galloping Pony, an inn and tavern not considered to be of the finest reputation, but John had stayed in worse.

Entering the tavern, he quickly shut the door so as not to spoil the tavern's surprisingly warm interior. The gloomy room was mostly empty aside from a few lowly individuals who considered drinking their day job, and the stale air reeked of the previous night's regulars. He made his way to the small bar where a gruff-looking innkeeper was wiping out mugs with a dirty cloth. After a brief exchange of words the man gestured to the side with his thumb. Only now was John's vision adequately adapted to the weak light to see a solitary man sitting in a corner booth. The forlorn individual slouched despondently behind a row of pewter mugs. John managed to get within three feet of the booth before the man bothered to raise his head.

"Mr. Whitaker, I did not know you frequented this fine establishment as well. Care to join me for a drink?" Bran wiped his mouth with the back of his hand.

John did not immediately answer, but instead paused to take in the young man's disheveled appearance. John had known Bran Gruffudd since he was five years old. In the best of times Bran did not have a reputation for being a snappy dresser, but he was looking pretty rough even for Bran.

"It is a little early, lad—even by my standards—but what the hell—Bartender! One for me too."

The bartender brought John his own mug and another for Bran.

"Seems like you had an early start," observed John.

Bran scrunched up his face as if to indicate deep thought. "Hmm, not sure if I ever stopped. Sort of been living on this bench for a while."

John worked the ale around in his mouth and then gave it a good looking over. He preferred liquor, but this was not really that disagreeable considering it was ten in the morning on a Wednesday. He shifted his gaze back to Bran. The young man had about three days' worth of stubble and desperately needed a bath. "Tell me, lad, how are you doing?"

Bran gave a low snort and waved his hand at the empty mugs in front of him, as though he was exhibiting a prize hog. "I have been better. I am assuming you know about father, and Rachael, and the baby?"

"Of course," said John. "I have handled Alun's affairs for almost twenty years." Silence filled the room before John continued, "Bran, I am so sorry for your loss. It cut me to the quick when I heard. Your father was a very good friend for a very long time. I sent you a letter at Fort Pitt shortly after the outbreak, but it must have just missed you. It was not until last week that I even heard a rumor you were back in town. Honestly, I am surprised you have not been to see me before now."

"Well, I have been busy," snorted Bran. He took a moment to flip a dried piece of bread crust into one of the empty mugs. "I am sorry. It has been a rough several months."

"No need to apologize, lad."

"I am assuming you are here to speak to me about my father's estate?"

"Yes, we do need to discuss an estate," said John, "but not the one you are thinking of."

"What is that supposed to mean?" asked Bran.

John set the mug on the table and ceremoniously pulled a large envelope out of an inside coat pocket.

"Tell me, Bran, what do you know about your father's family?"

Bran was slightly taken aback by the change of subject but he welcomed the opportunity to talk about anything that might take his mind off his current misery. "Quite a bit as a matter of fact. My grandfather was a Welsh baron. It is a really old title. If I am correct, it is one of the oldest in Britain. It was established in the 1400s and was officially recognized as a part of the Peerage of Great Britain in the 1500s. My Grandfather Llywelyn was the 11th Baron Gruffudd. He had two sons."

"—and your father was the younger son?" interrupted the lawyer.

"That is correct," said Bran. "My father was younger than Uncle Llew by about two years."

John was surprised at Bran's lucidity, especially since he had obviously been drinking since the sun rose, but like his father, Bran could always hold his drink.

"I know your father served as a British army officer in the colonies during the French and Indian War, and he ended up staying after the war, but do you know much about what happened to your uncle after your father left?"

"Not really," mused Bran. "Father would exchange letters with him about four times a year, but I was not always privy to their contents. The last I heard, my uncle was living in southern Wales on the family estate. I think it is about a day's ride past Cardiff."

"Your uncle did not have any children?"

"No. In fact, I do not think he ever married," answered Bran. He was beginning to wonder where this cross examination was going.

"Then that squares with what I know. It also means your father would have been your uncle's heir." It was more of a statement than a question.

"Yes, I suppose so," responded Bran.

"Thank you. I need to update you on a few things. As your father's attorney, this morning I received a letter. It was postmarked London. It came from a London solicitor by the name of Brooks. Per this Mr. Brooks, your uncle died about twelve months ago. The letter gives no indication as to the circumstances, but it does clearly state your uncle left no other heirs. The letter came to me because, as you stated, your father inherits your uncle's estate and title in the eventuality of his death."

Even in his alcohol-fogged state Bran could see where things were going.

John finished explaining. "Because of your father's recent passing, everything now passes to you. If my math is correct, you are now the 13th Baron Gruffudd. Not the luckiest number in the world, but you cannot have everything." He raised the final remnants of his mug in a toast, but Bran was too distracted to notice.

Bran's attention finally turned back to the man in front of him.

John continued, "Now, I suppose you could always choose to vacate the title. I am no expert on British peerage law, but I am fairly confident the title would just become extinct. There undoubtedly would be monies that would make their way to you once assets were slowly sold off."

"Or, I could move to the ancient land of my fathers and assume my uncle's title and position," said a now very sober Bran.

John nodded, "That is absolutely an option, and considering recent events, it might be a good choice. That is not to say it would be an easy transition. Just getting there would be a task, not to mention you will be entering a culture and a society that is mostly foreign to you. Now, you do have the benefit of thirteen generations of noble blood running through your veins, though some are bound to look down on you for being an American. But you have your father's grit and determination; I also have no doubt you have the brains and education to pull it off. By the way, do you speak Welsh?"

"Yes, I speak Welsh, as well as French. My father made sure I learned at a young age. Though I am pretty sure English is the main tongue spoken in that particular part of Wales."

John looked directly into the young man's eyes. "If anyone deserves a second chance, Bran, it is you, and it looks like the Almighty may have just sent one your way."

4

Cardiff

Bran stared at the portly, rosy-cheeked man sitting across from him in the stage coach. It had been quite a few miles since Bran had comprehended anything coming out of the man's mouth. The stranger's lips opened and closed, and Bran had the mental image of a child making the jaws of a nutcracker doll go up and down so fast it was on the verge of breaking. Bran was baffled; how could one man know so much about stage coaches? First, it was ten minutes about this brand new stage coach line from London to Cardiff, Wales; and then it was on to some man named John Beasant and the marvelous improvements he had made in the area of stage coach turning systems. But when the man moved on to recent enhancements in stage coach braking technology, Bran began to consider different ways he could throw the stranger out the window without unduly upsetting the coach's two female passengers. Then there was that part about being a British lord. He was not sure if such an action would be considered rude or chivalrous, so instead Bran resigned himself to watching the man's mouth in hopes a fly might find its way in. The only part of the one-way conversation that interested Bran was a monologue about new advancements that prevented coach wheels from falling off. Bran thought the man was joking at first but then realized he was completely serious. Did people ride around in vehicles whose wheels might fall off before now? He could not imagine any American tolerating that for long. This was probably why the British were so good at building ship, everyone was scared to travel by land.

Fortunately, Bran was rescued by the simple fact that they arrived at their destination, if it could truly qualify as a destination. Cardiff was the largest town in southern Wales, though with its roughly eighteen hundred inhabitants, it was not exactly an urban mecca. It contained the usual mix of people that occupied most towns scattered up and down the south coast of Britain: fishermen, merchants, farmers, and small-time manufacturers. Cardiff also had a functional enough natural harbor that probably could become first rate if anyone applied the proper amount of funds and manpower.

Bran let the ladies descend first. They were followed by his friend, the stagecoach connoisseur. The coach lurched slightly, resettling itself on its axles as the corpulent man exited.

Bran had considered pushing on to his new estate, Caer Cigfran, but since he was not scheduled to arrive until the next day, he thought it best to spend the night in Cardiff. Plus, a good night's sleep would mean he could arrive fresh. He wanted to make a good first impression on the estate's household and whoever else might be waiting to receive him.

The lobby of the inn was minuscule. It was essentially a small foyer with a crudely constructed counter in one corner. Opposite the counter, a precariously balanced staircase wound its way up to the second floor. Bran contented himself with the front landing while two of his fellow passengers secured their rooms for the night. Once it was his turn, the whole transaction took only a minute to complete. The proprietor, a surly man who barely spoke, was only interested in a means of payment. He did not even request the young American's name. Before Bran knew it, he was following a pair of hotel urchins who expertly navigated his two trunks up the rickety stairs and into his semi-squalid room. The small quarters had a musty smell, as if he was the first person to set foot in the room for the past fifty years. The boys dropped the trunks with a crunch that made Bran grimace. A lone ray of sunlight coming through the window caused the disturbed dust particles to look like a newly arrived swarm of gnats. Bran could not help but let out a cough as he gave each boy a shilling; then with a tip of their dirty little hats they were gone.

Bran awoke with a start. He had only meant to take a short nap. The formerly sun-filled room was now shrouded in darkness. Sliding his stockinged feet to the floor, he sat silently on the rigid cot. A few feeble rays of moonlight splattered their way through the dirty window. The weak beams of light made a strange paisley pattern on the floor but did little to illuminate the room. Bran sat quietly, letting his eyes adjust to the dark surroundings. He scratched an insect bite on the side of his neck. *Nice*, he thought. Apparently he had a cotmate. Once he could see adequately, he groped his way to the opposite side of the room. An ancient collection of candle drippings sat on a small table, but he had no way to light it.

Barely able to see, Bran extracted an old, worn, gold pocket watch. He had to be careful to prevent the cover from popping off the old relic. Holding it up to the window he was just able to catch the reflection of the moon. *Had he really been asleep for over three hours?* As if suddenly conscious of the elapsed time, Bran's stomach protested with a loud gurgle.

One of the women in the stagecoach, whose daughter lived in Cardiff, had told him the inn was not where you wanted to eat a meal. The information seemed like a helpful bit of intelligence at the time, but due to the nature of his accommodations, it was now a no-brainer. According to the lady there was a nice public house down the street named the Lazy Dog. Apparently, it had a good atmosphere and served a meal tastier than three day-old shepherd's pie.

Bran considered changing into something more befitting his newly obtained nobility; but since no one yet knew who he was, he simply threw his faded greatcoat over his dusty, well-worn travel clothes and headed down to the street.

Stepping into the darkness, Bran instinctively drew his coat tightly around his shoulders. Darkness now overwhelmed the long narrow avenue. Occasionally the moon would peer from behind a cloud for just an instant, only to beat a hasty retreat. What had been a thriving artery of commerce upon his arrival now sat silent and hollow. He could hear the occasional crash of a door or distant muffled shouts, but otherwise all was quiet.

Looking like another lonely sailor on a moist Cardiff night, Bran wound his way down the thoroughfare. He was about halfway to his destination when he heard a clatter in the alley to his immediate right. Unsure of what caused the disturbance, he paused. He considered walking on, but the soldier in him did not like the idea of an unknown something at his back. Unable to ascertain the originator of the noise, he moved closer. The cloud-shrouded moon did little to illuminate the inky blackness. Combing the darkness with his eyes, he braced his nerves. He half expected a dog or cat to suddenly charge out of the gloom. But as his eyes adjusted, he realized there was a young girl standing in the shadows. Bran could not see her very well at first, but then she slowly stepped into the moonlight.

She was pretty enough, but no older than fifteen, and rail thin. Her long blonde hair was far from clean, but it appeared to have been teased out with a brush to make it look more glamorous. Under her left eye was a dark bruise. The moonlight gave her a slightly paranormal appearance.

The girl stepped towards Bran and slowly began to open her coat. "Care for a nightcap mister?" She asked in a soft voice that contained a nauseating mix of fear and seduction.

She was close enough for him to smell the stink of her breath. Bran's eyes went to the bruise. It was no doubt a gift from her pimp. His anger began to swell, but then pity overtook him. Bran took a step closer to the girl.

She moved towards him with fearful anticipation. "Where to, mister?"

Bran stopped and withdrew a two-pound note. He handed it to the girl. "Here, take this, and take the night off." He knew better than to think she would get to keep the money, but maybe it would spare her from any unfortunate engagements that evening.

Confusion temporarily clouded the girl's countenance; then realizing what she had been given, she turned and sprinted up the street.

Bran paused for a moment to consider his own upbringing. What was it that separated this poor lost soul from the women in his own life? Not much, he concluded. In most cases it was a few family connections, one's upbringing, a pile of precious metals in a bank, and the grace of God that made all the difference.

Bran's stomach let out another growl and he was reminded of the purpose of his little nighttime venture.

He had partaken of better food, but the overall meal still could be described as surprisingly satisfying. The food was only passable, but a lively atmosphere, good service, and an excellent Madeira all combined to make it a pleasant meal.

Stepping back into the night, Bran took a moment to breathe on his hands before shoving them deep into his coat pockets. In the warm tavern, fatigue and alcohol served to dull his wits and make him sleepy, but now he was back outdoors, and his senses began to return in full. A heavy mist had taken root in the intervening hours, and the occasional light cast an iridescent glow through the gloom. He was fifty paces into his return journey and the raucous noises of the tavern were already fading. Bran was about to quicken his pace when another, less attractive sound greeted his ears.

Although subtle, it was the unmistakable sound of something hard striking human flesh. Bran paused; his ears searched the night for the source of the disturbance. Inside, his contented soul longed for the sound to be a trick of the night, but then he heard it again, only this time there was also the sound of a woman's whimper.

The miserable sound emanated from an abandoned building a mere twenty paces down the street. Bran intentionally lightened his footfalls as he approached the building. The scarred remnants of a weather-beaten door loosely hung by its hinges. Fearing the aged hinges might betray his presence, Bran eased the door open inch by inch. He was able to slide through the opening at the same moment his ears took in a more pronounced slap followed by the commensurate whimper.

The room stank of rat feces. He also thought he could discern a faint odor of vomit. As soon as he was inside his eyes fell on a lighted doorway at the far corner of the room. No door hung in the opening and a flickering yellow light played across the opposite wall. Grime and filth covered the floor, but a newly streaked path led up to the opening. It did not take an expert to see a person had been unwillingly dragged into the room.

Gently probing for loose floorboards, Bran slowly made his way to the open doorframe. He used his hand to push a batch of loose cobwebs from his face. He had just taken position against the edge of the opening when he heard a scratchy male voice speak.

"Get on your feet. Have you forgotten you are nothing more than Haymarket ware? Besides, who takes care of you?"

A faint sob followed.

"Answer me!"

"You, Tommy!" It was a woman's voice, and it was weak, cracked, and full of fear.

"That is right, and you better not forget it. Now give me that money. Not like you did anything to earn it. You never do anything. Not sure why I even keep you around."

"But someone gave it to me."

"More likely you stole it. Canna have you steelin' from people, Poppet. Might damage my reputation."

Bran cautiously peered around the doorframe. The girl he had seen hours earlier was propped against a wall at the room's opposite end. Her left eye was swollen shut and her arms encased her legs. Every few seconds her body would tremble convulsively. Bran was sure she could not see him. He was not sure if she could see much of anything right now.

Bran's position put him behind the man, but somewhat at an angle. The girl's attacker was a few inches shorter than the American. He had a square jaw, and he wore his oily, black hair in a tight bun. He was attired in a charcoal coat, black pants, and unusually large shoes laced with gaudy silver buckles.

The man slowly extracted a small silver device from the inside of his coat. Bran estimated the object to be the size of a fat carrot. With a snap of his wrist the device telescoped into an 18-inch truncheon.

Even in the darkness Bran could see terror fill the girl's eyes.

"I should have done this a long time ago; I cannot afford to have the rest of my young ladies gettin' ideas," crowed the man. "Tommy's girls start gettin' a bad reputation, and the next thing you know, I canna care fo' my family. After all, I donna want my little girls growin' up to be like you, full of disease and the devil. Sort of ironic with you being named Mary—that is—with Mary being the name of the Lord's mother." The man laughed with a cackle, "Of course, you ain't no virgin!"

Resigned to the blow, the girl named Mary collapsed into a fetal position. Her unwillingness to protest, fight, or attempt to flee said volumes about the state of her physical and emotional condition.

The man raised the truncheon, ready to impart his brutal instruction. But as the weapon reached the apex of its travels, it froze, unwilling to travel any further.

"WHAT THE—"

Bran's hand closed around the man's wrist, fixing it and the fiendish implement in space. The astonished stranger instinctively turned towards his attacker, only to have Bran violently torque his arm to the side. The man shrieked in pain and the truncheon jerked loose. The handle of the weapon inadvertently found Bran's eye socket. Bran let out a grunt, but still managed to keep both eyes on the man. The pimp used Bran's momentary misfortune to retreat into a nearby corner. Massaging his aching arm, the man assessed the uninvited visitor who had just chosen to disrupt his little party.

"You just made a big mistake!" the man named Tommy hissed. "Who do ya think ya are?"

"I am her neighbor," growled an enraged Bran.

The man's face twisted into a sneer. "Dirty Mary donna have no neighbors. She lives in an alley."

"And I thought you were some sort of Biblical scholar," mocked Bran. "Are you telling me you have never read the story of the Good Samaritan?"

Tommy's face betrayed his confusion.

"Never mind," snorted Bran, "no reason to cast pearls before swine." It was taking every ounce of his strength to maintain his self-control. "I see you can dish out a beating, and as a result you probably think you are pretty tough, so I will tell you what I am going to do. I am going to beat you within an inch of your life. But do not worry, when you reach the point you cannot take any more, I will show you the same mercy you were about to show this young woman."

Anger clouded Tommy's countenance and his jaw clenched. His face took on the aspect of a rabid dog as his eyes furtively searched for a way of escape. Sensing no way out, the man charged.

Caught off guard by the man's impetuous bull rush, Bran did the only thing he could do. Clenching his teeth and tightening his neck muscles, Bran delivered a devastating head-butt. He simultaneously felt and heard the man's soft nasal cartilage crater under the impact. Shrieking, the man staggered backwards. The pimp's nose burst like an overcooked sausage. Already reeling, the man stepped on the fallen truncheon. The mis-step was just enough to cause him to pitch over backwards. With a thunderous crash, the back of his head slammed into the wall, and his neck snapped with a crack. The man lay motionless on the filthy floor, aside from an involuntary twitch in his left leg.

Bran slowly walked forward. His brain told him caution was in order as the man might be engaging in a ruse, but he knew this was not the case. Pressing two fingers against the man's carotid artery, he felt nothing. The man's leg was now still. Bran used his hand to cross himself and then turned to the girl. He lowered himself to one knee.

"Are you alright?" he asked softly.

The girl let loose a cockeyed nod. Bran was not sure if it was a yes or a no.

"So, your name is Mary, is it?" This time the girl's nod was a distinct yes.

"Can you stand?"

The girl answered by gingerly pushing herself to her feet. Bran could see one eye was swollen shut.

"Guess we officially have one pair of good eyes between the two of us." Bran knew it was a poor attempt at humor given the circumstances. He massaged his own swollen eye as he awaited a reply.

The girl did not say anything.

Bran squatted down to retrieve the dead man's truncheon. Collapsing the metal weapon, he shoved it in his coat pocket. As he slowly stood again, he could see Mary eyeing the dead man.

Her normally milky skin had gone even paler, and it contrasted sharply with the scarlet inflammation on the side of her face.

"Is 'e dead mister?"

It was Bran's turn to just nod.

"Good, 'e was a bad man."

Bran was somewhat surprised by the indifferent nature of her statement. For the very first time she fully turned her attention to Bran.

"Mister, were ya really gonna beat him like ya said?"

Bran's face was grim. "As attractive as it might have seemed in the moment, that's not my way."

"Then why threaten 'im like that?" Mary asked confusedly.

"Fear causes a person to make mistakes. I was simply seeking to gain the advantage. The same way the man sought to use fear against you, I attempted to turn his own weapon back on him. Unfortunately, fear can also cause unpredictable behaviors. That was almost my undoing a moment ago."

The girl looked satisfied with his answer, but then touched her forehead. "You 'ave blood," she whispered.

Bran had no idea what she was talking about. His confusion was obviously apparent to his companion.

She again mimed a wiping motion, but this time in a way that was more pronounced.

Wiping his sleeve across his forehead, Bran brought it back down only to observe a dark crimson stain. "Charming," he said. Apparently, the dead man had left him with a souvenir from the head-butt.

"Well, Mary, we had better get out of here. I do not know much about this Tommy fellow, but I do not think we want to be found with his dead body, regardless of who he is. Also, I am assuming it is not going to be safe around here for you anymore." Bran knew it was a ridiculous statement. It was not like the girl's life had been devoid of risk when this animal was alive.

"Mister, what do you think I should do?'

Whether he liked it or not, Bran knew the moment he had assaulted the pimp that the girl had become his responsibility. He paused momentarily, unsure how to answer her question, but then he had an idea.

An hour later it was settled. After asking a few discreet questions, Bran was able to make his way to the nearby parsonage. A short conversation with the vicar and his wife was adequate to put matters into motion. He guessed the handful of coins he plied one by one into the clergyman's hands also helped bring the negotiation to a rapid conclusion.

The arrangement was such: The priest and his wife would care for the girl for several days, in secret, until she was able to travel, at which point they would put her in the priest's ancient trap and take her up to Caer Cigfran. If she did not show up within the week, Bran would be back. He was explicit on the last point.

Bran figured he could have his new housekeeper offer her a job as a scullery maid, or something of that sort once she arrived. Not that he really knew what a scullery maid did, but it seemed like a good place to start. It would not be much, but it would be respectable work and a chance to start anew.

Problem temporarily solved, Bran went back to his room at the inn. Five minutes later he was asleep.

Bran awoke to the sound of someone banging on his door. After making it back to the room, he had removed everything but his shirt and trousers before collapsing onto the cot. That seemed like only moments ago, but Bran could see the sun was already up. Now that his brain was coming to terms with being awake, he could hear the voice of a man.

"Open in the name of the law!"

"Great," Bran said to himself. He sat up and used his right hand to softly examine his eye. Not only was it tender but it was still swollen shut. Bran could only imagine what it might look like by now. He swung his feet over the edge of the bed and gingerly made his way to the door. No sooner had he unlatched the barrier than two large men roughly seized him by the arms.

"You are comin' with us, and don' try anythin'."

Bran began to protest but realized that was probably better left for someone who was empowered to make decisions, so bare feet and all, Bran was trundled out the door.

Four hours later he found himself leaning against a wall in a small cell. He could have sat upon the faded cot that occupied the other side of the cubicle, but it was already occupied by some unidentified type of insect vermin. The only other object in the cell was a bucket. Bran was simply grateful the bucket was empty, and despite a certain level of discomfort, he was set on keeping it that way. There was one other unoccupied cell across from him, and it appeared to be an exact replica of his own. He was pretty sure that bucket was not empty.

The two men had partly pushed and partly dragged him down the street. After a cursory search of his personage, they dumped him in the cell. Several times he had called for someone, but to no avail. Finally, after some time, he heard the scrape of a wooden crossbar being lifted from its bracket. That was immediately followed by the squeaky groan of a heavy iron door being pushed aside. A rather plain, sandy-haired man in a cheap black suit came around the corner. In his hand was a sheaf of papers, and on his face sat a rather conceited grin. He looked at Bran.

"Well, well, what do we 'ave 'ere? I am not sure who ya think ya are mister, but you 'ave gotten yourself in a tad bitta trouble 'ave you not." It was a statement, not a question. He glanced down at his collection of papers as if unsure why this particular criminal had run afoul of the law.

"Murder, and of one of our most upstanding citizens no less."

Bran's face screwed up in rage, but this was just what he had expected. He'd had four hours to think things over, and it was naive to think a criminal like Tommy had not been greasing the fist of someone in authority. In a small town like Cardiff it would be impossible to hide one's true colors.

"Listen, you have this all wrong."

The man's eyebrow went up and he cut Bran off.

"You sound like a Yankee. Well, that explains a lot. Not going to 'elp you out being from over there. Think you can just cruise through our town attacking people? That is not the way it works around 'ere. We are a nation of laws if you did not know, not some colonial outpost. Besides, we found the weapon in your coat."

Bran silently swore to himself. *Why had he picked up the man's weapon?* His only satisfaction was in knowing the girl was safe, but then he realized if he could not get to his new estate before she arrived, she would be on her own again. That concern rapidly fled his mind when he realized they might decide to simply hang him here and now without a trial. Anxiety rapidly supplanted annoyance.

"What's your name, Yankee?" The man's question jarred

Bran's attention back to his interrogator.

"Bran Gruffudd."

The official paused, and for the first time Bran could see the man's confidence begin to waiver. In a slightly less brash tone the official asked, "I don' suppose Lord Gruffudd of Caer Cigfran is a relative of yours?"

"No," replied a seething Bran—the man visibly relaxed—"I am Lord Gruffudd."

The little man froze—but for a moment—and then hastily fled the dungeon without another word.

Bran was incredulous that the man had run off and left him on his own again. He was pleased his name prompted a response of sorts, but he still could not fully cast aside the grisly image of himself swinging from a weather beaten Welsh gallows, so he did the only thing he could do given the circumstance; he waited.

The next person he saw was a portly man with a red nose and bushy mustache. The man was well dressed but also had the look of someone who had put his clothes on in a hurry. Bran thought the man was the spitting image of a walrus. The newcomer was followed by the same two beefy men who were present at his arrest. The other official was nowhere to be found.

This new man had barely stridden through the door when he began to greet Bran in a nasally, sycophantic tone. "Lord Gruffudd, I am oh, so sorry. I am George Sykes, the lord mayor of Cardiff. There has been a terrible mistake, as you can imagine."

Bran glared at the man, "Figured out who I am, have you?" Bran was making no effort whatsoever to hide his irritation.

"Uh, yes," the man stammered. "About the same time Mr.

Price was speaking with you, one of your grooms from Caer Cigfran arrived. They had been expecting your arrival first thing this morning. When you did not arrive, they sent someone looking for you."

Bran snorted, "I hope you told him you had his lord locked up in jail? Or did self-defense suddenly become a crime in Wales?"

"Of course not," squawked the man in a high falsetto. "I mean . . . well . . . what I mean to say is . . . I did not know you were you . . . and besides, we all knew Tommy would eventually get his just deserts." The man paused for a brief moment to catch his breath and decide if what he was saying made sense. "My lord, what can I do for you?" The lord mayor could no longer hide the desperation in his voice. "Perhaps you would care for a ride to Caer Cigfran in my personal carriage . . . and then maybe we could forget about this unfortunate little affair?" He added the last part of his statement in a voice barely above a whisper.

The young baron scowled at the man but did not speak. All that could be heard was the soft scuttling of rats in the corner. Bran watched the man's cheeks slowly transition from pink to puce. When Bran slowly growled his response, the lord mayor flinched. "Yes, that would be appreciated," but then Bran paused to give his shirt a subtle sniff, and in a slightly ameliorated tone he added, "but first, I believe a bath and change of clothes are in order."

5

Caer Cigfran

For goodness sake Cristyn, would you please stop fidgeting? You know that is not how a young lady is supposed to behave." Despite her many years in Wales, the older woman's voice still carried the faint Irish lilt of her childhood.

Cristyn Davies glanced at her companion. She knew her friend was not really upset with her, but it was about the tenth time she had received that particular piece of instruction in the past two hours.

"But Mrs. Clarke, are you not jittery?"

"If you are referring to my old bones not fitting together quite like they used to, then perhaps a little. But you should know better than to make such disparaging remarks about your elders."

Despite her growing agitation, Cristyn could not help but smile at the older woman whose attention remained fixated on her embroidery. "Mrs. Clarke, you know to what I am referring. His lordship should have been here hours ago. What do you think is delaying him?"

"Sweetheart, I appreciate your spirit, but you have much to learn. First, I would not spend too much time attempting to understand the inner workings of a man's brain, especially a man you have never met. It is a vain pursuit. Usually they are not even sure why it is they are doing what they are doing. As for not arriving at the appointed hour, I would not read into it. It could be any of a thousand reasons. He might have had too much to drink last night and had a late start; the wheels might have fallen off the carriage; or perhaps he met a young thing at a tavern and is even now trying to decide if perhaps he should abdicate his newly-found title, take up fishing as an occupation, and raise fat, ruddy-faced babies by the seashore."

"Oh, Mrs. Clarke, you are teasing me."

The smallest of smiles creased the older woman's face. "Perhaps I am. Just remember, although men can be very capable when it comes to the big things in life, they tend to be utterly hopeless with the smaller things. Ask them to go off and conquer a continent, and no doubt they will do it quite admirably; but ask them to show up on time to a dinner party on their own, and well, you might as well cancel the party. I distinctly remember a time I sent my darling reverend to the market to buy a loaf of bread. Three hours later he returned with three chickens. Live chickens at that. The vicarage did not even have a chicken coop."

It was Cristyn's turn to smile. She knew most people imagined the severe looking woman to have no sense of humor, simply based on her looks. Those closest to her knew this was far from the truth. She possessed a wit capable of skewering a wild boar.

"Sweetheart, I really cannot understand why you are so nervous. His previous lordship was a pleasant enough sort. I would not imagine his brother to be all that much different. I expect he will be very similar to any other lord of the manor.

He will eat, sleep, hunt, and engage in aristocratically sanctioned dissipation. I do not really see how any of that will impact you."

Cristyn knew her friend was being deliberately disingenuous in her appraisal of the situation, but it was also her way to make light of serious matters.

"I think the fact the man will be my new guardian probably ought to count for something," countered Cristyn. "What if he is some sort of lecherous ogre?"

"I would not worry too much about that. You are pretty spry, so I am sure you could stay one step ahead of him. But you do know there is an easy way to rid yourself of that problem."

"Yes, yes, if I just married it would all be better."

"Exactly," replied Mrs. Clarke. "There is no reason why you should not have at least one baby on each knee by now. Remind me, how many proposals have you refused so far?"

"Only two."

"Only two! I like the way you say that. You know, marriage proposals are not meant to be like biscuits on a platter, where you choose and pick at your own leisure."

"I realize that," sighed Cristyn. She was getting tired of revisiting this same topic every fortnight. "But I also think it is disingenuous to count the proposal from my cousin as an honest proposal. You yourself said the man was a pig."

"True, but do not forget you said 'no' to Lord Wallflower as well."

"Wendover," corrected Cristyn.

"Yes, whatever his name is. After all, the man is an earl in his own right, not to mention he will inherit his father's dukedom someday. Remind me of your major issue with him?"

"Oh, he is a fine enough man. It just did not seem right. He is a little too young and too . . . English, if you get what I am trying to say."

"No, you will need to enlighten me," responded the older lady. She had put down her embroidery and fixed Cristyn with a piercing stare. One eyebrow perched slightly higher than the other.

Cristyn fidgeted uncomfortably. "You know, Eton, Oxford, and gentlemen's clubs."

"Humph . . . so what is your plan, find some Frenchie to marry?" When Cristyn did not take the bait she continued, "I still think you should take my suggestion and move to London. At least you would have a bigger selection of promising young gentlemen to turn down. And you never know, you might meet some little, fat Belgian viscount worthy of your affections. Maybe then you could satiate your little foreigner fetish."

"I do not have a foreigner fetish," exclaimed an increasingly exasperated Cristyn. "All I am saying is, if I marry, it will not be to the standard—"

"English, aristocratic, self-important half-wit." The older woman finished her sentence while putting forth a subtle grin.

Cristyn gave a wry smile. "Not quite sure I would have phrased it that way, but that is probably an apt enough description. And as for London, you know how much I love the country. I think I would go crazy if I spent even a week cooped up in that filthy city."

"Yes, I know that my dear, but remember you also have not yet earned the right to life on a leisurely country estate. That is supposed to happen after you have made a good match, and produced an heir for Lord Half-Wit. Once you have done that, you can do whatever you want. You may not like the system we have, but that is the way it works."

A soft but firm rapping at the door precluded any further comment.

"Come in!" answered Cristyn. She let out an inaudible sigh of relief at being rescued from Mrs. Clarke's inquisition.

A well-dressed, elderly man entered the room. Cristyn was not sure how old Rogers was, but she was guessing close to seventy. He would have been a tall man in his day, but time, age, and the incessant nature of his duties had taken their toll. No matter how hard Rogers worked to maintain that ramrod figure, it was no longer possible. Even in the short time she had been living at Caer Cigfran, Cristyn noticed he had further begun to acquiesce to the physics of aging.

Rogers had served the family for many years and Cristyn was pretty sure this would be Rogers' third Lord Gruffudd. She was not sure why he had not been retired before now. Heavens, he had earned it. It was probably a combination of the butler's stubbornness, and the stubbornness of the baron he had served for so many years. She had been witness to just one run-in between the two proud and estimable men. In that particular instance it ended as one might expect. Rogers achieved his ends, whereas his master still had the self-satisfaction of thinking he had had his way.

The butler addressed her in the slow succinct way for which he was known. "Lady Cristyn, would you and Mrs. Clarke care for your luncheon now, or would you prefer to wait a little longer lest his lordship arrive?"

Cristyn could sense tension in Rogers' voice. Unlike her own apprehensions, she knew his anxiety stemmed from being forced to keep the staff at the ready for hours on end. She shot a glance at Mrs. Clarke to see if she had an opinion on the matter, but she was already again engrossed in her embroidery.

Besides, the thin woman seldom ever ate.

"One more hour, Rogers. If his lordship has not arrived by then, we will go ahead and eat. Feel free to let the servants eat in the meantime."

Rogers bristled ever so imperceptibly. He did not like others telling him how to run his staff, even her ladyship. Cristyn was well aware such comments irritated the man, but after the harassment dished out by Mrs. Clarke, it felt good to needle someone else.

As soon as the butler departed she stood. She hoped a turn around the room might prevent the previous conversation from reigniting. Cristyn stole a quick glance at Mrs. Clarke, but it appeared the older woman was not interested in resuming her former barrage at present.

Cristyn could tell the day was getting on by the shadows in the garden outside her sitting room. Not that she could see them that well; the 300-year-old house was essentially a small castle. Thick sandstone walls framed small windows. The unusually small openings may have provided an adequate deterrent against disgruntled peasants, but they did very little to provide the occupants with a scenic view of the grounds. Her thoughts were again broken by another soft tap on the door. She bid the person to enter. It was Rogers again.

"My lady, one of the grooms has been keeping watch over the main approach to the estate. He just returned on horse to say a carriage has turned up the lane and is heading this way."

Cristyn rose to her feet while instinctively straitening her dress. "Rogers, that is more than likely him. Please turn out the staff. We will meet the rest of you out front momentarily." The butler again departed and Cristyn extracted a small hand mirror from a bureau. She took a moment to examine herself as she pushed a few reddish-blonde tresses away from her face.

"I would not try too hard my dear," observed Mrs. Clarke, "with a face and figure like yours you might end up causing the old codger to fall in love with you."

Cristyn reddened and hastily shoved the mirror back in the drawer. "Mrs. Clarke, you are not making things better."

"I realize that, sweetheart. I just do not want you to do anything to make matters worse." With that she let out a soft chuckle. "My apologies, I am making sport of your anxiety and that is unkind. We have dawdled long enough. How about we go meet this decrepit Lord Gruffudd?"

As Cristyn stepped out through the manor's broad front door she paused to take a deep breath. It was an unseasonably warm, early spring afternoon, and a gentle ocean breeze swept over the hilltop. In the distance, she thought she could hear the familiar call of a seagull which might have found itself too far inland.

The household staff was already turned out. Rogers and the housekeeper, Mrs. Mills, had them firmly in hand. Each servant stood in order of their household precedence, each wearing their duty uniform, with perhaps a tad extra spit and polish applied. Cristyn and Mrs. Clarke took their place near the front entrance, a few steps from Rogers and Mrs. Mills.

The thing that initially struck Cristyn when she saw the coach for the first time was its gaudiness. There was way too much gold paint to go along with the funny little flags off of the back, but it did not stop there. Both the coachman and footman wore ostentatious lime uniforms that bordered on the ridiculous. It was not the kind of thing a person of quality would own, but rather someone trying to elevate himself and failing miserably. Then she had a ghastly thought, *or possibly some foolish American trying to live up to his preconceived notion of an impressive entrance.*

Fortunately, her thoughts were not allowed to wander further because at that moment the coach arrived at the top of the drive. By the time the coach had come to a complete stop, the footman already had the stairs down and was opening the door.

What happened next caused Cristyn's breath to catch in her throat. Out of the coach stepped the recently deceased Lord Gruffudd. From the faint squeaks next to her she knew Mrs. Clarke was having a similar reaction. As she squinted her eyes to block out the glare of the expiring sun, she realized it was not a ghost. The man was the spitting image of the former Lord Gruffudd, albeit a good twenty-five years younger. Then her eyes fell on his left eye. The man had about the blackest eye she had ever seen. Gracious, it looked like he had been on the losing end of a tavern brawl.

Despite his bruised appearance, the man was extremely good looking and immaculately dressed. He wore a navy-blue coat, tan pants, and navy boots. On his head sat a matching top hat. Cristyn could not help but smile at the almost comical way the man's eye matched the rest of his attire. "At least he knows how to creatively accessorize," she whispered to Mrs. Clarke.

"Never mind that, my dear. I am thinking you might want to go pull that brush back out of the drawer. Or better yet, I might want to borrow it myself."

Mrs. Clarke's comment came at the same moment Cristyn heard Rogers mutter something imperceptible. For the briefest moment, she considered turning and asking the butler to repeat himself, but then she saw what had the old butler rattled. The new Lord Gruffudd was working his way down the long line of servants like it was a receiving line, shaking each person's hand and saying hello. He was currently partway through the lower servants. He had just finished with the outdoor staff and was moving on to the maids. From here Cristyn could see some of the maids giggling.

Rogers spoke again, this time in a slightly louder tone, "Lady Cristyn, do you not think we ought to—?" but Cristyn held up her hand to cut off the question while simultaneously stifling her own laughter.

"It is all right Rogers. This is all very new for him. We will only embarrass him if we interrupt him now. I am sure the staff will have to get used to some unorthodox ways until he has a chance to get his sea legs."

Bran could not believe how many servants there were. Not that he was sure what he was expecting. Growing up in Philadelphia they always had some domestic help, but never more than three servants: usually a maid, a cook, and perhaps a gardener. But goodness, there must be twenty or more servants here. He rapidly worked his way down the line introducing himself. He was already feeling terribly self-conscious and out of place. He had hoped to arrive early. Instead he had arrived late, sporting a black eye, and in the lord mayor's ridiculous coach. The fact that a few of the maids were giggling under their breaths only made it worse. It was not the first time in the past week Bran wished he had done a little more research before setting foot on a foreign shore. He had heard Wales described as the frontier of Britain, but this was nothing like the western frontier to which he was so accustomed.

Bran finally made his way to the end of the line at which

point he noticed a middle-aged woman, an ancient butler, an uncommonly attractive young lady with strawberry blonde hair, and an elderly woman next to her. It was the young lady who spoke first.

"Lord Gruffudd, welcome home to Caer Cigfran. I am Cristyn Davies and this is Mrs. Clarke. Your brother—" She hesitated for the briefest moment trying to match Bran with his place in the family genealogical line.

"No, he was my *Uncle Llew*," interjected Bran. "My father—Alun Gruffudd—was his younger brother. Father would have inherited his title except he too recently passed."

Cristyn's smile dissolved into a frown. "Oh, I am so sorry to hear that. You have my condolences."

"Thank you, that means a lot"—and then knowing he ought to return the respect—"and the same to you, for the loss of your—?"

This time it was Cristyn who politely interrupted to fill in the missing information. "Your Uncle Llew was my guardian. He assumed that role about three years ago when my own dear father passed away. He was a good man. His passing was mourned by all." Cristyn paused for a moment and then continued, "But from the sound of it, dear Mr. Brooks could have been a little more thorough in the information he provided you. In fact, based on how little he told you I am a little surprised you came at all."

Before Bran could respond, Cristyn gave him a smile that caused him to momentarily loose his train of thought.

"But never mind, my lord, you are here. I am sure you must be famished from your journey. If you would care to come inside I think Cook has prepared a light afternoon repast for us. I also imagine you could do with a drink to wash the dust of the road from your throat."

Bran smiled back, "That would be nice, thank you. I had a bit of a rough morning so I did not get a chance to eat any breakfast." Then realizing he had neglected to introduce himself to the two other people standing next to them, he turned to address the two senior servants.

Before he could say anything, the butler jumped in. "I am Rogers, my lord, and this is Mrs. Mills, the housekeeper. If you require anything, I think it goes without saying."

"Thank you, Rogers. If you would not mind having my trunks unloaded from the carriage and taken up to my room that would be greatly appreciated. Once that is complete, feel free to send the lord mayor's coach team on their way. I am sure the old windbag—I mean lord mayor—will probably have need of them soon." Bran turned just in time to see the smallest semblance of relief flash across Cristyn's face. Not sure what it was about, and not wanting to ask, he silently followed her into the house.

6

New Acquaintances

Bran followed Cristyn and Mrs. Clarke into the manor's great hall. Once his eyes adjusted to the dim lighting he paused for a moment to take in the cavernous room. While not large when compared to other stately English country homes, the room resonated with an element of historic grandeur. Each wall was paneled in dark wood, and the centerpiece of the hall was an enormous, twelve-foot fireplace. Carved into plaster above the fireplace were the crests of all the families with whom the Gruffudd family was associated by marriage. Above the smaller crests was the all too familiar Gruffudd family coat of arms with the red dragon of Wales on top of a field of royal blue and white.

The table was already set, and Bran helped both women into their chairs before settling into his own. A footman emerged with their food.

Each of the three individuals turned their attention to their meal. Eventually what began as a relaxing silence became more and more uncomfortable. The distant tick of a grandfather clock became increasingly pronounced.

Cristyn broke the silence. "My lord, if you do not mind me

asking, please tell us a little about yourself. Your uncle shared a few things with us, but most of those were about your father and not yourself."

Bran took another sip of wine trying to decide how much of his past he wanted to delve into, but it also occurred to him that this lovely, blonde-haired young lady, who spoke with the mildest of Welsh accents, was the closest thing he had in this country to family.

"As you are probably aware, my father was a British army officer, but after fighting against the French in the French and Indian War—you would know it as the Seven Years War—he met my mother and decided to stay in the colonies. America is a land of vast unexplored frontiers, so my father parlayed his war fighting experience into a career in surveying. Growing up we lived in Philadelphia, but I have just as many memories of accompanying my father on long sojourns through the woods. After attending college, I followed my father into the profession. I spent several years surveying vast parts of western Pennsylvania and eastern Ohio, and then another couple of years serving as an army officer."

Bran paused to take a bite of food.

"So, tell us, my lord, would you consider yourself a foreigner?" inquired Mrs. Clarke.

Unfortunately for Cristyn, her friend's question caught her right as she was taking a sip of wine. Before she knew what was happening, wine began to trickle out of her nose. Horror stricken, she frantically searched for her napkin, which was inopportunely sitting on the floor. She dove for the cloth implement.

"My lady, can I help—?" Then seized by a momentary insecurity that perhaps he was not addressing her by the appropriate title, Bran haphazardly blurted out, "I mean, you are a lady, are you not?" Realizing his error, his face went scarlet.

"Do not worry, my lord, she is very much a lady," said an impassive Mrs. Clarke. "That is just her party trick. You should see what she does at Christmas."

Bran and Cristyn nervously stared at each other for a moment, as if unsure what to do or say next. Finally, Bran's face stretched into a broad smile and a second later the three of them were laughing heartily.

Eventually the mirth subsided and they continued their meal.

"My lord," asked Cristyn, "At the risk of sounding impertinent, I was curious why you chose to leave your former life behind? As you stated, that is a significant transition."

Bran hesitated in his answer, "I think the short answer would be, aside from the opportunity to assume my uncle's title, certain events back in America made it clear I needed to escape."

"Understandable," replied a sympathetic Mrs. Clarke. "Even great men run afoul of the law on occasion. Just look at old Socrates. Came up with all that great stuff, but then was arrested, tried, and forced to drink hemlock."

Cristyn glared at her companion.

"—Mrs. Clarke"—interrupted an embarrassed Bran—"I think you misunderstand. I was not running from the law. I simply needed a change of scenery."

"Whatever you say, my lord," said an unfazed Mrs. Clarke. "Half the people around here are miscreants anyway. You would fit in just fine."

Bran hurriedly changed the subject. "Lady Cristyn, I was wondering if you would mind telling me a little bit about yourself. For example, how did my uncle become your guardian?"

"I suppose that is a fair question." She then took a moment to dab the corner of her mouth and collect her thoughts. "I was raised on a large estate approximately twelve miles from here. My father was the Marquess of Gyr. His estate was one of the richest in Wales. My mother on the other hand was the third daughter of an Irish earl. Mrs. Clarke was her lifelong friend."

Mrs. Clarke smiled and nodded slightly as if to bring credence to the comment.

Cristyn continued, "Aside from my mother dying when I was still an infant, I lacked for nothing growing up. My father was a kind and loving man who saw to my every need. When I was about seven years of age, Mrs. Clarke's husband passed, and shortly thereafter she agreed to serve as my governess. Once my education was complete, she stayed on as my lady's companion. It was as a child that I first had the opportunity to meet Uncle Llew. Not that he was my real uncle, but that is what I called him as a little girl. He and my father were childhood friends and even attended Cambridge together."

Cristyn stopped for a moment to let the footman refill her glass and then continued, "The nature of my father's estate did not allow it to pass to a female heir unless there were no other heirs of the male line remaining. My father did have a male heir. It was my cousin Caradoc who was next in line. Unfortunately, my cousin is a less than honorable man. Father knew this. He knew if anything ever happened to him prior to me marrying, I would be put in a difficult situation. Of course, I would have a handsome allowance and dowry, but I would also be under the complete control of my cousin. Father imposed on his old friend—your uncle—to agree to be my guardian should anything ever happen to him. Uncle Llew agreed. Then a little over three years ago my father became ill and died. Uncle Llew became my guardian and Caradoc inherited my father's marquisate. Unfortunately, matters did not quite settle there. Caradoc still thinks I would make him a good wife. He has proposed on two occasions, and I turned him down both times. He comes by weekly to solicit my attentions. It was not so bad when your Uncle was alive, but you can imagine how much worse it has been since he passed and I have been on my own."

"Do not be too hard on the man," encouraged Mrs. Clarke, "you cannot fault his taste. No doubt you will make some lucky man a fine wife."

Bran did not follow with any additional questions. He was still working to take everything in.

"My lord, there is something else you should know as well," added Cristyn. "Has anyone ever told you how your uncle died?"

Bran paused for a moment to finish chewing his food. "The solicitor I met in London said something about my uncle committing suicide a few minutes before he was supposed to fight a duel. I plied him for a few more details, but he did not have much more to offer."

He was just beginning to fully grasp how little he knew about anything in this strange new world he had entered.

"The man your uncle was supposed to fight was my cousin, Caradoc." Cristyn stopped for a moment to let the full weight of the information sink in.

Bran set down his fork as his face slowly dissolved into a frown. "But what were they dueling over, and why would he have killed himself?"

Cristyn thought for a moment. "Regarding your first question, no one is fully sure what instigated the affair. I lived under the same roof as the man and I do not even know. Though, you will not have to go far to hear a number of fanciful rumors. Everyone from the parlor maid to the butcher has a theory. It goes without saying, some are more interesting than others. Regarding your second question, your uncle's suicide came as a shock to everyone in the district."

"Why the shock?" inquired a puzzled Bran.

"Because it makes no sense for him to have killed himself. First, it was not in his character. Lord Gruffudd was the type to meet his challenges head on, not give in. If you told me a year ago he was going to die from suicide, I would have laughed at you for being out of your mind. But there is also a second reason. You may not be aware, but Lord Gruffudd was reputed to be the finest pistol marksman in this part of Wales. People were astounded that my cousin even accepted the challenge. It was assumed he was signing his own death warrant. People used to say the only person who could ever defeat Lord Gruffudd at pistols was Alun Gruffudd, your father."

Bran smiled. His brain flitted back to memories of firing pistols with his father. He remembered his father killing a deer at a hundred paces with a pistol. He also remembered the old story told by one of his father's war friends. The man liked to regale people with how Alun had shot two running enemies simultaneously with two different pistols.

"Unfortunately," Bran added, "I never truly inherited that particular family skill."

Rogers chose that moment to enter the room and interrupt the conversation. "Pardon me, my lady; the landau is ready and waiting outside the front door. There are only a few hours of daylight left, so if you were wanting to give his lordship a quick tour of the grounds, now might be a good time to do so."

Cristyn glanced back over at Bran.

He smiled at both of them. "Yes, that sounds splendid."

7

Over the Cliff

Bran rested his arm on the side of the landau. With his chin nestled on his hand, he stared at nothing in particular. The sun had recently set, and what used to be clearly distinguishable trees on the top of the nearby ridge were rapidly becoming an amorphic collection of shadows. A team of beautifully matched palominos pulled the landau. Their coats took on a dusky gray hue in the fading light, and the rhythmic clopping of their hooves made Bran's eyes heavy. He stole a glance at Cristyn and Mrs. Clarke opposite him. The two women were sharing a whispered conversation that occasionally would result in subdued laughter. Due to their staying on the estate, the driver opted not to light the two lanterns flanking the landau. The horses knew their stabling and fodder were near, and the driver's sole responsibility was to keep the team's gait even. Bran's attention returned to the murky landscape, and his rearward facing position allowed him to survey the countryside as it slowly dissolved into darkness. The breadth and beauty of the estate left him awestruck. Every little hill they had crested on their tour seemed to reveal another tenant holding, scattered sheep, and a small patchwork collection of crops. This is not to say it was the same as his home back in America. Jagged rocky outcroppings, coarse grasses, and brown hues gave the land an ancient aura. Only once over the course of their journey did they stop. About forty minutes earlier, a vicious thunderstorm had materialized out of nowhere and buffeted the picturesque landscape like a rolling artillery barrage. Scurrying for cover, the landau had found refuge under a massive oak tree. Then as rapidly as the storm appeared, it was gone.

The distant echo of shouting men tore Bran from his preoccupation. Craning over the side of the landau, he was just able to distinguish bouncing lights in the distance. They looked like a family of fireflies dancing in a summer meadow. Bran was familiar with the sight and knew the yellow globs were actually men running with lanterns.

"Pick it up a little bit, driver. I want to see what is going on ahead of us."

The driver gave the reigns a gentle snap. Bran was momentarily thrown off balance by the acceleration but remained standing in an effort to see around the driver.

Second by second the cries of the crowd became louder and more pronounced.

"What is it, my lord?" asked a concerned Cristyn.

Mrs. Clarke did not give him a chance to respond. "It is probably the French, my dear. They undoubtedly used up all their noble necks and are now in search of some of ours." She used her hand to gesture the tightening of a hangman's noose.

Cristyn gave her an exasperated look. "Is that why they chose to land in rural Wales, and why all the voices appear to speak with Welsh accents?"

Bran hushed both women. "I am not sure what is going on, but it looks like there might have been an accident. Men are using their lanterns to try and peer down the embankment." Sensing they were at a good place, Bran tapped the driver, "That is good, pull up right here and wait with the ladies." Before the wheels could come to a full stop Bran leapt over the side. As an afterthought, he tossed his hat into the landau and then took off jogging down the road.

Bran's initial thought was how sticky the road was, considering it had not rained for long. His boots tugged at the ground, and loud sucking sounds announced his approach. The mud forced him to stop running, and he transitioned to a brisk walk. Nearby an owl let out a loud hoot, all-the-while indifferent to the affairs of men.

The nearest man heard him approach. He quickly took in Bran's appearance and greeted him with a hasty, "My lord." Bran knew there was no way the man knew who he was, but rather he was making inferences based on Bran's attire and arrival in the landau. Then to Bran's surprise the man followed the greeting with, "My lady."

Bran turned quickly to see Cristyn standing next to him, her beautiful robin's egg-blue dress splattered with mud. He raised an eyebrow but then turned his attention back to the man next to him. "What happened?"

"We are not fully sure, my lord." The man spoke in clear enough English but his voice carried a discernible West Country accent. "Near as we can tell somun was drivin' a farm cart down the road shortly after the rain storm and got too closeta the edge. The soil musta giv'n 'way and cart, driver, and horse went down the embankment. There has been a 'ol lot a rain as o' late, and this bit o' road 'as always been dodgy."

Bran looked down the hill. The lanterns were ineffective at illuminating anything beyond fifteen feet, but the sounds told it all. Mixed with the terrified screams of a horse, he could hear the deep throated shouts of a man in severe distress.

Bran quickly turned to the group. "Does anyone have some rope?"

A small man in a patched brown vest removed a pipe from his mouth and spoke in an irritatingly slow manner. "Ney, gotta house nearby though. I could getta rope."

"Get every bit of rope you have and bring it back right away," commanded Bran. "Every second will count." He turned to the rest of the group. "If anyone else can get their hands on some rope quickly, do so now! We are going to need a lot. Also, if any of you have a gun and a knife, bring them too." Bran barely finished speaking when three men dashed off into the darkness. The man next to him pressed something into his hand.

"Here's a knife, my lord."

Bran shoved it into his boot. Tearing off his jacket and handing it to Cristyn, Bran turned to the remaining farmers. "The rest of you men help me get these two horses unhitched from the landau. However, keep their collars and the rest of their harness attached. We will need something to attach the ropes to." It took a few minutes of sliding around in the mud to get the horses freed and to lead them near the embankment. Bran shouted orders at the two men shepherding the horses. "Back them up to the edge, but do not get too close; give yourself about ten feet." Right about then, a few of the men returned with various pieces of rope. Bran surveyed the motley collection of cords. Pointing at two of the largest ropes, he gave instructions to two burly hands waiting eagerly nearby. "Take each of these ropes and affix them to the horses. Bring the loose ends to me." While the men headed off as instructed,

Bran used the time to fashion one of the smaller ropes into a crude climbing harness around his waist and thighs.

Cristyn immediately caught on to Bran's plan. "My lord, do you really think you are the best person to be lowered like a worm on a hook into that—" she stared over the side of the road "—darkness?"

He pretended not to hear her comment. One of the farm hands brought him the free ends of the ropes. Bran fastened the first rope to his climbing harness. He took the second rope and attached it to a lantern. Turning to the group he shouted, "Did anyone bring a gun?" An older man with a white beard stepped forward.

"Here you go, my lord. It is primed and ready to go. Does your lordship know the best place to shoot a horse?"

"Unfortunately, I do." Bran grasped the gun in his free hand.

He turned to the men holding the horses. "All right lads, give me some tension. As soon as these lines are taught, start slowly lowering me down the slope. I will need to assess the situation before anything else can be done. I want to be able to pull up short of whatever mess I might find. The last thing I need is to get tangled in it." The nearest man holding a horse gave Bran an understanding nod.

As Bran slowly slid over the side of the embankment, he immediately began to struggle against tangled roots and mud. With his left hand he guided the loose rope with the attached lantern, and with his right he carefully maneuvered the descent, doing his best to keep the musket barrel out of the mud. Little by little the situation came into view. After a few more feet, he shouted for the men above to halt. He pivoted his body, and taking hold of the lantern, he took a moment to examine the chaos.

The hill descended at a forty-five degree angle for about two hundred feet and was covered in mud and rocks. Right below him sat the remnants of what, in its day, appeared to have been a formidable tree. Now all that was left was ten feet of trunk coming out of the slope at an upward angle. How in the world such a stalwart tree ended up growing in such a bizarre place, Bran would never know.

Resting against the tree were the remnants of a farm wagon. As near as he could tell, the wagon had careened down the slope until it slammed into the ancient oak. Partially pinned between the wagon and the tree was a man, and to the right of both was a horse lying on the slope. The horse was still tangled in the harness and one of its legs stuck out at a grotesque angle. Every few seconds the terrified horse would struggle against its bonds, and when she did so, she would slide a little further down the slope. Whenever this would happen, it increased the pressure the wagon put on the trapped man. Unfortunately, Bran knew what had to be done first. He loved horses, but the mare could not be saved. He shouted up to his handlers. "Move me down and to the left, slowly!"

Bran heard a resounding "Aye, my lord!" come down the embankment. A few seconds later he started moving. He did his best to walk along the slope as his support rope carried him along. Bran shouted out a few more adjustments until he was just above the horse's head. It seemed like every time he moved he blocked the lantern, which sent eerie shadows across the grisly scene. He was finally able to wedge the light between two large rocks where it would not be in the way.

Bran was no stranger to killing horses. He briefly thought back to the time he had been forced to shoot his horse after it broke its leg during a particularly arduous surveying expedition in the Western Pennsylvania wilderness. The worst part was that it took him two weeks to walk back to civilization after he had lost his horse. He had learned a lot of lessons that day, but right now was not the time for reminiscing. Bran knew that the best place to shoot a horse was found by mentally drawing a line from the ear to the opposite eye. You did this for both sides and then fired a well-placed round right where they intersected. Bran prayed he would not have a misfire, and that there would be enough powder to finish the job. Also, in light of only having one round, he knew he was only going to get one attempt. Bran swore to himself. Considering how much the horse was heaving back and forth, this was not going to be easy. He positioned his feet so he could steady his arms. Bran was able to use a rock on the slope to somewhat brace the gangly weapon. While speaking softly to the frightened animal, he lined the musket up on its target. The horse stilled for a moment at the sound of Bran's soothing tone. "Sorry girl, it will all be over in a moment." With the horse momentarily calmed, he pulled the trigger. The musket gave a sharp report. Bran was temporarily blinded by the flash in the dark and by the cloud of black smoke. The stench of gunpowder filled the air. When the smoke cleared, he knew the old musket had done its job. The dead horse lay limp on the slope, its weight still tugging at the harness. He could also hear the trapped man's continued groans. Bran called up the slope to be lowered a few more feet. Once he was in proximity to the harness, he deftly pulled the knife from his right boot. He made sure his legs were not where they might get tangled in the harness, then he made a few quick incisions with the knife. The natural tension placed on each strap by the horse's weight made the task of cutting easy. Bran was not even to the last strap when they broke. The horse's carcass immediately began to slide down the slope, accelerating as it went.

Bran did not waste time trying to see where the horse landed. He was already turning his attention to the next problem, the man trapped by the wagon. Bran gave a few more directional orders to the team above and was able to work his way over to the man and the wagon. The freed horse solved the pressure problem, but Bran also saw it created a new challenge. As long as the horse's weight had been pulling down on the wagon, the resulting pressure kept the wagon relatively secure in its place. Now that the horse was gone, the wagon was starting to wobble. Bran was afraid if it came loose from the old tree trunk it might carry the man with it. Bran also had another problem. He had only two ropes, but three things needed to be moved: the wagon, the hurt farmer, and himself.

Bran knew the next order of business was to get the wagon off the injured man enough to give himself room to work the man free. He recovered the lantern. This time removing it from the rope completely, he found a place in the wagon where he could again wedge the small light. Bran then tied the second rope to the closest wheel axle. Once it was secure, he made his way over to the trapped man. Bran put himself in a position just above the injured man. He braced himself against the tree and removed his own rope. About eight feet from the end of the rope he tied a knot. Rope in hand, Bran climbed down beside the man; he was in bad shape. Even in the faint lantern light, Bran could see most of the color was already receding from the wrinkly face. He was able to speak to the man for the first time. "Hello friend, how are you faring?" The man grunted out a few indiscernible, accented syllables. Bran reassured the man as he looped the first rope around the man's chest forming a sling of sorts. "Hang in there, we will have you out of here in a minute." As soon as Bran finished tying the sling he shouted up the hill. "Alright, pull up slow and easy on the rope. I will tell you when to stop!" At first nothing appeared to happen, then little by little the wagon started to pull away from the man. When he could see about a six-inch gap, Bran told them to stop.

Bran quickly shimmied his way up the tree until he was above the knot. Grabbing the rope with both hands he stood on the knot. The man remained secure in the rope sling below him. He issued his next order. "Slowly bring the first rope up. Not too fast, and be ready to stop if I tell you!" A moment later he and the man began to ascend past the wagon. Looking down he saw the man finally clear the wagon. Bran let out a sigh of relief. He was about to issue the order for the horse to keep pulling them up, when the unthinkable happened. The wagon started to dislodge from the tree.

Somewhere in the recesses of Bran's mind he deduced the loss of pressure against the tree had caused the wagon to shift its center of gravity. But regardless of what was causing it, Bran now faced a much more urgent problem. As soon as the wagon fell, its immense weight was going to pull the horse right off the top of the hill, and worse, the horse was going to come down right on top of him and his new friend. Bran knew he had seconds to act. He could see the wagon's mud-covered support rope five feet to his left. He tore his cravat from his neck and wrapped it around his left hand. Pushing off with both feet, he jumped and grabbed hold of the wagon support rope. The cravat gave him just enough traction on the slippery rope to keep from sliding off. It also prevented a potentially nasty rope burn, which he could ill afford at the moment. Dangling by his arms, Bran felt a momentary slippage as the horses above compensated for the increased weight. *Bloody hell, this is going to hurt*, Bran thought to himself. Holding the rope with his right hand, he extracted the boot knife for the second time. He then began sawing away at the rope, making sure he cut below where he was holding. All the while he could see the massive wagon below begin to slip further off the tree trunk. He could hear the men above shouting as the horse continued to be pulled towards the embankment. A second before the wagon fully broke loose from the tree, Bran sliced through the final strand. As soon as he knew the rope was severed, he threw the knife away and frantically re-doubled his grip on the now unencumbered rope. It was just in time. The loss of the wagon's weight pulling against the rope caused the straining horse above to surge forward, rapidly pulling Bran up the slope for about twelve feet before the horse above regained its footing. Desperately clinging to the rope, a battered, mud-coated, and exhausted Bran shouted the order for both men to be slowly brought up. Thirty seconds later, he and the injured man lay safely back on the muddy road.

8

Laverbread

The hatchling hammered away at the final few pieces of egg. Blackness gave way to a soft glow, which was soon overcome by a rush of bright light. Blinking its semi-blind eyes, the chick slowly pushed free of its cocoon. With an undignified crunch the small wet creature fell into the bottom of the nest; sticks and twigs assaulted its matted feathers. Thick mucus encased every inch of the bird's body; stiff limbs resisted every movement. Seeking reassurance from the sun, the small creature peered into the sky. However, indifferent to the small bird, the life-giving orb slid behind a bank of clouds. The hatchling lay still, fighting to hear the call of its parents, but all that came was a mournful howl as the wind whipped past the cliffside aerie.

High above the small bird, a giant red dragon wound its way down the cliff face. The hulking beast moved with unlikely agility. Its smooth scaly hide slid over the granite edifice with no more difficulty than a snake easing itself across a forest trail. Four inch claws devoured the rock, and step by step, the monstrous reptile neared its prey. But then, thirty feet from its objective, the serpent momentarily lost its footing, and a small avalanche of gravel pummeled the edge of the nest.

Startled out of its stupor, the hatchling beat its wings in a futile effort to forestall its impending doom; but the infant bird was months from fledging. In a desperate effort to escape, the chick scampered over the nest's side, and flung itself into the abyss.

Bran jerked awake with a start. "Blazes!" he muttered to himself. His whole body throbbed in response to the sudden movement. He felt like he had been keelhauled. But then his mind flashed back to his crude assent of the embankment the night before. He smiled ruefully as he examined the underside of his arms. They were devoid of flesh in many places. Yes, keelhauled was probably more of an apt description than he would have liked.

There was a knock at the door, and it separated him from the painful memory of the previous evening.

"Come in." His dry, sticky mouth was just able to utter the words.

A tall, young man whom Bran gauged to be in his early twenties, poked his head into the room.

"I am here to wake you per your request, my lord."

"Request? When did I make that request?" grumbled an exasperated Bran.

"Last night, my lord, before you retired for the evening."

Bran groaned as he attempted to move his sore limbs. "I believe retired is too generous an assessment. I would describe it as hauling my battered carcass into bed."

The servant smiled subtly at his master's earthy assessment. "Only you would know, my lord."

Bran fought to gain a more dignified position. He settled on propping himself against the large mahogany headboard with the aid of a stack of pillows. *Gracious*, he was discovering new aching muscles by the second.

"By the way, what is your name?" asked Bran.

The servant began to peel back the shades on a nearby set of windows. "My name is Thornbush, my lord; I am one of your footmen."

"Was it you who helped me to my room last night?"

"No, my lord, that was my twin brother."

"Then you are both named Thornbush?"

"Yes, my lord."

"That is a bit confusing, is it not?"

"Yes, my lord. We are both technically Thornbush, but my brother answers to the name Joseph. That is his given name. My brother also wears a small brass dragon pin on the facings of his coat. That was something your uncle thought up to keep the two of us straight."

"Well if your brother gets to go by Joseph, then how come you got stuck with Thornbush?"

The footman grimaced. "It is because my given name is Paulette."

"But is not that a woman's name?" questioned a somewhat incredulous Bran.

"It is, my lord."

"But then how the devil—?"

"My brother is a few minutes older than me, my lord. My mother was not anticipating there being two of us. She had settled on a boy's name and a girl's name. The girl's name was the same as my mother's recently deceased sister."

"Hmm," muttered Bran. "So, you are telling me you became the living memorial to your mother's deceased sister?"

"Something like that."

"If it makes you feel any better, Thornbush, you are the

ugliest woman I have ever seen."

"You never met my aunt, my lord."

Bran burst into laughter only to have an aching rib cage stymie his mirth. "So, tell me Thornbush. When is breakfast?"

"Breakfast is served whenever his lordship is ready for breakfast. There is not a specified hour."

Bran mentally chided himself for asking the question. Despite a bruised body, he was feeling ravenous.

The footman exposed the last window and turned back to face his master.

"My lord, do you require anything else before I leave? Perhaps a spot of tea or help getting dressed?"

Bran wanted to say, "Maybe you could carry me downstairs," but he settled on, "Thank you, but I am sure I will manage."

The servant turned on the spot and departed.

Bran twisted himself diagonally in the bed so he could fully extend his hands above his head in a good stretch. He felt every muscle in his body protest, but it was a good pain nonetheless.

He gave himself a few more minutes to awaken adequately, at which point he slid his feet around to the floor. He then managed to hobble over to his two large sea trunks lying in the corner. Both were constructed of maple and were covered with deer hides. Someone had already unpacked his garments. Each item either lay neatly folded in the bureau or hung inside a nearby wardrobe. He was grateful this particular servant had taken the initiative to press most of the items. His newly shined shoes sparkled in the morning sun. He may have felt like hell, but at least he would look the part of the lord of the manor.

Fifteen minutes later, an immaculately dressed Bran gingerly made his way down to the great hall.

Settling in his seat at the table, Bran noticed a large quantity of letters precariously stacked on a silver tray to his left. He estimated there were at least thirty of various sizes and colors.

He barely had time to unfold the napkin in his lap when a footman appeared holding a teapot. Bran was about to say, "Hello again, Thornbush," until he saw the small dragon pin on the man's coat. He changed tack. "Good morning, Joseph."

"Good morning, my lord."

If the servant was impressed Bran knew his name, he gave no indication.

"My lord, the pot only contains hot water. Unsure of how strong you like your tea, I left your leaves in the tin. I hope that is satisfactory?"

"So, I am assuming that means there is no coffee?"

The footman's puzzled expression supplied Bran with the answer he was seeking.

"I am sorry, my lord, I do not think we have any coffee, but I will check with the cook if you would like."

"Do not bother." Bran had foreseen this eventuality, and he possessed his own stash of coffee beans inside one of his trunks. His mother, a coffee drinker and an American patriot, called her coffee the "king of the American breakfast table." If Bran's father wanted tea, she made him leave the house to drink it. That being said, Bran never acquired a taste for tea.

"Perhaps in the near future I will show Cook how to properly roast and prepare the beans. In the meantime, Joseph, please make me some tea, but make it nice and strong."

"Yes, my lord." The footman was obviously pleased to be relieved of the task of searching for coffee. He was not fully sure what a coffee bean even looked like.

After he finished preparing Bran's tea, Joseph vanished only to return seconds later; this time he bore a covered dish in each hand. He gingerly set each plate down in front of Bran, and with a well-practiced flourish he swept away the metal covers. Bran's eyes quickly took in the all too familiar sight of fried eggs, bacon, sausage and—

"Excuse me, but what the hell is that?" Bran's eyes fell on a black patty covered in a fried, brownish crust. "It looks like burnt dirt."

Joseph was unperturbed, "Laverbread, my lord."

"Lava what?" but before the footman could answer he added, "I do not believe it, Cook tried to fry my coffee beans."

"Not at all, my lord," consoled the footman, "it is just seaweed." He made the statement as if this one simple proclamation would set all matters right.

"Seaweed! Then why is it not in the ocean where it belongs?"

"My lord, it is a local delicacy. Lava seaweed in rolled oats and then fried."

Bran snorted but did not pursue the matter further. He was mainly annoyed this piece of information had been left out of his upbringing . . . probably had something to do with his mother not being Welsh. The fact it looked disgusting might also have been a factor.

Bran began to dig in, and the footman informed him there was extra food and plates on an old gnarled buffet situated at the side of the room. Finding himself in the middle of an embarrassingly large mouthful of food, Bran simply nodded his understanding.

In no time he wolfed down three eggs and quite a few pieces of bacon. He was now chasing it down with his second cup of tea. The burnt seaweed was left unmolested.

Despite his voracious appetite, he managed to wade through the first few letters in the stack. Most of them dealt with nonurgent matters relating to the management of the estate.

He was just finishing a tedious letter discussing the price of wool when Cristyn waltzed into the room. She was wearing a pink dress with a faint floral pattern. Her strawberry blond hair was up, and one renegade lock was bouncing freely against her neck.

"Good morning, my lord. I am surprised to see you up and about so early considering last night's excitement."

"The same could be said of you, my lady."

"Yes, but I believe you did all of the work."

"Well, if you want the truth, apparently last night I handed out some overly zealous orders as to the hour I desired to be awakened this morning."

A smirk flashed across Cristyn's face, but she said nothing.

"Will Mrs. Clarke be joining us this morning?" inquired Bran.

"Oh no, my lord, she usually takes breakfast in her room. She likes to give me at least one meal per day in peace."

"I admire her consideration," said a stoic Bran. "Also, as a gentleman I felt it was my duty to leave you with all the burnt sea plants this morning. By the way, if you did not know, it is called hot lava weed."

Cristyn giggled. "Do not like the laverbread, my lord? You will hurt Cook's feelings, you know. She prides herself on her laverbread."

Caught off guard by the comment, Bran looked abashed but then found his voice, "In the army I choked down many an unrecognizable meal with the aid of a large cup of black coffee, but since I do not seem to have any—coffee that is—I had better not risk it. Besides, if Cook wants to pride herself on a dish garnished with oats, my suggestion would be Dutch apple pie with a nice oatmeal streusel."

Cristyn chuckled. "I am guessing your lordship has not yet met Cook."

Bran shook his head and went back to his reading. Cristyn dug into her breakfast.

A few minutes later Bran set the letter down.

"My lady, I do not suppose you know a man named Savage?"

"I do not, my lord. Is that his real name, or is that how people describe him?"

"I have no idea, could be both I suppose. According to this letter, Mr. Savage is a banker. Whether he lives up to his name, I have no way of knowing. But he would like me to come to London at my earliest convenience." Bran let out a soft sigh of frustration. "Another trip to London after having just arrived here is not exactly what I had in mind, but Mr. Savage seems to infer we must talk sooner as opposed to later. Perhaps I could push it out a week or two? Besides, he signs his name like a woman. Must be an interesting chap."

Bran casually tossed the letter on the table and turned his attention to his ward.

"By the way, my lady, I apologize for last night's antics. I hope you did not find the affair overly taxing?"

Cristyn pushed one of her strawberry curls out of her face and smiled. "Not at all. It was the most exhilarating thing to happen around here in some time. But if anyone was going to be overtaxed it would be you. I hope you did not injure yourself too badly."

"Oh, no, I am perfectly fine," He could feel his back cramping even as he told the white lie. "I imagine I could have been a little less impetuous, but shooting horses on muddy hillsides is how I like to finish every afternoon carriage ride. It tends to invigorate torpid limbs."

"You know, my lord, you have your uncle's sense of humor." She said it with a grin.

"My father used to tell me the same thing on occasion, but it was usually right after he would tell me to 'knock it off.'"

They paused the conversation as Bran poured Cristyn a little more tea.

"On a serious note, my lord, what you did was quite heroic. I overheard one of the maids talking about it this morning in the hall. Apparently, the whole neighborhood is a buzz."

Bran's face warmed slightly and he hid his embarrassment behind a feigned cough. He shifted subjects.

"There is also a letter here from Lord Gyr. He has invited us to a dinner party at his house toward the end of the month. I will not lie, it is a tad bit uncomfortable considering, well, you know what I mean." Bran flipped through the letter a second time to see if he had missed anything, all the while drumming his fingers on the table.

Cristyn said nothing.

"You are awfully silent . . . what do you think? Would you mind accompanying me?"

Bran looked up only to see Cristyn's face was devoid of color.

"My lady, are you all right? Did I somehow upset you?"

Cristyn cut him off. Her voice had taken on a flat, somewhat scratchy tone. "Please do not go, my lord. He is an evil man. The further you can stay away from him the better. I warned your uncle, but he would always laugh and tell me it was not a woman's place to worry about such things."

Bran fidgeted in his chair uncomfortably, not quite sure how to respond to such a declaration.

"I just do not see how I can refuse the invitation. You would know better than I, but there does not seem to be an excess of gentlemen and ladies in these parts. All I know is that he and my uncle were supposed to fight a duel, but in fact never did. I do not see how that is my concern. After all, it is not my place to serve as judge and juror over this man, especially having never met him."

Cristyn took a drink of water and daintily dabbed her mouth with a napkin.

"I will accompany you, my lord." She made the statement with cold resignation in her voice. "But please promise me you will be careful?"

Bran accepted her acquiescence with a simple, "Thank you." Then in a somewhat feeble effort to recover the mood of the conversation added, "I would also appreciate it if you would give me the pleasure of the evening's first dance."

She gave him a weak smile and nodded her ascent.

"Good, then it is settled." He was suddenly conscious of a false cheeriness in his voice. "Now as for this morning, I was considering a visit to the man I assisted last night in order to see how he is recovering. Any idea where he might live?"

"I heard one of the farmers say the man was living with the Fox family. Their farm is not hard to find, and one of the grooms should be able to provide you with directions."

"Excellent. I will head over there shortly. Also, right after lunch I am scheduled to spend some time with the butler, Rogers. Anything I should know—or tips—before I sit down with him?"

Cristyn thought for a moment. "My only suggestion would be to listen to the man. He has been running this house longer than either of us have been alive. I believe it was your grandfather who first hired him. That being said, he is a person of strong opinions and has very established ways of doing things. If you feel like you want to push back on something, it might be best to be non-committal for now. You can then resist later when you feel more confident and positioned to do so."

Bran nodded appreciatively. "That is quite helpful. Anything else?"

"Yes, he will point out your need to hire a valet."

"A man-servant?" asked Bran.

"Yes, your uncle had one, but he left shortly after your uncle's passing."

"Is that completely necessary?" asked a disconcerted Bran. "I am more than capable of dressing myself. Been doing it for well over twenty years as a matter of fact."

Cristyn gave him a wry smile. "Undoubtedly you are, my lord, but not only will you find it socially expected, but I think you will find the right valet to be an asset beyond measure. The right man will help ease your transition."

Nonplussed, Bran opened his mouth as if to speak but then closed it again.

Sensing no comment was forthcoming, Cristyn continued, "My lord, before you depart, there is one other thing. Mrs. Clarke and I will be visiting the local children's home this afternoon. The home was very important to your uncle, and I am sure the people who oversee it would love to meet you. You are more than welcome to join us if you find yourself available."

"I would be happy to. What time will you be leaving?"

"About three o'clock."

"Three o'clock, it is."

After polishing off his final few drops of tea, Bran pushed his chair back from the table.

"Now if you will excuse me, my lady, I probably should head out before Cook comes up here herself and makes me eat the seaweed."

9

Bull

When Bran arrived at the stable, the groom brought out a lovely white mare named Sage. The young man was also able to supply Bran with general directions to the house where the injured farmer reportedly lived. To Bran's embarrassment, he failed to make his way into the saddle on his first attempt. The groom came hurrying over.

"My lord, please let me assist."

"I am fine, just a bit sore," responded Bran a little more gruffly than he intended. Then as if to demonstrate his own virility and skill, he launched himself into the saddle with a grunt.

Bran loved to ride, and although he missed Jackie, he felt an instant connection with the mare as he sent her into a gentle trot down the lane. At first his body protested, but after a few minutes the gentle sway began to loosen his muscles.

Once he felt as if they were both adequately warmed up, he turned the horse into a nearby field and urged her into a gentle canter. Bran removed his hat to allow the breeze to blow through his hair.

Ah, this is the life, he thought. For the first time since being in

Britain he felt truly himself. Seeing a wide stretch of flat meadow in front of him, he sent the horse into a full gallop. Bran lowered himself in the saddle, all the while clenching his hat in his left hand. Ahead, he caught sight of the ruins of a small boundary wall. Bran did not slow. A few seconds later his knees instinctively tightened around each side of the horse as the mare cleared the rocky outcropping with plenty of room to spare.

Unfortunately, Bran did not fare quite as well as the horse. The jolt of the landing sharply reminded him that he was not at one hundred percent. A moment later, he eased up on the reigns, bringing the horse back to a gentle trot. "Good girl!" He affectionately patted the horse on the side of the neck.

A short while later he was within eyeshot of his destination. It was a two-story, gray, stone farmhouse that sat on the far side of the meadow. Even from a distance, Bran could tell the house was made from the same sandstone as his own estate. As he approached his destination, the building seemed to shrink. He realized that from a distance the small windows gave the house a false appearance of grandeur.

Bran leaned on the pommel as he surveyed the front of the house for something resembling a hitching post, but when he came up short he settled on an old, gnarled oak tree about twenty feet from the front door. Once he was sure his knot was adequate to prevent Sage from wandering the neighborhood, he made his way to the door. The weather had joined with the years to give the door a rough-hewn appearance. In the middle perched an old, rusty knocker. He lifted and dropped the heavy antique. It let loose an eerie, hollow, cracking sound and to Bran's horror, the old device snapped off cleanly in his hand. *Bloody hell*, he muttered to himself. He furtively looked around as if he expected some nearby bystander to decry his guilt, but then common sense took hold. He briefly considered chucking the metal relic into the bushes, but immediately thought better of the idea.

"Coming, coming!" A woman's baritone voice resonated from behind the door. Bran could also hear the barking of at least two dogs. The next thing he knew the door flew open and a solid looking, middle-aged woman filled the doorframe. Her face and hands were covered with ash and flour. Bran assumed she had been baking bread.

The woman boomed her greeting, "Yes, how can I help—?" but setting her eyes on Bran she faltered. In a much softer, though still husky voice, she added, "Lord Gruffudd, to what do we owe this pleasure?"

Bran was still amazed at how everyone seemed to recognize him so rapidly, but then he recalled a few comments about how much he resembled his uncle. "Good morning—Mrs. Fox?"

"That is correct, my lord."

Bran gave her a grin that revealed his white teeth. "Mrs. Fox. I am sorry to drop in unannounced, but I heard the man who fell victim to the wagon accident yesterday was staying here. I simply wanted to inquire regarding his health."

"Of course, my lord. Where are my manners? Do come in. Can I get your lordship some water or a cup of tea?"

Bran held up his hand, "Oh, no thank you, I—" Only then did he realize the woman was staring at the piece of metal in his hand. "I am so sorry, I seem to have successfully broken your door," confessed Bran abashedly.

The woman laughed. "It is me who should be apologizing, my lord. That old thing breaks at least once a month. I would have rid us of it long ago, but Mr. Fox thinks it makes the house look more impressive like. Here, give it to me."

Relieved of the source of his embarrassment, Bran's eyes shifted to the small room that obviously served as both kitchen and dining area. The room was tidy but lived in. At the far side, he could see the large bread oven that had obviously been Mrs. Fox's focus before his unexpected arrival. She led him into a small adjacent compartment which now served as a makeshift bedroom. Bran was not sure if this transformation had occurred before or after the previous night's accident. The room was lit by a small solitary window roughly five feet from the ground. A narrow shaft of white light projected onto the opposing wall. Half the room was filled with tightly packed straw on which a faded patchwork quilt was spread. On top of the quilt lay a man.

Pausing before entering, Bran took in the injured man. He was immediately struck by how much the man resembled an English bulldog. The man had a large, bald, round head with drooping jowls set off by closely cropped mutton chops. The facial hair only served to accentuate his canine similarities. Bran was not sure if the styling was intentional or simply coincidental. The top of the man's bald head included a number of skin folds that only served to complete the caricature.

The man seemed to be dozing, but as Bran walked through the doorway he opened his eyes enough to take in his visitor. Instantly recognizing his rescuer, the man came awake and attempted to straighten himself into a more dignified manner on the pallet.

In a strong Scottish brogue, the man spoke, "My lord, I do apologize, I would try to rise, but as the good Lord said, 'The spirit is willing, but the body is weak.'"

Seeing the man's distress, Bran immediately raised his hand

to put him at ease.

"Relax, friend; you have been through a lot. Let us dispense with the formalities so your body can focus on the more important task of healing itself." Despite the man's injuries, Bran was struck by the profound happiness that radiated from his eyes.

"Has the doctor seen you? What is the prognosis?"

The man chuckled, "Much better than it could have been, thanks to you, my lord. Apparently, the doctor is surprised I fared as well as I did, considering my age and what happened. Not even a broken bone, just lots of sore muscles, a sprained shoulder, and a large amount of wounded pride." The man let loose a grin that displayed a prominent gold tooth.

Bran returned the smile. "I am so happy to hear you are faring well. I am sorry, but in all the excitement, I do not think I ever learned your name."

The man's eyes furrowed in embarrassment. "My apologies, my lord. The name is Alastair McCance, but most folks just call me Bull, on account that I look like a bulldog."

Bran smiled at the comment. "Pleased to meet you, Bull." Then not sure how to ask his next question, Bran did his best, "I am curious, but how exactly did the accident happen? That is not something you see every day."

The smile left the man's face but not his eyes. "I was a fool. As you might have gathered by now, I am no farmer. However, I was taking some casks of ale to the village when I went around a nasty turn. The road was slick with mud and the horse lost his footing. This caused some of the casks to shift. By then we were so close to the edge it caused the already soaked road to give way. The cart went over and it pulled the horse with it. Fortunately, that tree stopped our descent. Of course, that was where you found us."

Bran was struggling to fully follow the man's story through his accent. "I see. Sounds like it was bad luck and could have happened to anyone." Bran paused to scratch his nose and then continued. "You mentioned you are not a farmer, and the way you handled that wagon full of barrels implies you are definitely not a whisky smuggler—so what are you?"

The man brightened at the prospect of moving on to a more pleasant, less embarrassing topic. "I've spent most of my time as a gentleman's gentleman, my lord. My most recent posting was with the Duke of Denver. I served him as valet for fifteen years."

Pride radiated from the man's face, but then the smile abated. "Regretfully, my mother-in-law became ill. My dear Alice, before she passed, made me promise I would keep an eye on her mum. The old lady lives very close to here. There was no way I could carry on my former duties while also caring for the old lady. The Foxes were kind enough to give me work and lodging."

Bran stood stroking his chin with his hand, half lost in thought. He turned his attention back to the injured man.

"Bull, this will seem somewhat spur of the moment, but I am told I am in need of a valet. I am not quite sure I even know what one does, but everyone seems to think I am in desperate need, as a matter of fact. Would you be interested in such a post once you complete your recovery?" Then feeling like he needed to sell it further added, "I would be happy to have you moved to the manor for the duration of your convalescence. Granted, a lowly baron might be a bit of a come-down after a duke, but I daresay it would probably be better than riding farm carts down cliffs." He added the latter with a grin.

Bull responded with gusto. "Of course, I would be humbled to fill the position. I am sure I could start soon, and the duke gave me a quality reference; besides, the Foxes just hired a new hand, and I was beginning to feel like was just getting in the way."

Bran walked up and very gently slapped Bull on the uninjured shoulder. "Excellent! I will arrange to have you moved up to the manor tomorrow. In the meantime, just focus on getting better."

As Bran rode back to the manor he reflected on his good morning's work. *Not even noon and I already found myself a valet. Bran, maybe you will make an aristocrat yet.*

10

Grace Meadows

Sally! Goodness gracious, where have you gone off to?" exclaimed Eliza Lewis.

"Right here, mum." Sally, a slim redhead who was no more than thirteen staggered into the kitchen toting an enormous oak bucket. She walked splay legged and at every step sent large quantities of water slopping onto the clean flagstone floor.

"Oh good, you already fetched the water," said a smiling Eliza; "And do not forget to clean up those puddles when you are finished. The last thing we need is Mr. Paulson stumping in here only to break his neck."

Eliza knew the comment was unnecessary. Sally was extremely responsible for her age; in fact, if she were honest, Eliza could have used about four Sallys. After all, Eliza Lewis had fourteen children, and she needed all the help she could muster. In truth, they were not technically her children, but it was best not to tell that to Eliza. A stout Welshwoman who was rapidly approaching fifty, Eliza's indefatigable stamina was legendary. Perhaps the only thing she was better known for was the love she bestowed on each of her little charges. For the past thirty years Eliza had cared for ten plus children seven days a week. To say she did it alone would have been a misstatement. Of course she had Sally who, despite her diminutive size, was a tremendous help. Sally was technically the oldest child in the brood, but Eliza seldom treated her as a mere child. Then there was Mr. Paulson, the crotchety old sailor with a peg leg, who had faithfully been at Eliza's side for some fifteen years; and while he was quick to snap at village tradesmen, it could be argued he loved each of the children more than even Eliza. Many wondered why the two devoted compatriots simply did not just get married, but Mr. Paulson was always quick to state that Miss Lewis was holding out for a man with a handsomer peg. If Mr. Paulson had a fault, it was probably his occasional tendency to let language of the saltier sort slip into his conversations with the children; though he had done better ever since the little Bobby Milner incident.

Reverend Hughes had been visiting Grace Meadows Children's Home for tea, and part way through the meal the elderly priest accidentally knocked his little china cup onto the floor. Three-year-old Bobby quietly sat nearby playing with his blocks, but at the sound of the smash he let out a high pitched, "Damn the bastard!" Mr. Paulson found himself on verbal probation shortly thereafter. Not that the incident deterred Mr. Paulson. He preferred to confine himself to his typical duties, which included tasks like milking the cows, chopping wood, and fixing all the things little children are so adept at breaking.

"Sally, I expect her ladyship will be here any moment. You know she always comes at the exact same time every Wednesday. Punctual she is, her ladyship. She also mentioned at church she might attempt to bring his new lordship. I heard he takes after his uncle. Please see to wiping off the faces of the younger children. Some of them just ate."

Sally had barely finished wiping down the last toddler when Eliza heard a gentle knock at the door. Pausing to re-adjust her large apron, Eliza made her way to the entrance. She catapulted the door open with the exuberant slam for which she was known.

"Lady Cristyn and Mrs. Clarke! How good of you to honor us with your presence as always. Welcome back to Grace Meadows."

"Good afternoon, Miss Lewis," said a rosy-cheeked Cristyn. She was flushed from the exertion of the long walk from the manor.

Mrs. Clarke was fanning herself rapidly and simply nodded her breathless greeting, as if any attempt at vocalization might be the death of her.

Cristyn turned slightly. "Miss Lewis, may I introduce Lord Gruffudd. He has already heard so much about the amazing work you and Mr. Paulson do, and he positively begged to join us today."

Bran leaned forward in a subtle bow.

Eliza returned the courtesy by lowering her ample girth into a shallow curtsey.

"Come in, come in," said Eliza with gusto. "As always, it is a privilege to have such esteemed guests." The small group made their way inside.

"It is I who hold you in high esteem if half the things I hear about your work are true," said an effusive Bran.

Miss Lewis flushed visibly. "That is kind of you to say, my lord. We are just trying to do His work"—she lifted a finger upward—"He has a special place in his heart for orphans you know."

The main living area was surprisingly large, and Mrs. Clarke quickly found her way to a small couch where she collapsed with a highly audible sigh. The rest of the group paid her no mind.

"Miss Lewis, is it true you keep fourteen children here at the home?" asked Bran.

"Yes, my lord, though it would not be quite right to count dear Sally. She is really my second set of hands."

Sally flushed at the compliment and it was not difficult for Bran to identify the crimson-faced girl in the corner who was feeding an infant a bottle.

"Miss Lewis, perhaps it might be good to take a moment to tell his lordship a little about the home and the work you do," interjected Cristyn.

Miss Lewis beamed, "Of course, my lady. Would you care to sit down?"

Each person found a place to sit amongst the hodgepodge of well-loved furniture. Bran found himself sitting in a particularly straight-backed, wooden chair.

"Well, my lord," began Miss Lewis, "when I was a wee girl, I became an orphan myself. Back then, the town did not have any kind of formal children's home. I was one of the fortunate ones, and a kind foster family raised me. However, there were many who were not so blessed. As a part of my good fortune, I had the opportunity to attend church each week. Through the work of the church, I had my first opportunity to begin helping other children who were in similar need. After all, the Bible says, 'It is better to give than to receive.'"

"So true," concurred Mrs. Clarke, who had revived herself enough to partake in the conversation.

Eliza continued, "The previous rector envisioned starting a children's home for the town. He had already engaged a few of the more prominent families to financially support the cause, but he approached me to see if I would run it. Well, you can imagine how flattered I was at the age of seventeen to be given such an immense responsibility; and to make a long story short, I have been doing this ever since, going on thirty years."

"How many children have you put through the home over those thirty years?" asked Bran curiously.

Miss Lewis did not hesitate, "Eighty-seven children, my lord, including the ones we have now."

Bran's eyebrows shot up. "And all of those orphans came from this small community?"

Miss Lewis shook her head, "No, I am happy to say the work we have done has become so well known that we tend to collect children from the surrounding areas. We also have some children whose parents or parent are still living. Little Sarah Everspring would be an example. She is three years old and her mother died during childbirth. However, her father is a poor fisherman who lives about eight miles from here. He has no way to work and care for her. We watch over the girl, and he comes and sees her every single Sunday."

"And where does your funding come from?" asked Bran. "I do not imagine caring for so many children can be cheap."

"You would think money would be a concern, but it really has not," said Miss Lewis. "Reverend Hughes and the previous rector have both been great advocates for the ministry. A lot of folks in the community do their part, and of course her ladyship's father and your uncle were both large benefactors. The building we now occupy is quite new and was built for the express purpose of caring for the children."

"Well, I hope you know I can be counted on to continue my family's support," offered Bran magnanimously.

"That is very kind of you, my lord, and as always, it is not taken for granted. However, I do not think you will find another investment which will yield a larger return on your money."

"I am sure there is not," replied a smiling Bran. His mind momentarily flashed back to the mysterious banker's letter.

"Lord Gruffudd, would you be interested in meeting some of the children? The older children are currently out on the lawn playing ball, but a few of the younger toddlers are playing in the other room, and of course Sally is holding little Amos Schofield. He is only six months old and the newest addition to our happy clan. A jolly fellow he is too. I have never known a happier baby."

Sally let little Amos suck the last few drops out of his bottle, though the look on his face indicated he found the portion entirely lacking.

"Let us start with not-so-little Amos," laughed Bran.

Sally staggered over with the large baby.

Bran was not sure who weighed more, Amos or Sally. Bran stuck out his hand and the chubby youngster immediately grabbed hold of his finger. He had never seen such a fat baby. Corpulent little Amos had fat roles in his cheeks, in his neck, and not to mention about ten knees.

Bran was still laughing. "Do any of the other children get to eat with this fellow around?"

"A person would wonder," said a genuinely concerned Miss Lewis. "That young lad does know how to put it away. We feed him twice what a normal child eats, and he still gives us dirty looks as if we are cheating him. His story really is a sad one. His mother was a woman of the streets who was drifting through town. She came into the church one day and Reverend Hughes started talking to her. After much cajoling by the Reverend, she confessed she planned to dispose of the baby once it arrived. Reverend Hughes told her of our modest little enterprise, and she hung around just long enough to deliver and hand off the child."

Bran stroked his chin. Miss Lewis' story sparked his own set of thoughts.

"Miss Lewis," inquired Bran, "is there any chance you could use some additional help? Perhaps another young woman around age fifteen to sixteen?"

"She would be an answer to my prayers, especially if she came with your recommendation."

"I am not sure I can provide her with a full recommendation," continued Bran, "but when I passed through Cardiff on the way here, I was presented with an opportunity to assist a young woman who was in some peril." He paused for a moment, considering how to proceed in light of his audience. "Let us just say, like this boy's mother, she has her own troubled past, but I would like to see if the course of her life might perhaps be redirected."

If anyone in the room was surprised by the statement, none seemed to show it.

Mrs. Clarke waded into the conversation. "Seems like an excellent idea to me. Better for a young girl to be taking care of babies than making them. Besides, if you take care of enough babies, it will make you less likely to want to make more of them before the time is right."

"When could we expect this girl to arrive?" asked Miss Lewis.

"I do not know exactly, in a few days I hope," said Bran. "A man was not too kind to her, and by the time I was able to assist she was in pretty rough shape. She is currently staying with the vicar and his wife in Cardiff, that is, until she is able to make the journey. Of course, I would be more than willing to offset any living expenses that may be incurred."

"Oh pooh," exclaimed Miss Lewis, "as I told you, my lord, money is not an issue. I eagerly anticipate the help, and I am sure Sally does as well. Besides, it will give little Sally a companion close to her own age."

"My lord, do not worry about the details," interjected Cristyn. "When she arrives, I will ensure she gets what she needs and is sent down to Grace Meadows."

"Excellent," said a beaming Bran. He was feeling quite smug that he had managed to bring closure to one matter while assisting someone else in the process. "So how about I get to know big Amos here a little better?" He held up both arms, ready to receive the infant.

The women all glanced at each other. Little Sally was on the border of panic, caught between traditional etiquette and the clear request of a peer of the realm.

Cristyn intervened. "My lord, perhaps it would be better to leave the children to us women."

"Oh, let his lordship hold the baby," declared a slightly irritable Mrs. Clarke. "Besides, I have always thought it was a load of poppycock, that is, men not engaging with the little ones. It is not as if they do not have a part in making them. Besides, I am sure the little guy will appreciate the male interaction. Nothing but a bunch of hens around here."

With no one else having a response, Sally handed over the child.

"My lord, he is a bit of spitter, and he just ate, so you might want to be careful which way you point him," said a fretting Miss Lewis.

"Understood," chuckled Bran. "Keep the musket barrel pointed down range."

Bran carried the baby over to one of the larger chairs where he sat down and attempted to give the child a horse ride on his knee. It was not lost on him that every woman in the room was eyeing him nervously, all the while attempting to look relaxed. Mrs. Clarke was the only one who seemed pleased. She eyed Cristyn as if to say, "It could be yours, you know."

Somewhat satisfied that the new baron was not about to dash the baby against the wall, the other women turned their attention and conversation to each other.

Bran was having a thoroughly good time with the child, and his mind began to slowly flit back to his own child whom he had never truly known. He had been so excited when he received the letter telling him Rachael had given birth. There was something about babies. They possessed a mixture of absolute dependence coupled with complete freedom to do what they wanted, when they wanted.

As if reading Bran's thoughts and taking them as a cue, little Amos chose that particular moment to make a little more room for his digesting dinner. It was a sound none in the room could miss. The odor of rotten eggs quickly found their way to Bran's nose, and his watering eyes met Amos' smiling ones. The baby's countenance was one of triumph and glee. It took Mrs. Clarke to rouse the women from their stupefied state.

"Well, who is going rescue his lordship?"

The statement hit little Sally like a hot poker, and she spurred into action. Five seconds later she hurried little Amos out of the room.

But Mrs. Clarke was not done. "I do not know what you are all surprised about. You fill a little baby full of food and then bounce him up and down, it is bound to come out one end or the other."

Cristyn was now looking at her companion as if to say, *that is enough*, but Mrs. Clarke mistook the look as disbelief.

"Do not give me that look my dear; you were a bit of a smelly baby yourself if I remember correctly."

At a loss for words, Cristyn's face turned crimson.

Bran successfully stifled a laugh.

"And do not try and deny it," continued Mrs. Clarke. "There was this one time when your father was showing you off to Lord Hightower. I thought you were going to clear the room. I swear it took days for your father to air out that coat."

Miss Lewis decided to rescue her guests from themselves.

"My lord, how would you like me to introduce you to Mr. Paulson and a few of the older children?" Eager for an escape, Bran quickly followed her out the front door.

A few minutes later Miss Lewis returned, but without Bran. She did not hesitate in rejoining the conversation.

"So tell me a little bit about this lord of yours, my lady. He does not quite seem like the normal type."

"It is because he is foreign," interjected Mrs. Clarke.

"I thought he was from the colonies?" responded a confused Miss Lewis.

"You are correct," replied Cristyn exasperatedly, "but to your previous comment, he is different. However, he is different in a good way. Lord Gruffudd seems to have all the nobility of an aristocrat, but a lot less of the baggage that seems to come with the really old families. My guess is he will learn what he needs to learn, but hopefully not enough to truly change him."

"My lady, what does he think of the situation related to his uncle?" asked Miss Lewis.

"I do not think he knows much about it," replied Cristyn. "He only arrived yesterday and we have not really had a chance to delve too deeply into any subject. I am not even sure if it is my place to speak of such matters. Due to its sensitivity, I am wondering if I should defer the topic to Reverend Hughes."

"Yes, my lady, that is probably very wise. Reverend Hughes has a way with words. Besides, some things are best left between men."

From there the conversation meandered its way through a variety of other topics for the better part of an hour. It only came to an end when Bran re-entered the house.

"Lady Cristyn, Mrs. Clarke, I think it is time we left these fine people alone. Caring for fourteen children is difficult enough without me getting in the way."

As the group made their way up the path from the house, Cristyn leaned over to Bran.

"My lord, forgive my impertinence, but did you know you have grass stains on the knees of your trousers?"

Bran glanced down nonchalantly. "I suppose I do."

11

Besieged

The rifles over the library mantle rattled like old bones. Bran lifted his eyes from the letter in front of him to see if any of the aged weapons would fall to the ground. *Getting closer*, he thought to himself. The thunderstorm ponderously advanced on the estate like an approaching army. A draft sailed across the surface of the desk, threatening to extinguish the candle fixed to the tall brass candle holder. Bran cupped his hand around the candle just long enough to allow the small flame to regain its strength. He was about to return to his letter writing when a soft tap sounded at the door.

"Come in." He did not bother to look up. The hinges put forth a mournful moan as the heavy door swung slowly inward.

"My lord, am I disturbing you?"

Bran hastily put down his quill and rose to his feet. "Lady Cristyn, my apologies. I thought you were Rogers bringing me some coffee."

She remained in the doorway. "I apologize for interrupting, my lord, I—did you really already teach Cook how to make coffee?"

Bran grinned sheepishly. "I did. A man must have his

priorities. Cook could definitely be described as irascible, and she had a degree of apprehension at first, but eventually her desire to please me overrode her hesitations; but I am also fairly confident it was not my coffee penchant that brought you to come see me."

Cristyn looked like someone who was fighting to recover the thread of their thoughts. "No, I came down for three reasons. First, I wanted to thank you for taking the time to visit Grace Meadows today. It meant a lot to Miss Lewis and Mr. Paulson."

"Oh, it was nothing. I rather enjoyed the outing."

"That is kind of you to say, my lord, but it was not nothing to those folks."

"I am glad I could help. Though, to be honest, I do not think I am ever going to get used to my presence always causing such a stir."

Cristyn smiled sympathetically. "If it makes you feel better, your uncle was the same way, and he was groomed for this role from the day he was born."

"Actually, that does make me feel better. It makes me feel like I will learn some things, but do not have to learn them all, or at least not today. Besides, I suppose that is what tomorrow is for."

Cristyn paused momentarily to ensure nothing else was forthcoming. "I thought you would also like to know the girl, Mary, arrived shortly before sunset this evening. The vicar and his wife drove her up from Cardiff as you said they would."

"Excellent," effused Brain. "What did you think of them by the way? I am referring to the vicar and his wife." Bran's face betrayed the slightest sign of a grin but Cristyn did not appear to notice.

"I do not know if it is my place to pass judgement, especially with the vicar being a man of the church. That being said, I would not describe them as cheery people. The only time either one smiled was when I gave them a few more coins for their trouble."

"Hmm, is that your way of saying they each still looked like they were sucking on half a lemon?"

Cristyn stifled a laugh.

Bran pretended not to notice. "At the time, I thought it simply had to do with the unpleasant manner of our meeting, but your description makes me question my initial assessment. It shows you that charity is often the most elusive of the three heavenly graces. Why? I am not fully sure."

"It is probably because charity requires the most outward action as it relates to our fellow man," responded Cristyn. "Faith and hope, on the other hand, can be more easily dismissed as internal matters of the heart."

Bran grunted. "Funny how that works. People tend to be obliging until you actually ask them to do something. Tell me, did our two cheerful friends give any indication if they would be traveling back tonight, or did you offer for them to stay here? I would want to steel myself lest I run into them in the hall."

"I believe they were going to stay with Reverend Hughes tonight before they returned home in the morning."

"Our local vicar, correct?"

"Yes, my lord. I am sure you will meet him soon. He was a good friend of your uncle and is a singularly uncommon man."

"Then I will look forward to meeting him. Hopefully he is friendlier than the dour vicar from Cardiff."

"You do not have anything to worry about there, my lord. It would be safe to say those two men are as far apart as the East is from the West. However, I am fully confident Reverend Hughes will make them feel very much at home."

"And what about the girl?" asked Bran.

"I was surprised how well she looked. Despite their less than affable personas, her caretakers appear to have done what you asked. She little resembles the pitiful soul you described to me and Mrs. Clarke on the return journey from Grace Meadows. One of the maids has a vacant bed in her room. Mary will sleep there tonight, and in the morning I will ensure she is promptly taken down to Grace Meadows. I imagine Miss Lewis will keep her so busy she will not have a chance to dwell on her less than pleasant past."

"It is a good lesson, you know," supplied a pensive Bran.

"What is, my lord?"

"That people tend to take on a persona that is reflective of how they are treated. Treat a man like a prince, and eventually he will start acting like a prince. Treat a person as rubbish, and eventually they will believe that too. Humbling really. Hopefully it is not too late for poor Mary."

Cristyn was moved by the obvious emotion in Bran's voice. She refrained from interrupting his thoughts. Neither spoke again for some time.

It was Bran who interrupted his own ruminations. "Thank you for taking care of this matter. You will find I do not like seeking assistance with my problems. I tend to try to fix them all myself, even when others could do a better job. It is a personal flaw. One of many as a matter of fact. But I am droning on. I know it is getting late. Was there something else you wanted to tell me?"

"Yes, I wanted to also let you know the staff has finished preparing a room for Mr. McCance's arrival tomorrow. Were there any other special preparations we should be aware of?"

Bran wrinkled up his face slightly. "Mr. McCance, who is that?"

"Bull, my lord. You did hire him as your valet, did you not?" She was unable to fully hide her amusement. "I would be quite sad if it was all a misunderstanding. I was looking forward to having him around. You really threw Rogers off balance, by the way, when you announced you had already hired a valet. I think it was good for him—Rogers that is."

"Oh, of course. I forgot his name was McCance. But you speak as if you know him."

"I do. Mr. McCance—Bull—used to serve the Duke of Denver. The duke was my father's friend. Not a close friend, mind you, but they did attend Cambridge together, and our families always seemed to find themselves together at various events."

"Who is the Duke of Denver, if you do not mind my asking?" In a world that was all about connections, Bran was fully aware he had none.

"I honestly do not know as much as you might expect. I do know he is a distant cousin of the king, and he is currently serving as the Under-Secretary of State for Foreign Affairs."

"Is that the nation's chief diplomat?"

"If you mean the Foreign Secretary, then no, it is different. But I do believe the duke does report to Lord Grenville. My understanding is that Lord Grenville deals in the lofty matters of state, and the Duke of Denver handles those foreign issues that are less than seemly, but necessary."

"Seems like an odd sort of job for a duke, does it not?"

"Maybe," said Cristyn, "but it is a job that comes with tremendous power and influence, especially in regard to many of the more veiled activities on the continent. The duke is not a man to be trifled with. I can see him being very good at that sort of thing."

"You mean things like spies and subterfuge?"

"Yes," said Cristyn.

Bran was not sure if she meant the comment to be an insult or a compliment towards the man.

"You know a lot about politics. Is that common—?"

"—For a lady?" Cristyn finished his sentence while her face warmed slightly. "Politics and affairs of state have always interested me, but my father used to discourage it. He said it was not a suitable interest for a woman of my station. He would sometimes catch me reading his newspaper. Those instances would usually result in a long lecture that I would endure dutifully. However, they did little to assuage my curiosity. When I moved here your uncle was less particular about such things, which probably had to do with being a confirmed bachelor. In fact, I think he enjoyed having someone to whom he could discuss such issues. I will admit I very much enjoyed the conversations."

"What is he like?"

"Who? Uncle Llew?"

"Well yes—but I was wondering specifically about the duke."

"Oh, I do not know, my lord. Based on the few times I have interacted with him I would say he is sensible, no-nonsense, but also a little cold, and somewhat conceited." She blushed slightly, in fear that she might have said too much.

"Hmm," said Bran, "he sounds like your perfect aristocrat." He flashed a smile and was pleased to see her respond in kind.

"Well, my lord, it is late, and I must be retiring for the

evening. Do you require anything else?"

"No, I am fine, and I apologize for keeping you up. It may not seem like much, but every little thing I learn is helpful."

With that she said goodnight and departed.

Bran pushed his armchair back from the desk and sat with his hands folded under his chin. The same pesky draft wafted a few remnants of Cristyn's perfume over to the desk. The sweet scent brought back memories. He sat for some time contemplating all that his new role entailed, both the anticipated and unanticipated.

Oh Rachael, what would you think of me right now . . . and this? He waved his hand as if he were presenting the room. *I know, you would probably be laughing hysterically. You should be here to help me. You were always the people person.*

His concentration was broken by a thump against the large French windows behind him. As if on cue, a flash illuminated the otherwise dim room and was almost immediately followed by a thunderclap. He walked to the window. *I hope that is not you trying to tell me something, my love.*

With a quick snap, he undid the latch and gazed out over the gardens. The rain was perilously close, and more lightning lit up the horizon. He stepped outside to momentarily experience nature in its full fury.

Despite the wind, Bran smelled the man's cheap cologne a split second before the crook of the man's arm wrapped around Bran's neck. Caught completely off guard, Bran instinctively tried to wrench the arm away, but he had no leverage. His vision was already swimming and he knew he only had seconds. With a vicious downward strike he slammed his right fist into the attacker's groin. A grunt and an immediate lessening of the pressure told Bran he was on target. With a quick spin and jerk, he sent the attacker careening into the other French window. Glass shattered and mullions splintered as the man careened into the library. Before his attacker could regain his feet, Bran was on him like a savage. But just as he was about to send a fist into the rising man's jaw, a different fist hit him across the side of the face. Bran reeled and lost his balance, slamming against the heavy oak desk in the process. Before he could recover, two sets of strong arms grabbed him and hauled him backwards until he was pinioned in the large desk chair. Bran heard the familiar click of a pistol being cocked; a reedy, red-headed man stepped from behind the chair. The weapon was pointed at Bran's head.

"Settle down, your lordship; we will only be here for a few minutes."

At the sight of the weapon Bran ceased his struggling.

"That is better," said the red-head. Then turning to his companions, he ordered, "Get to work, we don' have all day. It has to be here somewhere, and make sure you dunderheads do not look in the same places as last time."

Perplexed, Bran sat quietly, watching the strange events unfold around him. In addition to the man holding the pistol, three other men began to ransack his library. The focus of their attention appeared to be the room's largest bookcase. One by one, large leather-bound volumes were ripped from the shelf and hastily rifled through. Bran cringed as valuable titles were abused and discarded like street refuse. With each passing second, both Bran and the searchers' patience dwindled. The fact the room was only lit by two remaining candles made their task all the more difficult. The flickering yellow light made the room feel like a ghostly chapel.

"Why are you looking over there, you moron? We looked

over there last time." The man's voice was full of condescension.

The recipient of the rebuke was not about to back down. "Shut ya gob, ya don' even know what ya talkin' 'bout. Worry about ya self."

Exasperated, the man with the pistol turned his attention to the quarreling looters. He took a step forward as if to demonstrate his irritation. "Knock it off. You are not getting paid to bellow at each other like a pair of old bulls fighting over a cow. Remember there is a bonus if you find it."

The momentary distraction was all Bran needed. In one motion, he grabbed hold of the brass candlestick on the desk and sent it slamming into the man's pistol hand like a crude mace. Bran could hear the splintering of finger bones, and the pistol discharged. The man let out a cry as loose plaster fragments sprayed the room. Again, on cue, the storm decided to make its arrival known. Water began to flood through the broken opening in the window, and the relentless drumming of the rain sounded like a herd of galloping horses. Bran was getting ready to charge another attacker in a hasty sally when a sharp gust of wind snuffed out the two remaining candles. The room was plunged into darkness. Only the frequent flash of lightning cast momentary illumination on the otherwise inky chamber.

Bran began to slowly move around the room, using the random flashes of light to try and gain the advantage. His opponents were doing the same. At one point a fortuitous flash of lighting allowed him to barely dodge a small porcelain vase hurled by one of the intruders. The enamel-covered piece of pottery shattered on the floor behind him.

Suddenly, the door of the room opened and the light of the

hall shone into the room like the beam of a rock-bound lighthouse on a stormy night.

Cristyn stood silhouetted in the doorway. Her voice registered confusion and concern. "My lord, is everything alright?"

"Cristyn get out of here!" Bran shouted.

She froze, momentarily paralyzed by the ghostly drama unfolding in front of her. Her hesitation cost her, and the intruder closest to the door grabbed hold of her arm.

"Aren't you a pretty little one? HEY LARRY, look what I got?"

Unimpressed by her attacker, Cristyn sent her right heel crashing down on the bridge of the man's foot. More out of surprise than pain, the man reflexively let go of her. She lunged out of his reach, but stumbled in the darkness and went crashing into a nearby credenza.

Bran's voice was full of panic now. "Cristyn? Cristyn?" When she did not respond, he rapidly moved in her direction. He was halfway across the room when he caught sight of another man on his left. This attacker was brandishing a fire poker. Bran hastily searched his surroundings. Setting his eyes on a slender maple end table, Bran hoisted the small piece of furniture by its legs. The man hesitated as he took in Bran's ad hoc tactics, but then he continued his advance. The fire poker came down like an ax, and Bran held the table like some crude shield. The thin wood top fractured, showering Bran in a rainstorm of splintered fragments. Still holding the remaining table leg, he drove it into the man's face. The man fell backwards, poker clattering across the floor. Bran dove for the discarded weapon. It was a race between him and the make-shift weapon's previous owner. As both men's fists closed around the iron implement, Bran slammed his opposite fist into the man's stubble-strewn jaw. It was not a clean strike, but it was enough to cause the man to withdraw. Newly armed, Bran rose to his feet. His first thought was Cristyn. But to his relief he saw the trailing hem of her dress slip out of the room. *Good girl*, he said to himself. But victory was short lived.

Pivoting to face his next potential assailant, Bran was just able to glimpse the red-headed man bringing a marble bust down against the side of his head. Bran's cranium felt like it was cloven in two, and his knees buckled under him. He fell backwards, grasping for anything to help maintain his footing. His right arm upended an ancient suit of armor and sent it to the floor in a thunderous cacophony. Already the room was beginning to spin. Bran was on the verge of losing consciousness when he saw the final fragments of the large French window in front of him crash inwards. He maintained his wits just long enough to see a man resembling Sergeant Abbott burst into the room. The man brought a heavy walking staff down on the nearest assailant. A moment later Bran lost consciousness.

12

Reverend Hughes

The wizened clergyman reclined in the large, faded armchair. He was not a big man to begin with, but as he sat in the massive chair he almost looked childlike. Out of the side of his mouth hung an old pipe, and the occasional puff of smoke billowed into the air. His head was covered in wisps of white hair. He wore delicate, round, wire-rimmed spectacles, and his face was covered with a white beard of the short-boxed style. Some even said he resembled an elderly leprechaun. On top of his crossed legs sat a worn leather volume; but at this particular moment the priest sat fixated on the patient in the bed in front of him.

Reverend Elis Hughes stared over the top of his glasses and contemplated Bran Gruffudd. He thought him a comely young man; his thick dark hair, combined with his sinewy physique, gave him a ruggedly wild appearance. The experience of seeing Bran lying in the antique four-poster, covered in expensive linens, was somewhat akin to walking into the parlor of a duchess only to come across a wolf nestled in front of the fireplace.

After examining the young nobleman the previous night,

the clergyman could tell this had not been the man's first scrap. His body was replete with old scars, characteristic of someone who had known the rougher side of life. Whether they were the product of growing up in a tough neighborhood, or souvenirs of a dangerous occupation, he had no way of knowing.

Then there was the little exploit where he had saved Bull McCance from the wagon accident. The priest had not been present at the affair, but he had talked to more than a few of the local farmers who had been at the scene. The average man does not fling himself down a mud-strewn embankment in the dark with a rope in one hand and a gun in the other.

Lastly, there was Reverend Hughes's own interaction with Lady Cristyn following the robbery. Despite being a bit bruised herself, the young lady was far more concerned about his lordship. If asked to describe the connection between her and Lord Gruffudd, he probably would not have used the word attraction. Not that anyone would have blamed her. No, the word he would have chosen was affection. A little surprising considering the relatively short time they had known each other. But in addition to the man's own qualities, he suspected the similarities Bran shared with his uncle were a contributor.

The aged clergyman took another puff on his pipe. *All right lad, enough sleep; time to rejoin the living. You have had your rest.* Reverend Hughes was not excessively worried about the long-term health of his patient. Lord Gruffudd was both young and strong. But he had been out for ten hours, and head wounds were tricky things. One time the priest had treated a shop keeper who had slipped and hit his head on the side of a counter. While not a sharp blow, the man had fallen over dead a week later. On the flip side, he knew a farmer who weighed no more than eight stones who took a blow to the head from a plow horse. The concussion knocked him clean out, but two days later the farmer was back plowing his field with no ill effects other than a nice-sized knot. Yes, head wounds were tricky things.

Reverend Hughes was delicately leafing through his book when his eye caught the momentary flicker of Bran's eyelids. The priest marked his place in the book and set it on the table next to him. Turning his full attention to his charge, he waited patiently. A moment later both eyelids opened. Despite Bran's somewhat disoriented state, his eyes were full of life. Reverend Hughes knew at that moment the young man would make a full recovery.

Bran curiously scanned the room. He had the look of someone who was not quite sure how he had arrived in his current circumstance.

In an effort not to rush the young man, Reverend Hughes took a moment to ream out his pipe. Only when the task was complete did he again turn his attention to Bran. "Your lordship, I am glad you chose to return to us; you had us worried."

Now fully aware of his companion's presence, Bran addressed the collared man in a thick voice. "My apologies, reverend; you seem to have me at a disadvantage."

Even as Bran spoke a sharp pain pulsed through his temple. He closed his eyes in a futile attempt to ward off the pain. Once the throbbing abated, he turned his attention back to the vicar. "Forgive me, I do not quite feel myself right now."

Reverend Hughes chuckled, "It is no wonder. That was quite a bash you took. Fortunately, you have a hard head. If I had to guess I would say you take a great deal after your uncle in that regard. But my apologies, we have not been formally introduced; I am the Reverend Elis Hughes, and I am very pleased to finally meet you."

Bran was slowly regaining his wits. "Pleased to meet you, reverend. Am I correct in assuming your presence means things were questionable for a while?"

The priest was in the middle of filling his pipe full of tobacco, and Bran's comment took him slightly off guard. When he fully processed what was just said, a friendly grin spread across his face.

"If you are implying I am here to perform Last Rites, then I can happily say you are mistaken. I am an Anglican priest. We do not do that sort of thing. We prefer to let people die in peace. Besides, in addition to the local vicar, I am also the village doctor. That is, ever since old Dr. Peters died twelve winters ago. Not that it surprised any of us. The man was positively ancient. His old hands used to shake worse than Mrs. Owen's backside at a parish dance. We have had a hard time filling the post ever since, so for the time being, I am doing my best to fill the void."

Bran had a bemused look on his face, as if he was attempting and failing to take in everything that was just said. The priest used the opportunity to give his pipe a couple of gentle draws to get it started. It was a minute or two before Bran spoke again. "So, should I call you reverend or doctor?"

"Your lordship is welcome to call me whatever he wants. Your uncle on occasion would call me a few things I do not care to repeat, but our relationship was also unique. If you want to be the same as everyone else, then reverend will suffice. But enough of that; how are you feeling, my lord?"

"Like a donkey kicked me in the head."

"A donkey might actually have hurt less," said the priest. "A donkey's hoof is not made of stone."

"So, what is my diagnosis?" inquired Bran.

Reverend Hughes hesitated in answering so that he could take a few more puffs on his pipe. "You suffered a severe contusion of your left temporal lobe. You can blame an old bust of Scipio Africanus for that. Fortunately for your brain, ol' Scipio fared worse when he met your head than he did when he met the army of the Carthaginians. The fact that you are speaking clearly is a sign that you are well on your way to a healthy recovery. However, an unfortunate side effect of your injury is that I do not expect you will ever walk again."

Bran's eyes bulged out. "What! Are you serious?"

The priest laughed, "No, I am just teasing you. I expect you to make a full recovery. You already did the hard part. I am referring to the waking up and talking part, that is."

Bran rolled his eyes only to discover that hurt too. He was desperately trying to get a bead on the funny little man that seemed to relish the role of both healer and tormenter.

"So, you are my priest?" asked the younger man.

"Well, that depends on you, I suppose."

"What do you mean?"

"By that I mean what church do you claim allegiance to, my lord? That is, unless you are a pagan, which I imagine is a possibility being that you came from America. Now by the off chance you are a papist, well . . . then there is not much I can do for you." He delivered the last line with an impish grin.

"I am an Anglican, I suppose," said Bran. "My father was an Anglican but my mother was a Puritan. I was sort of trapped in the middle."

Reverend Hughes acquired a doleful look. "You have my sympathies. I know plenty of both—not to mention a few

Methodists—and in the middle would be the worst place to be."

"Are you always this cheeky?" Bran gave the man a rueful grin.

"Absolutely. Have you met many members of the clergy? They tend to be a depressing lot. I refuse to join the crowd."

Bran's mind was awash with questions. "Reverend, I do not know if you are the right person to ask, but do you have any idea what happened last night?"

"Well, my lord, I do not have all the information, but I probably know enough to satiate your curiosity for the moment. I spoke with her ladyship, and it sounds like the two of you interrupted some burglars."

"Lady Cristyn mentioned a series of recent robbery attempts. I guess these were very particular thieves," said Bran. "It did not seem like they were finding what they sought."

"Very strange indeed. I had forgotten about those other two incidents. She also says you acquitted yourself quite well. With four intruders, your hands were more than full. Had it not been for the sudden arrival of this Roger Stanton chap, we might have been carrying you out in a box."

"Roger who?" asked Bran, "I am not sure who you are talking about."

"Oh, I apologize. He is a Yorkshireman who showed up at the last possible moment to rescue your hide. Giant gorilla of a man, and not really known in these parts. Apparently, he had followed the four hooligans from the local pub after he overheard some of their conversation and deduced they were up to no good. Fortunate for you he did. But that is all I know. Her ladyship spoke with him, not me."

As if summoned by invisible force, there was at that moment a light tap upon the door. Bran let out a weak, "Come in."

The door opened and Cristyn slid into the room. The pensive look of concern clouding her face immediately evaporated when she saw Bran sitting up in bed.

She gave him a weak smile, "My lord, it is so good to see you awake. All of us were quite worried about you. I brought you some water in case you find yourself thirsty." She set a glass and a small pewter pitcher on a table next to the bed.

"Do not worry, I have a feeling when it is my time to go it will be by a means much less exciting than fighting a gang of thieves. I will probably stumble over a cliff or something." He attempted to laugh at his own humor, but Cristyn did not join in, so he let it go.

"And how are you, my lady?" inquired Bran. "You were in the thick of it too."

"Oh, I am well, my lord, though I am sorry I broke your credenza. It really was a nice piece of furniture."

Bran stared at her incredulously, at a momentary loss for words. "And you, you are sure you are alright? You did not hit your head or anything?"

"Yes, my lord, I am perfectly fine."

"And how about this Yorkshireman Reverend Hughes was just telling me about; how is he?"

"He is doing well," answered Cristyn. "I made it back to your library with both the footmen right as the last thief exited through the window. Apparently Mr. Stanton did a lot to curb their enthusiasm. By the way, Mr. Stanton said he needed work. I had never met him before last night, but I offered him some temporary employment, nonetheless. It seemed like it was the least we could do. I hope I did not act out of turn."

"No, not at all," stammered Bran. "What did you offer him, if I may ask?"

"I asked him what type of work he preferred. He said he was good with horses, and since we are short a groom, I suggested he give us a hand down at the stables."

Bran smiled, "Sounds like Providence if you ask me."

13

Quiberon Bay

Cristyn left the room and Bran reached for the water. He could not remember the last time he had drunk something. No wonder he had a headache. Finishing the glass, he turned his attention back to Reverend Hughes. The old priest was tranquilly puffing away on his pipe.

"So tell me, reverend, how does one end up becoming both a physician and a priest?"

Reverend Hughes took a particularly long draw on his pipe before answering. "I would like to say it is a thrilling story best suited for a warm fire and a bottle of Balblair, but that would be a bit of a stretch. And since we only seem to have the fire, I am happy to regale you with the short version if you are up to it."

"I do not appear to be going anywhere," agreed Bran jovially. "I have the feeling if I get up just yet, that young lady out there will have this Stanton chap lash me to the bed. Therefore, my time is yours; that is if you have the time?" It occurred to Bran that a man who does double duty as both a physician and a priest might have other things to do than sit around and entertain an invalid.

"I am all yours," replied the priest. "Besides, I have an overly eager young curate who knows where to find me should my services be needed."

Bran slid a few pillows behind his back for additional support, and the priest began his tale.

"Hmm, where to begin? I suppose the beginning is as good a place as any. I was my parents' only child, and my mother died when I was just an infant. My father did his best to raise me, but he also had the responsibilities of a thriving medical practice in Plymouth to occupy his time. My father was very well known, and some of his patients would journey from as far as Portsmouth to consult with him. That is by no means an insignificant trip, especially if you consider it was over fifty years ago. Well, my early years saw me under the care of my nurse, but as I grew older I began to spend more and more time at my father's side. I do not think we realize how much children are capable of learning through osmosis, and this was definitely the case in my circumstance. As the months passed, my days were equally divided between helping my father and pursuing my studies. One thing worth noting is that my experiences with my father not only taught me a lot about medicine but also a lot about people. Physical trials tend to peel the outer veneer off of most people. For some it brings out the best, and for others the worst. However, it was not until years later that I fully appreciated what that season taught me."

The priest paused for a moment to allow Bran to pour another cup of water. Once he could tell Bran was ready he continued his tale. "Finally, when I made it to the appropriate age, my father sent me off to formally learn the medicinal arts for myself. In fact, I do not think it ever even occurred to him that I might want to study anything other than medicine. But alas, it did not matter, and before I knew it I was off to the University of Glasgow. There I spent five years learning medicine. Glasgow had a superb school of medicine, but it also might as well have been a foreign land. You see, this was the very first time I was away from home, and a lot of growing up occurred. Like most men who have the opportunity to attend university, I am extremely proud of some experiences, and equally ashamed of others. Without going into too much detail, let us just say I was a very different person by the time I returned home. But despite both ups and downs, I emerged ready to enter into my profession.

"Upon my return, I expected to immediately join my father in his practice, but instead he acquired the notion that it would be good for me to see a little of the world before settling down. If he had known the far-reaching consequences of that decision, undoubtedly he would have chosen differently.

"One of my father's friends, a Captain Robert Duff, agreed to take me on as his ship's surgeon. In retrospect, it was extremely bizarre that I would go straight from university to crew member on a ship of war, but I honored my father's wishes with little to no objection. Like all young men, I had romantic notions of adventure and faraway lands.

"The ship was a fifty-gun forth rate called the HMS Rochester. We were assigned to a British fleet off the west coast of France. Among other things, our job was to blockade a French fleet out of Brest. Apparently, the Admiralty was concerned this particular fleet might have designs on Scotland. Initially, the experience was nothing like what I had envisioned. Blockade duty is long, boring work. Day after day, foul weather or good, we sailed the coast looking for all sorts of French interlopers. To make matters even less interesting for me, once a ship has been at sea for some time all illness tends to disappear. After all, a ship is a closed system. This is a horrible thing when people are sick, but great when they are healthy. Unfortunately, for an active young ship's surgeon with his heart set on high adventure, it was a tedious existence. I tried to satisfy myself with the occasional broken finger or sprained ankle. Every day was much like the previous, that is until our ship and its small squadron of frigates and forth rates spotted the French at Quiberon Bay—have you heard of the Battle of Quiberon Bay, my lord?"

Bran nodded in ascent. "Yes, the battle that broke the back of the French fleet during the Seven Years War, was it not?"

A look of satisfaction spread across the elderly priest's face, "Quite right. The fleet fared well that day, but it forever changed me." Reverend Hughes's eyes drifted, as if lost in thought. "I remember standing over this one particular man. I am not even sure what he did on the ship; maybe he was a gunner's mate. Regardless, he was speared by a splinter and there was blood everywhere. We are not talking about a splinter you might find in your finger. Picture wagon wheel spokes, tent stakes, and pieces of firewood, each one pointed or serrated. Now send them in all directions like some horrible wooden shrapnel. In a naval battle splinters are the true man killers.

"So anyway, this sailor kept looking at me to do something, but I knew if I pulled the massive oak splinter out, he would only bleed out and die faster. So instead I stood there like a helpless babe holding the man's sticky hand amidst the coalescing pools of blood, wondering where he would go when his final breath left him. But the worst part was his eyes. The man was covered in blood head to toe, but his eyes were milky white, and both were brimming over with fear. Not only did it occur to me that I had no idea where this man's soul was going when he expired, but it was also obvious that the man did not know either. Before the day ended, and even before all the blood was washed from the decks, I knew medicine was not the ultimate career for me. It took some effort to convince my father, but eventually I decided to help heal souls rather than bodies. I have now worn the collar for over thirty years."

Silence filled the room and the priest took another thoughtful draw on his pipe. Bran open his mouth to speak but his train of thought was shattered by the mental image of the ruined bodies he himself had witnessed on the battlefield.

Reverend Hughes finally spoke again. "How I ended up in Wales is a story for another day. Most of my time here has been solely in the capacity of priest, but I practice my former arts when called upon; and while I would not classify myself as the best physician in Britain, it has given me one more way I can minister to the people. When our Lord walked this earth He always met people's physical needs before He met their spiritual needs. Never forget that."

Bran sat in silence, reflecting.

"Also remember my young friend, just because the Lord calls you to something new does not mean you leave behind the person you were before. The natural tendency is to view our lives as collections of unique events that only occasionally have bearing upon each other. I prefer to view our lives as complex tapestries. Thousands of threads mix, twist, and diverge. Up close they often look haphazard or random, but take a step back and the true beauty of the creator's handiwork is revealed. The person we become is a summation of all that came before. Often it is the trials of yesterday's man that provides the strength and tools for tomorrow's man to thrive and endure."

Bran lay pensively, considering the priest's words.

"And on that note, it is time you got some more rest. I will be back this evening to check on your progress." With that, the old priest rose from his chair, gathered his worn volume, and departed.

14

A Much Missed Friend

Bran eased Sage into a gentle walk as they turned onto the carriage drive. His ears enjoyed the soothing "clip clop" of the horse's iron-shod feet as they struck the packed gravel. A thin vapor of steam encircled the horse's hot body. A minute later he could see the burly form of Roger Stanton walking out to meet him. The large groom deftly snapped a lead onto the bridle and gently, but firmly, took control of the horse. Bran slid out of the saddle with an easy grunt.

"Thank you, Stanton. It is good to see you. I apologize I have not had the chance to duck my head in before now, but this is really my first day out of bed. I think Reverend Hughes and her ladyship would have kept me cooped up for another ten days had it been their choice, but a man can only lie in bed for so long. Also, I wanted to thank you for saving my skin last week. I was in a bit over my head. Your timing was fortunate."

"That is kind of you, my lord, but I am sure you would have done the same. In fact, from what I hear, you have done the same."

"That is very magnanimous of you, but either way, I am truly grateful." With that, Bran turned to begin walking back to the house.

"My lord, if you have a moment, I have someone in the stables who would like to see you for a few minutes."

Intrigued by the mystery, Bran followed Stanton and the horse back to the main structure. As they entered Bran inhaled the strong scents of hay, feed, and horses. It took him back to his time in the stables at Fort Pitt. Once inside, they momentarily paused as the groom put the white mare back in her box.

"Do not worry girl, I will take care of you in a moment, but first I have something I need to show his lordship." The horse let out a slow whinny, as if she understood exactly what was just said to her.

"Right over here, my lord, in the last box." A half step behind the large man, Bran peered into the wooden cubicle. Devoid of windows, it took his eyes a few seconds to adjust to the low light. But a moment later he knew exactly what he was looking at.

"Jackie!" The shout escaped Bran's lips before he knew what he was doing, but he did not care. Instantly recognizing the voice of her long absent master, the horse came sauntering over to the gate. Before she was even halfway across the stall, Bran was inside with his arms clasped around the horse's neck and his face buried in her mane. The horse gently shook her head up and down as if to say she was every bit as happy to see him. Bran could feel tears trying to escape the corners of his eyes. He gave them a quick wipe with his sleeve.

Stanton leaned his bulky form against the gate and rested his chin on his folded arms. He grinned as he watched the long overdue reunion between man and beast. Then realizing he was forgetting something, he cried, "My lord, catch." With a quick flip, he pitched an apple in Bran's direction. Reflexively, Bran snagged the piece of fruit and held it up to the horse's mouth. With a single great chomp, she retrieved the proffered gift.

"I gave her some hay and oats when she arrived, my lord, but I thought I would leave the treats for you. There are a few more tasty morsels in the sack outside her door." Jackie was now licking Bran's hand as if to retrieve any lingering juices she might have left behind.

"Your lordship did not tell us she was coming," remarked the groom. "Did you know?"

"That I did," replied a smiling Bran, "but I had no idea it would be this soon. I figured it would be another six months at least."

"Why did she not travel with your lordship when you made the crossing over the Atlantic?"

"When I finally settled on leaving America, there were only so many ships to choose from. The earliest ships available only had room for me. It was a choice between delaying my departure significantly, or sending the horse along afterwards. I was a little worried about the possibility of losing her to thieves or some other misfortune, but then one of my father's merchant friends said he would be happy to put her on one of his ships as soon as space came available. He even said he would personally ensure the horse made it to the estate. Apparently my father had done him a good turn at some point, and he wanted to find a way to repay the favor."

Bran took a moment to run his hand through the horse's mane. "When did she arrive?"

"Just a little while ago," answered the groom. "A man from Cardiff brought her up. It looked like he rode her here and led his own horse behind. That way he had a relatively fresh horse for the journey home. He did not stay long. Rogers offered to pay the man, but apparently things were already arranged. I took the liberty of looking her over. She seems to be in good shape and none the worse for the journey."

Bran was half listening to what the groom had to say. He was slowly circling the horse, making his own detailed examination of his friend. After about five minutes he reached the same conclusion as Stanton; she was in good shape.

"My lord," continued Stanton, "please do not think me impertinent, but how did you end up naming her Jackie? I can see something like Nightshade or Shadow—"

Bran let out a laugh, "—but Jackie sounds like one's maiden aunt?" He chuckled again. "Well, I know you are hoping for something exciting, or possibly sordid, like the name of a long-lost lover."

The groom put forth a schoolboy's grin.

"So, I am sure you will be sorely disappointed to hear the truth. When I was about seven years old, my mother had a cousin who owned a farm nearby. We lived in the city, but we used to go visit frequently. On the farm was an old, worn out donkey named Jackie, and when I say worn out, I mean worn out. The thing had not done any work for about five years. It was only out of sentimentality that my mother's cousin kept the old beast alive. He told me it was the first animal he bought when he obtained the farm."

Bran absentmindedly stared at a swallow's nest high above the far corner of the box for a moment. It was as if the birds helped to crystallize the long dormant memory. "Well, I loved that old donkey. To a somewhat undersized seven-year-old, she was the least intimidating animal in the whole stable. She was also as docile a creature as you could imagine. I used to sit on her back as she carried me in circles around the yard. No saddle, no bridle, just an old blanket. It was as if the old girl knew she was doing one last thing of value in her life, and she was going to do it well. I swore then that if I ever got the chance to name my own horse, it would be Jackie."

It was Stanton's turn to laugh, "You are telling me that beautiful mare is named after an old donkey?" Then in a feigned hush he asked, "Does she know, my lord?" Thoroughly unable to contain his mirth over his own joke, Stanton laughed hard.

A sheepish smile blanketed Bran's face. "That is about it. When I became a surveyor, I used a few horses that belonged to my father. However, when my wife and I were married, she gave me Jackie as a wedding present. That is, I named her Jackie after she was given to me." Bran's face softened, "Whenever I look at Jackie, I remember the day Rachael gave her to me."

In respect to Bran's obvious sentimentality, Stanton stemmed his laughter. He fetched a little more hay and tossed it in the feeder. Meanwhile, Bran retrieved a handful of oats and gave them to the horse. "She is really just a baby, only four years old. I have not used her for anything particularly arduous up to this point. Mainly casual rides or medium length trips."

"What is her breed, my lord? She is obviously a prime bit of blood, but she looks a little different from most of the horses I have come across. She seems a little more compact than your typical English thoroughbred."

Bran smiled as he gave the horse another gentle pat on the shoulder. "That is because she is an American Quarter Horse. It is a breed developed in America."

"Why a Quarter Horse? She looks like a full horse to me." Stanton again guffawed at his own joke.

Bran grimaced but smiled nonetheless. "It is because they

are bred to be sprinters. They excel at the quarter mile road races popular in the northern states. Hence, the name Quarter Horse. They are also exceptionally agile. It is not uncommon for a farmer to use his horse as a laborer on weekdays but then race it on the weekend."

"Does she have some English Thoroughbred blood in her?" asked Stanton.

"She does," continued Bran. "The Quarter Horse is a combination of a few breeds. In addition to English Thoroughbred stock, they also have Indian pony blood in them. And when I say Indian, I am referring to American Indians. When the Spanish settled Florida, they brought with them what came to be known as the Florida Cracker horse. It is a smaller gaited breed known for speed and agility. Over time, various Indian groups started using the horse. They were some of the ancestors of the Quarter Horse."

"I heard of Florida" said Stanton, "but cracker?"

Bran did not hesitate, "It is because they would only eat crackers."

Stanton raised his left eyebrow as a disbelieving look spread across his face, "Really?"

It was Bran who had a laugh this time at the other man's expense. "No, they are named after the men who used to ride them. Cattle drivers in Florida used whips to drive the beasts. Whip cracker was changed to cracker, but I would refrain from calling your average person in America a cracker. It is also a derogatory form of address."

"So, is this horse fast?" asked Stanton.

"You are exceptionally fast, are you not, girl?" Bran scratched the horse's muzzle. Turning his head to Stanton he said, "Jackie's actually faster than most Quarter Horses. Her sire was a champion road racer in Virginia, and her dam was renowned in her own right. She can be a little impetuous due to her youth, but you are going to have a hard time finding a faster horse over short distances in all of Britain."

"Are you going to race her, my lord?"

Bran laughed. "No, racing probably would not be a good idea. I am sure she would do fine, but she would be unequally yoked to me." Bran held up both arms as if to emphasize he did not have the prototypical jockey physique. "If anything, she will be mostly for joy riding. I would take up fox hunting, except I always felt sorry for the poor fox. But, we have talked about ol' Jackie long enough. What about you, Stanton? Tell me a little about yourself."

"I do not know if there is much to tell."

Bran threw him a disarming smile, "Oh, come now. Everyone has a story. How about where you grew up? Who are your parents? What are your interests?"

A disconcerted look momentarily flashed across Stanton's face. Bran pretended not to notice. "Hmm, well, I grew up in a poor family in Yorkshire. It was just me and my brother. Money was always pretty tight. At an early age, I discovered an affection for horses. I suppose I liked them because they were strong and talked less than people. Eventually I found my way into the army."

"And where did you serve?" asked Bran.

"Mostly India," replied Stanton morosely.

"Did you like it there?"

"Hell no! From the day I landed I could not wait to leave. I could not stand the locals and it was so bloody hot. A big fella like me never does well in the heat. Every night I would fall asleep thinking of the chill wind whipping across the Dales. As soon as my enlistment was up, I was out of there. I thought about heading home, but my brother used to work 'round here, and he once told me there was lots of horse work to be had in these parts. I guess he was right."

Bran abstained from asking further questions. It was pretty obvious horses were the only thing Stanton really cared to talk about. "Well Stanton, I appreciate you keeping an eye on Jackie for me. I am also happy to know I have such an experienced horseman helping out at the estate. Do you think you will be able to stay a while?"

"I am not sure, my lord. It will depend on a few things. But in the meantime, rest assured your horses will be better cared for than you."

"I have no doubt," and with a jovial slap on the man's broad back Bran departed.

15

Bad Blood

The carriage gently rocked as it slowly found its way over the worn country road. The last vestiges of the sun retreated over the horizon, and the sky was aswirl with amber and opal hues. But as the light faded, so did the colors. For Bran, the state of his nerves was reflected in the darkening landscape. He was not quite sure why his insides felt suddenly blanketed in darkness, but for the first time since his conversation with Cristyn over breakfast almost three weeks earlier, he wondered if he had erred in his decision to come tonight. At the time it had seemed like the respectable, if not obvious, thing to do. Now the fingers of doubt plucked away at the back of his mind.

Bran stole a glance at Cristyn. If he somehow thought she was going to aid him in the fortification of his own resolve, he realized he was gravely mistaken. She sat staring out the side of the carriage, and her countenance carried a decidedly wan pallor. The knuckles in her hand shown white as they gripped the side of the carriage.

Mrs. Clarke, on the other hand, sat serenely with her eyes closed. Whenever the carriage found a small rut in the road, the older woman's head would gently loll from side to side. Bran was unable to tell if she was awake or asleep, but he guessed the latter.

In a soft voice laced with misgiving, Bran addressed Cristyn. "My lady, I am sorry. I can see now I should not have asked you to come. I cannot imagine how difficult this must be for you—that is—returning to the home of your childhood only to see it under the ownership of someone else."

She glanced up and gave him a weak smile. While not her normal gay self, he could tell his apology had the effect of injecting some life into her veins.

"I am probably the one who should be apologizing to you, my lord. You remind me so much of your uncle that I sometimes do you the disservice of forgetting you were dropped into the middle of a story belonging to others."

"That is alright, but it is our story now. We will find a way to forge ahead one way or another." The words came out of his mouth in a tinny, unconvincing manner; he suspected they were probably more to reassure himself than the young lady sitting across from him.

Cristyn gently shook her head. "No, I am doing you a disservice. I think in my desire to close off my own heart from the events of my past, I have not been as forthright with you as I should have been. Please understand, it has not been out of the desire to keep you from anything, but rather a lack of desire to speak of such things. My way of dealing with difficult circumstances has always been to build walls."

"That is only normal," Bran reassured.

"Perhaps it is normal, but it does so at your expense, my lord. When Theseus was dropped into the den of the Minotaur, he knew what he was about to face. I owe you the same. We have a few minutes before we arrive at our destination, so I think I need to do my best to unwind the proverbial ball of string as you prepare to navigate the enemy's labyrinth, and I should give you a little historical context regarding my cousin."

Since Bran did not interrupt she continued. "I have known my cousin for my entire life. Caradoc, that is his given name, was the only son of my father's younger brother. Though when I say younger, I am only talking by about sixteen months. Because he was born to his parents early on, and I was born to my parents later in life, a good eleven years separated us in age. If you asked me to describe Caradoc as a child, I would have described him as cruel. That is not to say he was the type who tormented mice or pulled the antennae off lacewings. No, he much preferred the suffering of other people. I have one especially vivid memory of walking out of church with him one Sunday. A farmer was giving one of his sons a particularly severe beating behind the building, and Caradoc just stood there licking a candy-stick and watching. What stuck with me more than anything was the pleasure I saw in his eyes. It seemed as if watching the boy's suffering was some sort of a treat for him."

Bran let out a quiet snort. Thinking he meant to interject a comment, Cristyn paused. After a moment, he realized she was waiting on him. "I am sorry, please continue."

"When Caradoc was seventeen his father died. His mother had passed away when he was still a baby, but upon his father's death, my own father became his guardian. However, he soon left to attend university, so little changed in our home. After he went away to Cambridge I began to overhear things. Caradoc apparently was in the habit of playing pranks on the other boys at school. I am not talking about balancing a bucket of cold water on top of a door. I am talking about publicly humiliating actions. Things that might even drive a man, or boy, to suicide. There was one event that nearly had him sent down. Father intervened to prevent the expulsion, but oh, do I remember the row they had afterwards! It was not until years later that I heard what precisely had happened from the sister of one of the boys who had also been at the school. I would be too embarrassed to repeat to you what I heard. I can just tell you I was shocked and horrified that a member of my family was involved in such a deed. I remember crying of shame afterwards. The strange thing is, I do not remember whose shame cut me the deepest: mine, my cousin's, or the boy he had abused."

Bran thought back to the bullies he had known growing up. He knew there were physical bullies and emotional bullies. As far as Bran was concerned, the latter were far worse. Not only did their innate sense to dominate others bring with it a unique degree of cruelty, but the mental and emotional damage was often much further reaching. He had known grown men who carried such wounds throughout the rest of their lives. Unlike physical scars that grew tougher over time, these types of injuries remained open, festering reminders of prior sins, often never fully healing, and occasionally even worsening over time.

Cristyn continued her tale. "By the time Caradoc finished at university my father knew something had to be done. The ridiculous thing is he ended up one of the top students at Cambridge. My father had a friend who was very senior at the East India Company. He arranged for Caradoc to take a job there. I am not exactly sure what put the idea into father's head. I think, in his mind, he justified it by making the argument that all my cousin needed was a little maturity, and what better way for him to gain this than by seeing the world? Though I am fairly confident that deep down, my father just wanted Caradoc out of his day to day life. The next several years were peaceful ones in our home. Father and I enjoyed many a happy day together. Then one day, my cousin returned completely unannounced. Not a single letter to proclaim his forthcoming return, and the strangest thing in the coming weeks was not his sudden reappearance, but the change to his aspect. As far as outward appearances were concerned the journey seemed to have achieved its objective. He seemed a very different person, for the better that is. But as time began to pass, both my father and I saw the truth. The cruelty that so marked my cousin had simply worked its way beneath the surface. To those around us he was all beguiling charm. However, my father and I could both sense that it was still there."

Bran was now listening intently, chin resting on his steepled fingers. Every once in a while he would give a slight nod as if to indicate he was following completely. He was becoming more troubled by the moment.

The timbre of Cristyn's voice began to rise slightly as she continued. "I could especially tell the change—which I would argue was for the worse—was starting to take a toll on my father. I am not sure if he perhaps had a greater awareness of things occurring in the shadows, or if he felt partially responsible for the person Caradoc had become. Now do not misunderstand me, my father was a wonderful man, and I in no way ascribe my cousin's deviant nature to any failure of my father's. I simply think some people are destined for a dark path in life. That being said, my father began to slip into deeper and deeper levels of melancholy. This melancholy was marked by pity. At first I thought my cousin was the object of his inner sadness, feeling perhaps like he—my father—had somehow let the young man down. But as time passed I realized the sorrow was directed at everyone else. Everyone whose lives my cousin had somehow stained through his contact. This is probably why my father chose this time to make certain legal precautions. Under the conditions of his estate, upon the event of his death his title, money, and my guardianship would pass to Caradoc, his only surviving male heir. He could do little about the entailment, but it terrorized my father to think of me under the control of his nephew and his malignant influence. It was at this time that my father approached your uncle and beseeched him to become my guardian in the event of his death. Of course, aside from a sizable allowance left to me, there was no way for father to prevent everything else from passing to Caradoc. Your uncle willingly agreed, and I will forever be in his debt because of it.

"My cousin was not aware of the arrangement, nor did my father have a desire to inform him. Unfortunately, and coincidently, about a week after the arrangement was finalized, my cousin came to my father and requested my hand in marriage. He uncharacteristically assumed a posture of great emotion, confessing his undying devotion to me. Father told me about the incident later on, and had he not known Caradoc's true nature, he might have felt inclined to be persuaded by the declaration. But knowing the serpent he was dealing with, father refused.

"Now bear in mind, despite his great misgivings regarding his nephew, my father had managed to maintain a relatively positive relationship with Caradoc, at least to the extent that Caradoc was concerned. I think my father still hoped to be a force for change in the man's life if he was part of his inner circle, as opposed to on the outside. But when father refused to give his consent to our marriage, it was as if a wall was instantly erected. Any obliging attitude towards my father was replaced by an attitude of pure animus. I cannot recall father and Caradoc ever speaking again after that night.

"Not long thereafter, my father became ill. It was a strange illness, and even the specialists in London were never able to put their hand on the cause. It probably could be best described as a wasting disease that resulted in rapid physical deterioration. My cousin was never linked to his death, but I always suspected he somehow had a role, if not directly, then indirectly through his debased influence."

Cristyn took a moment to remove a fine silk handkerchief from her bag and blow her nose. "Forgive me. Aside from your uncle, this is the only time I have spoken of these matters aloud. The whole thing is so ghastly, but when spoken aloud it seems to be magnified and more real. At least when it is just in my thoughts I can dismiss it like it is some sort of horrible dream."

Bran did not respond. He was reflecting on all he had just heard. The whole situation was much deeper and darker than he would have ever surmised. He was used to fighting named evils on the open battlefield, but this appeared to be something different altogether.

16

Lord Gyr

No additional words were exchanged over the few remaining miles of their journey. Bran's attention was pulled from his own reflections when he saw the illumination of the approaching lanterns leading up to the main house. Bran's estate was not insignificant, but it paled in comparison to what lay before him. Unlike the ancient earthworks, stone walls, and well-worn timbers of Caer Cigfran, this estate was of a newer age. The large Queen Anne style house boasted symmetrical wings coming off each side of the house. Even in the glow of the moonlight, Bran could see rambling gardens that stretched out behind the main structure.

Noticing Bran's examination of the surroundings, Cristyn commented, "My great-grandfather built Foxglove about a hundred years ago. It is much more like a house you would find in England as opposed to Wales. My great-grandfather was vain and preoccupied with his social status. He felt it necessary to show the crowd in London he was one of them."

Mrs. Clarke spoke for the first time. "The English seem to think they have the market cornered when it comes to subtlety. I would beg to differ. No offense, dear, but you would never find a house like this in Ireland. We Irish are too practical."

"And too poor," muttered Cristyn under her breath so only Bran could hear.

The carriage halted with a gentle lurch. Bran exited first and helped Cristyn to the ground, with Mrs. Clarke following behind. Cristyn wore a long-sleeved, white dress that bordered on cream. The sleeves carried a slight ruffle, and down the middle of the dress ran an ornate gold pattern of tambour embroidery. Bran noticed how the narrow sleeves helped accent her tall, slender form. Bran in turn wore a dark green tail coat over tan trousers. As he offered Cristyn his left arm he gazed up at the facade of the house. What should have been bright and inviting instead seemed looming and foreboding.

They ascended the steps and Bran could see the worried expression on Cristyn's face. In an effort to reassure her he whispered, "Just remember, as the poet reminds us, 'A little more than kin, and less than kind.'"

She smiled while keeping her eyes fixed on the door ahead. "How true, though I cannot help but think a more appropriate line might be, 'Once more into the breach, dear friends.'"

A moment later they were shown into the great hall. At a glance, Bran took in the entirety of the gathering. The company was an assorted collection of the local gentry, comprising more than twenty men and women. The surrounding country was quite rural, and he was surprised Lord Gyr was able to scrape together this many individuals of consequence to invite to his little soiree.

He recognized about half of the room immediately. All were people he had been introduced to at various times and places over the course of the preceding month.

There was Jeremiah Willingham, an exceptionally short, red-faced man. Bran had shared one brief conversation with the man a few weeks prior; it had been a conversation just long enough for Bran to learn three things about Mr. Willingham. First, he owned a small estate about three miles from Caer Cigfran. Second, the man loved to laugh, often for no reason. Third, the man loved his port wine. Bran suspected two and three were probably somewhat related.

Also present was Colonel Edwards, a retired British Army officer. He and Bran had come upon each other while riding one afternoon and had shared a rather lengthy conversation while on horseback. The colonel knew Bran's father by reputation, having served with some of the same officers in the British Army over the course of their careers. The colonel was especially interested in Bran's experiences both as a surveyor and as an Indian fighter. Bran intentionally skirted around portions of the discussion that related to the British support of the Indians.

Then there was Sir Thomas something. Bran could not recall the man's surname. He only knew the man by reputation. Apparently, he had made his money in mining and was given his title as a reward for services to the Crown. One hard look at Sir Thomas made Bran pretty sure those services were monetary in nature.

Rounding out the guests was Reverend Hughes and a handful of people Bran did not recognize.

Lastly, his eyes fell on his host who was receiving guests across the ball room, away from the entrance. From this distance Bran took in the man he had heard so much about just minutes prior.

If Bran were to create the caricature of a British peer, Lord Gyr would have fit the bill. The man had thick, dirty blond hair that contained just enough curl to be right at home with contemporary fashions. Thick, full sideburns swept down both sides of his face. He was impeccably dressed, but not in a way that he could be accused of trying too hard.

At the moment Lord Gyr was sharing a joke with Jeremiah Willingham's wife. As Bran and Cristyn entered the room they saw their host glance subtly in their direction.

Not one to flee from danger or neglect propriety, Bran gently steered the two women in the direction of their host.

"Lord Gruffudd, you will have to excuse me for a little while; I need to take a moment to visit the powder room," said Mrs. Clarke. A moment later the older woman was gone.

"She does not want to speak to our host," commented Cristyn. "She probably assumes that since you are with me she can hide in the shadows. If only I were to be so fortunate."

Lord Gyr quickly brought his conversation with Mrs. Willingham to a conclusion. Whatever the man's final words were to the woman, it had the effect of making the portly, middle-aged woman giggle like a school girl. She was still laughing when he gently put his hand on her back as if to shuffle her on her way.

Once clear of the substantial woman, Lord Gyr shifted his attention to the two newcomers. With what Bran deemed to be a forced enthusiasm, their host addressed Cristyn first. "Cousin, I am so glad you came. You look beautiful tonight."

"Thank you, my lord. It was kind of you to think of us." Cristyn's response was cordial but devoid of emotion.

Lord Gyr continued his overly effusive greeting. "I feel like it has been ages since I have last had the pleasure of your company, cousin. You really should come visit Foxglove more often. Surely you must miss it."

The intended barb struck home, and Cristyn said nothing more. Lord Gyr turned his attention to Bran. "And of course, you must be the new Yankee heir we have heard so much about. How fortunate for you to inherit your uncle's title and estate."

"Something like that," responded a nonplussed Bran.

"And I trust the transition from the frontier has not been too difficult? I find that most men do not enjoy change, even if it is for the better."

"Not at all," replied Bran. "It has really been a bit of a homecoming. I am sure it is very different from what your ancestors experienced when they first came to Wales. No angry, displaced locals to contend with." He gave the marquess a knowing wink. Both Bran and his host were fully aware that Lord Gyr's family descended from the Marcher Lords. This was the group of English lords appointed by King William I to create settlements in Wales and, in the process, pacify the Welsh barbarians. Bran could see the comment had the desired effect on Lord Gyr. The man still had a grin plastered across his face, but Bran could now see a hidden malice in his eyes.

Bran also stole a glance at Cristyn. He was hoping his jab had not offended her, since she came from the same family line as Lord Gyr. However, based on a subtle smirk, he could tell she had enjoyed his comment.

With the slightest edge in his voice, the marquess replied, "Well put. I am glad things are going well. You have inherited some lovely holdings. Of course, some of them are tamer than others." Lord Gyr lazily shifted his gaze to Cristyn, and then added, "but I am sure you will get the opportunity to take full advantage of them over time. In that I envy you."

This time it was Cristyn who flushed, some from embarrassment, but mostly from anger.

Conscious of the fact his repartee had unintentionally resulted in Cristyn's discomfort, Bran quickly turned the conversation to more pedestrian topics. A few moments later the conversation ended, and Bran and Cristyn made their way over to the rest of the company.

Bran muttered under his breath, "I am sorry about that. I did not realize things would deteriorate that quickly."

Cristyn responded in kind, "Remember what I told you in the carriage, my lord. His lordship feasts on the humiliation of others. He obviously perceives you as a threat, which in turn also makes you a potentially tasty morsel. He cares little where he treads."

"Hmm, well as we say in America, 'Don't tread on me.'"

An hour later the group was called to dinner, and to Bran's chagrin, he found himself seated between Mrs. Willingham and an elderly woman who was more interested in her various aches and pains than true conversation. In the end, it did not really matter since Mrs. Willingham was more than happy to supply ample conversation for all of them. Bran was not surprised to see Cristyn seated near their host. Mrs. Clarke, on the other hand, was at the far opposite end of the table.

Bran worked his way through the first few courses, content to listen to Mrs. Willingham go on about the grand remodel of her home. Apparently, this part of Wales was devoid of satisfactory draperies.

"I just do not think Mr. Willingham fully appreciates the difficult position he has put me in." Her voice was just loud enough to allow Mr. Willingham the privilege of listening in to the conversation, if he so desired.

Based on what Bran could observe of Mr. Willingham, the man seemed more absorbed with his abnormally large plate of roast lamb than he was concerned with listening to his wife talk about her décor problems.

The woman continued unperturbed, "I keep telling him that we cannot have draperies made of muslin. He also suggested wool, but gracious. There are enough sheep around here without hanging them on the wall. I told him we will need to go into London, but every time I mention it he complains about his health. And of course, a woman of my stature cannot travel to London on her own, especially on that dreadful stage coach."

Bran caught himself ruminating on the woman's intended use of the word stature. It was only then that he realized his host had asked him a question. Unsure of the nature of the inquiry, Bran bought a little time by dabbing some wine from his lips with his napkin. He then turned to address Lord Gyr.

"I am sorry, my lord. I did not catch your last question."

In the somewhat self-satisfied tone of a man holding court, Lord Gyr responded, "We were just discussing the recent decline of crime rates. Colonel Edwards had a former sergeant major who now works for Bow Street, and the colonel was discussing some of their methods. It is my understanding you might have an insider's perspective when it comes to the merits of British law enforcement. Is that true?"

Bran stiffened slightly, but based on the other guests' blank looks, he could assume they had no idea what their host was intimating. Bran answered Lord Gyr with an air of bored indifference. "My lord, my observations gave me the impression that the nation's police force, while moderately efficient in its methods, perhaps often lacks some of the intellectual sophistication necessary to be truly effective."

The colonel grunted his general agreement. This caused everyone else at the table to nod stupidly.

An attractive, blonde woman whom Bran had never met chose to change the topic. From the redness in her face it was obvious she had been enjoying Lord Gyr's merlot. "Lord Gruffudd, I heard that while you were in America you fought a war against the Indians. What was that like?"

Bran was not sure he liked the simpering tone of the woman's voice. "War is a horrible thing, ma'am. Those who think to romanticize it have never been touched by it."

His comments did little to dissuade his fellow dinner guest. "Oh, I know"—despite Bran being pretty sure she did not—"but what must it have been like to fight the *noble savage*? Was it romantic?"

His thoughts flitted back to the night when he was beaten unconscious by Maneto. He futilely attempted to recall the romantic moments, but he also knew this was not the time or place to delve into such things.

He changed tack. "My fellow Philadelphian, Mr. Benjamin Franklin, was once quoted as saying, 'Savages we call them, because their manners differ from ours, which we think the perfection of civility; they think the same of theirs.'" He paused momentarily to allow the audience to digest his words. "I have fought Indians who were merely defending their home or way of life. I have also fought Indians who killed children, raped women, and personified everything implied by the more common definition of the word savage. In truth, most of them are little different than you or me. I think perhaps the problem lies in how we define the term savage. A savage is nothing more than a person who relishes cruel deeds, takes pleasure in the pain of others, and behaves at odds with the most honorable tenants of society." Slowly turning his eyes towards his host, he concluded with, "Even the most civilized societies are replete with savages. The difference between us and more primitive cultures is that our savages are often more adept at clothing themselves in the habiliments of civilized men."

Bran's unknown admirer was not finished with him yet.

"But, Lord Gruffudd, you must have some stories you would like to tell. For example, were you ever . . . what is the word . . . scalped?"

Bran's eyes bulged slightly. He could hear the colonel responding to the comment by choking on a piece of food. Bran paused before replying. "Just the one time, ma'am."

The woman appeared delighted. "Were you really? It must have been a frightful experience for you. Tell us, what was it like?" There was a voyeuristic glee in the woman's eyes.

"Terrible ma'am, a wretched affair, blood everywhere," expounded Bran flatly.

The whole room grew extremely quiet.

"But, what happened?" implored the woman.

Bran had gone back to eating his meal. "Happened to what, ma'am?"

"To your hair, my lord."

Bran feigned confusion. "Why? Is there something wrong with it?"

"No, after the savage cut it off." The woman was slightly exasperated but expectant.

"Oh, that . . . it grew back."

It was Lord Gyr who interrupted the interrogation. "Well, was not that interesting? Lord Gruffudd, I think I speak for all when I say we are glad you are a man of great follicle resilience." He then quickly shifted the conversation elsewhere, much to the chagrin of Bran's admirer.

Over the remainder of the evening Cristyn was pleased to

see that both men chose to engage in an unspoken détente. Nor was she disappointed when her cousin chose to turn his attentions away from her. She knew it was an attempted affront, but she was too emotionally drained to care. Only once did she meet Bran's gaze. He was on the receiving end of another one of Mrs. Wallingham's passionate soliloquies, and he managed to shoot Cristyn a playful look that said *help!*

She managed to stifle a laugh as she instead giggled into her goblet.

Bran smiled back, mouthing the words, *hang in there.*

You too, was her silent reply.

Fortunately for both of them, it ended up being a short evening. Mrs. Clarke fell ill halfway through dessert, and Bran was all too willing to use the interruption as an excuse to depart.

Lord Gyr watched the last carriage roll away. As soon as it began to fade into darkness he stormed back into the house, throwing his suit coat at a footman. "Do something with this." The man nodded subserviently, and the marquess headed directly to his private study. Slamming the door shut behind him, he made his way straight to the whiskey decanter. He poured himself a couple of fingers, threw it back, and then filled it again. *What a bunch of fools,* he thought. He strode over to a large leather armchair in the corner of the room. On the way, he gave the bell pull a yank. He could hear the tinkle of the corresponding bell in a distant corridor. Lord Gyr languidly threw himself into the chair, yet managed not to spill a drop of whisky. He took another long pull at his drink, and a moment later he heard a sharp but controlled tap at the door.

"Come in!"

A butler with salt and pepper hair entered the room. Despite it being well after three in the morning, the man greeted his master with clear, precise diction. "You rang, my lord?"

"Yes, I need to talk to Simmons at once. Send one of the grooms to go find him."

The butler showed the faintest glimmer of emotion. "At this hour, my lord? I am not even sure where he would be."

Lord Gyr slowly responded as if he were speaking to a small child. "Yes, at this time. It is important. Besides, you know as well as I do he will be at one of the pubs. Also, I am going to be heading up to London in the morning. Please tell my man to get my things together. We will be staying at my club for a few days as I take care of a few matters."

The butler momentarily paused, unsure if any additional instructions where in the offing.

Lord Gyr waved his hand dismissively. "Now hurry up. I would like to get a little sleep tonight." The butler rapidly retreated from the room.

The marquess made his way to a large desk on the far side of the study. Taking a seat behind the desk, he proceeded to remove a goose feather quill from the stand. Dipping it in a nearby bottle of ink, he began composing a short letter. After a few minutes, he crumpled up his work and flung it into the fire. He then proceeded anew. Every few minutes he repeated the same ritual until his composition met his expectations. He barely had time to pour another drink when he heard a sharp tap on the door.

"Come!"

The door seemed to barely open as a small, wiry man slunk into the room. He sported a short but bushy beard, and his eyes constantly scanned to and fro. Lord Gyr always thought the man looked like some rodent emerging from his hole for the first time. Just as silently the door shut, and the newcomer spoke in a gravelly voice.

"You desired to speak to me, my lord?"

Lord Gyr would normally have given the man a sarcastic reply, but due to the late hour he restrained himself. Instead he got down to business. "Yes, I needed to talk to you. I have a job."

Simmons would have betrayed the smallest sign of a smile if it had not been for his beard covering most of his mouth. Even though Lord Gyr was a pain in the ass to work for, he always paid well.

The marquess continued, "This evening I happened to overhear that Lord Gruffudd will be journeying to London tomorrow on business. I want you to arrange with a few of your London associates for him to have an accident."

Worry crept into Simmons' eyes for the first time. This time the gravel left his voice and it took on a soft hiss. "My lord, killing a peer is a risky business." Then wondering if he should state the obvious he added, "People are likely to ask questions, especially considering his uncle died so recently."

Lord Gyr waved his hand dismissively. "You let me worry about that. Peers of the realm have unfortunate accidents every year. Not to mention London can be a dangerous place for the uninitiated. Besides, I have the details worked out." The marquess handed Simmons the letter he had been working on.

Simmons ponderously read through its contents and let out a quiet chuckle. "Excellent, my lord; I think this will work."

Annoyed that his subordinate would think it his place to comment on his idea, the marquess snapped, "Of course it will work. That is if you do not botch the job."

Simmons re-assumed his normal subservient manner, "I will do my best, my lord."

"That is all. Take care not to lose the letter. I have no interest in wasting my valuable time writing you another one. If you can pull this little job off like I hope you will, you can also expect a little extra something for you and your men."

This time Simmons conveyed a full smile. "Yes, my lord." Then as quietly as he had come, the man disappeared from the house.

17

The Bank

The hackney coach slid down the street with a smooth, rhythmical clack. Considering he and Bull had spent the past two days rumbling along in his carriage, the contrast could not have been starker. Bran scrunched his tall frame so he could gaze up and out of the mud-spattered window. Even in the fading light of day he could see the Old Lady of Threadneedle Street, more commonly known as the Bank of England. The sun's rays had long passed behind the imposing Portland stone edifice and its twelve columns. In twilight, everything bore a distinctly gray hue, and for the thousandth time Bran was reminded how far from home he really was.

It had been an uneventful trip to London. Bran was grateful for Bull. The valet took care of all the details, giving Bran the freedom to think and reflect. After checking into a hotel in Piccadilly, there was just enough time to clean up and change clothes before the two men caught a cab to meet with the estate's bankers. If all went well, Bran hoped to be heading home first thing in the morning. Normally, Bran would not have asked his valet to accompany him to such a meeting, but Bull knew London and Bran did not.

The hackney glided to a stop in front of an innocuous limestone building. The two men alighted, and Bran quickly paid the jarvie. A few minutes later they found themselves entering a large, second floor anteroom. The room sharply contrasted with the exterior of the building. It smelled like a library, and every wall was richly appointed in dark wood paneling that ran from floor to ceiling. Each section of wall held a single wall sconce and a pair of flickering candles. The three-dimensional nature of the moldings caused shadows to randomly flit around the room.

Bull whispered to his master, "My lord, does not this room remind you of a cathedral?"

Bran briefly reflected on the comment. "Yes, but a cathedral to an entirely different kind of god."

Upon entering the room, Bran took a moment to let his eyes adjust. Once fully aware of his surroundings, his gaze fell on an immaculately dressed man sitting behind a small desk at the far side of the room. Bull found a seat by the door, and Bran approached the secretary. The young man rose to his feet, but Bran beat him to the greeting, "Good evening, I am Lord Gruffudd, and I am here to see Mr. Savage."

"My lord, I am Thomas Ross, Mr. Savage's secretary." The man was deferential but matter-of-fact. "We were expecting you. If you are ready, please follow me."

The secretary led Bran through a set of large double doors. The room they entered was similar to the previous, except it was more personalized. A number of paintings hung on the walls. To one side was a casual sitting area made up of large leather chairs situated around a low-slung table. On the opposite side of the room was a large Chippendale desk. Behind the desk sat a pale man in a dark suit. He smiled at the newcomer as he entered. Bran noticed the smile was friendly, but not warm.

"Lord Gruffudd, so pleased to meet you in person. If you do not mind giving me one minute, I will pull the rest of the papers together. I should have been more prepared, but one of my meetings this afternoon went over. In the meantime, please feel free to make yourself comfortable. If you are thirsty, Ross would be more than happy to get you something." He gestured to a small bar in the corner.

"No need, I can manage," responded Bran.

After pouring himself a small glass of Scotch, Bran made his way to one of the arm chairs. He overheard the banker give his secretary a few instructions. "Please pull the second Gruffudd file. I thought I had it, but apparently not." The secretary briskly left the room and the banker made his way over to Bran. "My lord, I do apologize. I am usually more organized. Ever since that French rogue, Napoleon Bonaparte, took his army into Italy, it has sent the international markets into chaos. Every day I feel like I am fighting to simply keep up." The banker made his own way over to the bar.

With no knowledge whatsoever of international banking markets, Bran just responded, "I completely understand."

The banker had barely finished pouring his own drink when the secretary returned with the file. After handing it to his superior, he departed.

Mr. Savage continued, "But that is not why you are here. I greatly appreciate you making the trip. It is my understanding you passed through London about a month ago. Had I known, of course I would have sought you out and spared you the trip . . . but, well, you understand."

The two men sat down opposite each other. Setting his drink on the table the banker continued. "I was so sorry to hear about your uncle's death. He was a fine man. I knew him for many years. I am not sure you are aware, but our firm has carried the distinguished privilege of managing the majority of the Gruffudd family's finances for over one-hundred-fifty years."

The banker made this last statement as if he had been the one personally doing the managing for the past century and a half. Bran had a brief mental image of a baby stacking coins on a desk. The image brought a slight smile to his face, but Mr. Savage was too busy delivering his carefully rehearsed speech to notice.

"My lord, I hope you realize I would not have asked you to come all this way if it were not a matter of great importance." He paused as if to allow his weighty words the chance to sink it. "I am not quite sure where to start, so I will first give you the broad financial picture. Also, please forgive me if any of this is already known to you."

Bran crossed his legs and leaned back in his chair.

"As you are well aware, the Gruffudd ancestral holdings are some of the oldest in Wales, and in all of Britain for that matter. Despite lacking significant natural resources, your ancestors were astute men. Over the years they were able to multiply their fortune through a combination of frugal spending, timely investments, and shrewd marriages. In a period when many of the old families squandered away their fortunes, yours was an exception."

Bran smiled to himself as he thought back to his father's penny-pinching ways.

"To this day, if you were to ask me for the value of your estate, I would have a difficult time settling on an exact number. You may find that statement preposterous, but over the years your ancestors diversified their wealth across many investments. While I might know where all the money is at a given time, it is a completely different task to settle on its entire value. Some money is in real-estate, while significant funds are also tied up in a combination of home and foreign investments. The constantly fluctuating value of all these assets makes it hard to nail down a specific number. Additionally, I also know your uncle did a small amount of business with Thompson and Godley. They specialize in corporate investments."

Bran nodded his head, "I completely understand the challenges, but you must have an estimate of what I am worth. You are my bankers after all."

Mr. Savage portrayed the slightest hint of his feathers being ruffled by the statement. "Of course we are, my lord, but you must understand it is not quite that easy."

Bran was beginning to sense a darker undercurrent to the conversation. "Mr. Savage, I am not looking for an exact number so I can make a withdrawal later this evening. Please just give me your best estimate."

The banker clenched his jaw and Bran could tell the man was engaged in an internal struggle. Then without warning he said, "Your fortune—at least the part we managed— used to be about £180,000."

Bran was slightly caught off guard by the way the man blurted out the number, neither did he miss the qualifier, "used to be."

"Mr. Savage, please explain, 'Used to be about £180,000.' Am I right in assuming that is not the current value?"

In truth, Bran had had an inkling that something was amiss from the very moment he had read the banker's letter back at Caer Cigfran. He had hoped he was reading too much into things at the time. Unfortunately, the banker's fidgety behavior was doing little to assuage his concerns.

Mr. Savage retreated to the bar where he poured himself another drink. This time he did not even offer one to his client. He was obviously distracted, but Bran did not allow the diversion to distract him from his line of questioning.

"Mr. Savage, with all due respect, you are not being particularly helpful."

The banker sat back down in his chair. He threw back the rest of his drink and then turned to his client. Bran noticed the man nervously pawing the empty glass.

"My lord, first off I want you to believe me when I tell you it was not our fault. I am not intending any disrespect towards his previous lordship, but the idea was his alone. We did our best to talk him out of it, but he insisted. I am not sure if you knew your uncle well, but he could be a very persuasive man when he so desired."

Bran's face was turning a light shade of red. "Mr. Savage, I am usually a very patient man, but I am also a very direct man. There are few things I abhor more than beating around the bush, and so far you have managed to beat around an entire hedge."

"It is just this, my lord," the banker's voice had taken on the unmistakable beginning of desperation, "about two and a half years ago your uncle came to us requesting a VERY large sum of money. Of course we pushed back, partly because of the sum, and partly because of the difficulty we would have liquidating enough assets to get our hands on such an enormous amount of capital."

Bran's anger of a moment earlier was instantly replaced with a strange combination of dread mixed with curiosity. "How much money are we talking about?"

The banker inserted a clammy but well-manicured hand inside his coat pocket, from which he extracted a folded sheet of paper. He slid it across the table in front of him.

Bran hesitated for a moment, not quite sure if he wanted to read it. Finally, he reached for the paper. A moment later he gulped. "That is, a . . . well, a lot of money."

He looked up from the piece of paper to see the pained look on the banker's face. The man simply nodded.

"You have no idea what my uncle wanted the money for?"

The man shook his head.

"And I am assuming by your manner, we have never seen this money again."

The man again shook his head.

Bran leaned back in his chair and exhaled deeply. "So, if we have no idea where this money went, then I am assuming we have a bit of a problem?"

This time the banker nodded.

Bran steeled himself. "Well then, let us talk about this in practical terms. What does it mean for me and for the estate?"

Now that the bad news had been broken, the banker appeared to be slipping back into the role of composed financial custodian and advisor.

"My lord, there are a number of implications. The biggest is your ability to cover your estate's operating costs. The estate produces a moderate amount of income through its farms and a small amount of mining. However, these businesses on their own have never been adequate to cover all of your expenses. The estate has always been reliant on outside investments to bridge the gap. Your uncle was a man of moderate tastes, and to the best of my knowledge, was not prone to gamble. This means that over time the estate's capital gradually saw an increase. But now that we have been forced to sell off most of the outside assets, I expect the estate will begin to experience a shortfall within the next six months. The only way to cover this will be to sell off assets that belong to the estate itself."

Despite not being a businessman, Bran was listening intently. "What do you mean by, assets that belong to the estate itself?"

The banker was now fully back in his element. "I am referring to parts of the estate proper. Principally, this would include things like parcels of land, and your mines." The man paused to give Bran a moment to take it all in. He then continued. "Unfortunately, once you begin to sell off pieces of the estate, the whole situation enters a death spiral."

Bran could now see where the man was going.

"As you sell off more and more of the estate, your ability to cover your expenses becomes less and less, which means you have to sell off more and more."

"Did you explain all of this to my uncle before he took that massive withdrawal?"

Bran could tell it pained the man to again reopen that particular topic, but he did not really care.

"Yes, we did explain it to your uncle. He insisted that the use of the money was short term and bore little to no risk. He assured us he would have it back long before we had to touch the assets of the estate."

"And he gave you no hint of what it was actually going to be used for?"

"Unfortunately, no. I actually pressed him a number of times on the issue. He finally became angry and said it was a personal matter and that it was his money to do with as he damn well pleased. Your uncle was generally a stoic man, but when his temper became roused, let us just say there were few men who would want to cross him."

Bran nodded his understanding. "Going back to my previous question, what does this mean going forward?"

The banker paused for a moment, as if measuring his next words. "You are in a bit of a tough spot, my lord. As near as I can tell, you have two options. The first is to do what I have pretty much already laid out. Little by little you sell off pieces of the estate until nothing is left."

"And the second option?"

"You go ahead and sell the estate now." Sensing the younger man was getting ready to speak, the banker charged ahead so he could finish his thought. "I know what you are thinking. This estate has been in your family for half a millennium."

Bran did not like his use of that particular word image. It somewhat made the situation sound even worse, though it really could not get much worse at this point.

The banker continued upon his line of thought. "The estate has much more value if it is intact. Were you to sell it today you could get a pretty handsome price. It would not be hard to find some wealthy, aspiring merchant who is seeking to raise himself in the eyes of his betters. Caer Cigfran is known well beyond Wales. It would give you plenty of money to still live comfortably. My recommendation at that point would be for you to buy a nice town house here in London where you could live in a way that would probably be more than equal to your tastes."

Bran was thinking the whole matter over, even as the banker was still finishing his explanation. Bran knew he would sooner die than live a life of gentleman's clubs and dinner parties. The thought of selling his ancestral home also made him want to vomit. He could sense generations of Gruffudds rolling over in their graves even as he pondered the thought. Bran finally decided he had had enough of this discussion. He quickly rose to his feet. "Mr. Savage, I appreciate your time. While this has been a disturbing conversation it has also been enlightening. I am at least happy that I know what I am dealing with. You may expect to hear back from me soon with a plan of action."

The banker stood too, slightly taken aback by the abrupt way the meeting was ending. "Uh, yes my lord." Then somewhat gathering himself he added, "My only advice is to not linger too long over the decision. If you are in fact interested in selling, it is in your best interest to do so sooner as opposed to later."

Bran wanted to say he would be damned if he would ever sell the home of his fathers, but he also knew it was not the time or place for such a comment. Instead he exchanged a few final polite remarks with the banker, and then made a hasty retreat.

18

Countess

Bran exited the banker's office, his thoughts still swirling with everything he had learned during the meeting. He said goodnight to the secretary and walked over to Bull. The burly valet sat ensconced in a massive leather armchair, a small pair of reading glasses perched on the end of his nose. Bran thought it looked like Bull had stolen the eyeglasses off of a small child.

"Bull, from the look of this chair, I would say you are the first person to ever sit in it. There is barely a crease or crack in the leather."

Bull jumped like there was a wasp in his shirt. The valet hastily shoved the book he had been reading into his pocket, but he was less successful with the glasses. The small, wire-rimmed device clattered onto the floor. Bull's face registered embarrassment, as if he had been caught stealing sweets.

Bran leaned over and recovered the eyewear before handing them back to the valet. "I like the glasses, Bull; they give you a scholarly appearance. You could pass off as one of my tutors back at the college. I did not realize you were a reader."

Bull responded somewhat sheepishly. "I do not know if you

would describe me as a reader, my lord, but I manage to get by. I've only known my letters for a few years now. The old duke had a secretary who was quite a learned man. He had been a teacher or a private tutor at some point. He used to give me reading lessons when time allowed."

"What are you reading?"

"Milton, my lord."

Bran's eyebrows went up. "*Paradise Lost*? That was my mother's favorite."

"Yes, my lord."

"'The mind is its own place, and in itself can make a heaven of hell, a hell of heaven.'"

"Say again, my lord?"

"Oh, nothing. Just a line from your book."

"What does it mean?" asked Bull.

"Just that the same way the devil found he could not think his way out of his problems, I do not think I will be able to either."

A trace of concern crept into Bull's eyes. "Not a good meeting, my lord?" When Bran did not answer immediately Bull probed further. "You forget, I have been a gentleman's gentleman for many years. Seldom would a trip to one of these banks put my gentleman in a good mood."

"No, you are spot on, Bull. It is not good news, but neither can we let our circumstances rule us." With effort, he forced himself to smile. "And since there is also nothing I can do about it, we must, how do the English put it . . . keep a stiff upper lip. Besides, I am famished. What do you say we hail a cab and see if we can find something to eat?"

Bull started.

"Bull, are you alright?"

"Yes, my lord, but I almost forgot. While you were in your meeting, a messenger brought you a letter. I received it on your behalf. But do not worry, it has not been opened."

"That is strange," reflected Bran.

"My apologies, my lord, but I thought it best to collect the letter."

"I am sorry Bull, that was not my intended meaning. I only think it strange to receive a letter when we are out making a call in a strange city."

The valet put his meaty hand in his coat pocket.

"Let us hope this letter has better news than the last letter a man pulled out of his coat this evening," said Bran.

"Excuse me, my lord?" Bull's face betrayed his confusion.

"I am sorry, Bull, just a joke. Not a particularly funny one either." Bran unfolded the letter. It took only a few seconds to take in the short message. He handed it back to Bull. "Tell me what you think. It is from the Countess of Lambert. She says she must meet with me at once. Says it concerns the affairs of my uncle."

As Bull slowly read the letter on his own, Bran could not help but feel an ember of hope burn ever so faintly in his breast.

Bull handed the letter back. "Definitely a woman's hand, my lord. I do not know this particular lady, but I have heard of her. Sort of sounds like an odd time to receive visitors, though. Do you have any idea what it might be about?"

Bran had the look of a man lost deep in thought. "I am at a loss, but I hope it can shed some light on the events surrounding the meeting I just concluded. Any idea how this countess would have known we were going to be here tonight?"

Bull ruminated. "I cannot say, my lord. Perhaps she heard

you were going to be in town and asked at the hotel. I did mention to the manager we were heading to meet some bankers and might be back late."

"I am sure that is it," responded Bran. "What do you think Bull? Can you forego your supper for just a little longer?"

Bull nodded dolefully.

"Do not worry, Bull. We will get you something to eat soon enough. Besides, I would not expect you to be hungry after dining on Milton all evening."

Both men chuckled.

"By the way," continued Bran, "the address listed here is in Westminster. Do you know the area?"

"A little . . . I have been there a few times. Of course, the Abbey is there, as well as Buckingham Palace and St. James Park. It has been a while, but I remember the neighborhood being a mixture of both nicer homes and older, more run-down residences. It is also not too far from the river, though not much of London is."

"Well then, let us catch a ride," said Bran. "The sooner we talk to this mysterious countess who is trying to arrange secret rendezvouses with my valet, the better."

"Maybe she wants me to read Milton to her, my lord." Both men laughed as they wound their way down the large stone staircase to the street.

Twenty minutes later the two men found themselves entering southern Westminster. As they turned down a smaller side lane, Bull leaned slightly towards Bran. "I think we are about there, my lord."

Bran was already taking note of the neighborhood. Their cab had just turned onto a poorly lit street. A pair of mature willow trees further diffused any illumination on the avenue.

Once the cab departed, the two men fully took in their surroundings. They were on a cobbled lane flanked on both sides by tall, aged row houses. Each house had about twenty feet of garden between it and the road. Bordering each garden and the road were similar four-foot-tall wrought iron fences. Gates supplied entry to the pathways that led straight to the front door of each house. The gardens varied in their contents. Some contained considerable amounts of well-maintained vegetation, while others appeared to be completely neglected. The houses were obviously quite large, but a superficial inspection revealed that these houses were well beyond their prime. In their day, they could have easily housed a local aristocrat or ambassador, but now Bran was not so sure.

"Hard to picture a countess living in one of these, my lord."

Bran did not respond to the statement. He was scanning up and down the street. In the poor light, he was just able to make out a cul-de-sac at the opposite end of the avenue. This indicated the only way out to be the way they had arrived. Bran was not sure why he was so on edge. A few of the houses glowed with lit windows, but others were completely dark.

The house in question had a small amount of illumination shining from a window on the second floor. One of the rooms adjacent to the front door also boasted a light. Bran subconsciously fingered the tomahawk buried deep inside his coat. The weapon had made it difficult to sit comfortably in the banker's office, but now Bran decided the discomfort was well worth it.

As they approached the front pathway to the house, he suddenly pulled Bull into the shadow of one of the large willow trees. "Bull, this place gives me the creeps. I am going to go up to the house, but I would like for you to discretely hang out here. It is probably going to be an innocuous meeting, but experience is telling me not to commit my entire force."

Part of Bull wanted to debate his master on the plan, but aside from it not being his place, he also saw the wisdom in Bran's scheme. "Would you like me to find another hackney, in case we want to get out of here quickly?"

Bran shook his head. "No. Had I been thinking straight we would have kept the other hackney here. I also do not like the idea of you disappearing right now. I would feel better knowing you were nearby keeping watch from the outside."

"Aye, my lord."

"Well then, I had better be on my way. I do not want to keep this countess . . . whatever her name is, waiting any longer."

Bran stepped out from the shadows and took a moment to flatten the front of his suit with the palms of his clammy hands before he sauntered down the short path. He was on edge, and really for no apparent reason he could discern. At that moment, he felt someone or something snag his arm. He instinctively did a side step, jerking his arm away. Only then did he realize he had brushed against a rose bush. *A little bit jittery Bran ol' boy.* To his relief he made it up the steps and to the front door without being assaulted by any more flowers.

An old, worn knocker hung in the middle of the door. Its edges were rounded from use, but it still held the recognizable image of a dragon. Bran's thoughts flitted to the red dragon of Wales, and he hoped it was an encouraging omen. He rapped the metal against the door; the resulting crack sounded abnormally loud in the otherwise still night. He wanted to glance over his shoulder at Bull but decided against it. A moment later the door swung inward and he looked upon a thick, red-faced woman in a maid's uniform.

She greeted him in a cockney accent. "Good evenin', sir. Can I 'elp you?"

"Lord Gruffudd to see her ladyship."

"Come in, my lord. We were expectin' you. If you do not mind waitin' in the front parlor, 'er ladyship will be with you in a few moments."

Bran was shown into a medium sized room full of yellow upholstered furniture. A handful of candles lit the room, but even in the weak light Bran could not help but notice how tired the décor appeared. He walked to the small mantle by the fireplace and ran his hand over the top. A heavy coat of dust blanketed his fingertips. Bran nervously paced the room, his mind futilely trying to anticipate the infinite number of places the forthcoming conversation might go. He glanced at a large picture window facing the street hoping to glimpse Bull, but it was a futile exercise. Time and neglect had left a thin layer of filth on the outside of the window. The window panes acted like a mirror reflecting the room's small amount of candlelight. Bran was circling the room for a fifth time when his eyes fell on a lumpy, white pile in the far corner behind the settee. He walked over to the large seat and picked up one of several dusty, white sheets. Bran's brain was attempting to parse this latest clue when his thoughts were interrupted by a thunderous crash on the street side of the room. He reflexively dropped the sheet and turned his head just in time to see a rusted wheelbarrow slide across the floor; behind it lay a wake of broken glass and shattered window mullions. Bran's eyes fixed on the opening, which now appeared as a black hole in the midst of the remaining milky white shards of glass. His hand palmed his tomahawk, ready to meet this unknown threat.

To his astonishment, the wrinkled face of Bull appeared in the opening. "Time for us to go, my lord!" Sensing his master's confusion, he added an enthusiastic, "NOW!"

As if to reinforce Bull's imperative, the door on the opposite side of the room burst open and five men piled through the doorway. Bran had just enough time to see the gang momentarily trip over each other before he hurled his own body toward the jagged hole.

19

River Chase

Bran could feel fingers plucking at the back of his coat as he careened through the broken window. Pieces of glass continued to shower the flowerbed like raindrops. For the briefest moment, he thought his pants might snag on a splintered mullion, but then his feet hit the pavement and he was off at a full gallop towards the gate. Bull's stocky frame was already hoofing it up the street. The sound of more glass shards raining onto the ground told Bran at least one assailant was immediately behind him.

He also heard a loud tear and the curses of the other men as they struggled to navigate through the treacherous hole. Bran knew the first man was closing the distance even as he stretched out his hand to grasp the stout iron gate. Grabbing the closest bar, Bran used the rigid structure as a lever to help change his direction. The crude fulcrum sent him catapulting up the street. As an afterthought, he gave the gate a hard shove immediately before letting go. A thud and grunt followed. Bran wanted to turn his head to see if the man was down, but there was not time for such luxuries. His attention now switched to Bull, whose lead was shrinking rapidly. The Scot's sweaty head glistened in the moonlight. Bull was running for his life, but it was obvious that the servant was not a sprinter. Bran was not a runner either, but his long stride allowed him to cover ground in a hurry when the situation demanded it. Once he was abreast of Bull he could hear the stocky man's lungs working like a bellows. Bran chanced a glance over his shoulder. He saw a man being helped up by one of the other pursuers. At that moment, four more men exited the yard and peeled up the street. His little ploy had worked, but he and Bull still had plenty of trouble behind them.

As they reached the end of the lane, Bran had to commit to a decision, and there was no time to deliberate. A left would take them further into town and possibly closer to aid. A right went down to the riverbank.

"This way, Bull!"

The valet was right behind Bran and he could hear the man's leather shoes slide across gravel as he took a hard-right turn. Bull gave a grunt that made Bran steal a look over his shoulder. Feeling a wave of relief, he saw the valet was still on his feet, albeit with a slight limp.

"Hang in there, Bull, you are doing great; do not pull up lame on me now!"

All Bran caught was a somewhat muffled "No worries, my lord." They were now well past the corner and a hundred feet from the water. There was probably fifteen seconds of concealment before the pursuing mob had them in sight again. Bran's eyes immediately fell on a small cargo wagon with a tarpaulin bunched in the back. The wagon sat next to a warehouse's rotting side door.

"Bull, get in the wagon and under the tarpaulin now!"

Fortunately, the older man knew how to take an order and

did not hesitate. While his burly servant navigated the old cart, Bran sent his foot flying against the door. As he hoped, the wood gave way with a sharp snap, and it rebounded against the inside wall of the warehouse. Two seconds later, Bran slid under the tarpaulin next to Bull. For the briefest moment Bran thought the gambit was up. The sound of rapid, heavy footfalls came in their direction and slowed.

A husky voice bellowed, "Over here!"

Bran stiffened, tomahawk in hand. He could barely make out Bull's form next to him. Both men attempted to ready themselves for a fight, all the while intentionally quieting their breathing.

Then the husky voice continued, "It looks like they went in the warehouse. I do not think there is another way out, so they are just as well trapped. Smyth, you go stand by the water's edge so you can keep an eye on this door in case the bastards try to backtrack. But also keep an eye on the side of the building. There might be a window or something we do not know about." No more voices followed. The sound of footfalls began again and then faded away.

Bran risked a whisper to his companion. "Are you all right, Bull?"

Bull assured his master he was fine but then added, "Other than this dreadful smell, that is."

Bull's comment caused Bran to fully take in their surroundings for the first time. The entire bottom of the old wagon was covered in discarded fish parts. The heavy canvas tarpaulin made the fishy stench worse by the moment, but foul smells were the least of their concerns.

"I am going to risk a peak," Bran said in a hushed tone. "The longer we stay here the greater our likelihood of being caught." Muscles coiled and ready for action, Bran delicately lifted the corner of the tarpaulin. He started with just a few inches, but when he realized they were mostly alone, he dared to look more. The fresh air flowed into his lungs, sweeping away the noxious smells, but only for a moment. After taking a moment to canvas his surroundings, he slowly lowered the tarpaulin back down.

"Looks like we have just one man down by the water's edge. That is all I can see for now. I do not think our concealment is going to last once their inspection of the warehouse is complete."

Bull grunted his concurrence.

"I think I can take the man by the water pretty easily." Bran used the bottom of his coat to clean the edge of his tomahawk. "The trick will be to do it in such a way that he does not sound the alarm. I could easily kill the man from this range, but not knowing who these miscreants are, I would hate to take a measure that extreme.

Bull was not sure if he agreed with his master's sense of fair play, but he did not question the decision.

Bran took another moment to assess the situation. Arriving at a course of action he laid out the plan.

Raising the edge of the tarpaulin for a second time, Bran waited until the lookout was distracted by some yells echoing from a distant barge. As soon as he perceived he was in the clear, Bran slid to the ground. Body hunched and tomahawk hanging loosely in his right hand, he slowly began to stalk the lookout. The sound of a faint grunt behind him told him Bull was also now clear of the wagon. The plan was simple. Close as much distance as they could before the lookout detected them. Bran's responsibility was to take care of the lookout. Bull's was to secure a hasty means of escape.

Bran was within fifty feet of the man when the lookout began to turn. Bran instantly pivoted, pointing his left shoulder at the man. With a sharp snap of his wrist he put the weapon to flight.

The lookout identified the threat at the same time the tomahawk went airborne. With a speed and agility Bran would not have anticipated from a man his size, the lookout threw himself to the side. The intended target was the man's right thigh. He had hoped to incapacitate but not kill. It was the man's last second dodge that changed everything. Instead of hitting him square in the thigh, the weapon glanced off the side of the man's leg and rattled across the weather-worn deck planking. A cry of pain and the immediate buckling of the man's leg indicated the throw had not failed entirely. Raising his left arm and lowering his shoulder like a battering ram, Bran closed the last few remaining feet in seconds. The blow caught the already teetering man in the chest and sent him backwards. As the man reeled, he caught his foot on a bollard and went flipping over the side of the dock into the water. A muffled splash followed. Bran was relieved the man's outcry had been kept to a minimum. Heavy footfalls twenty feet down the dock told him Bull was already hard at work completing his portion of the mission. Bran recovered his tomahawk. The weapon had stopped a foot short of sliding into the water. By the time he rejoined Bull, the servant already had one mooring line detached from a medium sized dingy, and he was working on a second. A well-placed strike from the tomahawk severed the second line. Twenty seconds later both men were in the boat, and Bull was tearing away at the oars.

"Just keep her with the current," Bran ordered. "We will try and get to a more populated area, at which point we will ditch her."

As the boat silently slid through the water both men exhaled a sigh of relief. Unfortunately, the silence of the river was punctuated by cries from the dock they had just left. Bran turned to see five men piling into a dory. "Oh, hell," Bran muttered under his breath. Turning to Bull he encouraged the older man, "No pressure, Bull, but it looks like we might have company soon. If you need me to relieve you at all, just say the word." But even as the words escaped him, he knew there was no point. Bull's strong, thick arms were working the oars with a relentless efficiency he knew he was incapable of matching.

"Do not worry, my lord; I have always liked boats," but then with a grim look he added, "though maybe after tonight that will no longer be the case."

Bran turned to observe their pursuers. Despite Bull's skill with the oars, he feared the sharper prow of the dory was going to make it irrelevant in a few minutes. Their pursuers had already halved the distance. Every few seconds he encouraged the older man in his efforts.

"You know, working for you is a lot more exciting than my previous jobs."

"Do not give me that," rejoined Bran, "when I met you, you were rolling down a hill in a giant cart."

"Point taken," replied Bull sheepishly.

"And to think," continued Bran, "I was under the impression I would be coming to Britain to enjoy the leisure-filled life of a country squire. Instead I have felt a little more like Robin Hood."

Bull smiled, "I can be Little John. Besides, I went to visit Sherwood Forest one time; it was—"

Bran interrupted the reminiscing valet as their pursuers closed to within fifty feet. "Sorry, Bull, you will have to tell me about it some other time. We are about to have company." Bran rummaged among the remnants of an old wooden crate in the bottom of the boat. He was pleased to find a broken oar. The weather-worn device was about seven feet long. All that was left of the handle was a splintery mess. Holding up the oar he declared, "Robin Hood now has his staff. Just keep us steady Bull, and I will see if I can soften these guys up a bit." The valet nodded and Bran positioned himself in the stern of the boat.

As the pursuers came closer, Bran instantly perceived their strategy. A man in the bow had a grappling hook. Apparently, their goal was to grapple and then board.

"Preparing to repel boarders, Bull; keep rowing!"

A moment later the iron hook flew through the air. Bran dodged to his left as it thumped against the rear seat of the dingy. A sharp rearward tug on their vessel gave the signal the enemy was reeling them in. Bran waited for the tension in the line to build. A split second later he severed the line with his tomahawk. Looking behind him, he saw the men in the pursuing boat involuntarily fall backwards into their craft as the tension in the line suddenly released. Curses resounded as the men tried to untangle each other.

Bull yelled over his shoulder, "I am gonna put her in up here, my lord! I know where there are some stairs along the river. It is close to Downing Street. There are always soldiers around that part of the city!"

Bran signaled his agreement. A moment earlier he would not have thought they could make it, but the confusion in the other craft appeared to buy them just enough time to complete their escape.

"BRACE YOURSELF!" cried Bull. The wooden hull grated against the stone steps. Bran barely had time to grab the side of the boat lest he be thrown into the murky water. Bull did not wait for the boat to come to a complete stop before he threw the oars over the side and headed up the steps yelling, "Follow me!" Bran charged up the stairs behind him, his long shanks taking three steps at a time. The two men could hear the pursuers' boat scraping against their own. From the sound of the men's shouts it was obvious they were having difficulty working their way around the dingy. After a bit of scraping and yelling, the heavy feet of their pursuers bounded up the steps, but Bran and Bull were already hightailing it down the street.

Bull shouted directions between huffs, "Just down . . . this way. There are always . . . guards near Downing Street. We are . . . not far from . . . the Horse Guards." They started to pass a few people on the road now, and Bran could see some soldiers standing guard up ahead. He chanced a glance over his shoulder. The pursuers were still behind them, but he could tell even at a distance, the growing crowd of people had them concerned. "Slow up, Bull. I do not think they will keep chasing us now. Besides, we do not want to look like we are up to no good ourselves." Both men slowed their pace and eventually settled into a brisk walk, occasionally darting nervous glances behind them to check for their pursuers. Eventually the men melted away into the crowd.

Bull laced his meaty fingers behind his head as he fought to catch his breath.

"You are not going to die on me now, are you Bull?" Bran's voice was laced with sarcasm, but his tone still held a note of concern.

Bull turned, "No, my lord, I think I am all right. I am just not used to that kind of activity. I mean, I used to spend a lot of time running from the lasses back home, but that was quite a while ago." The Scot's red face let forth an impish grin.

Bran suddenly formed the mental image of a young boy with a large wrinkled head and thick sideburns running through the heather as a mob of girls, clad in colorful tartans, chased after him. The mental image, combined with lingering adrenaline, caused Bran to suddenly break into laughter. "How about I get you that dinner I promised you earlier?"

"That sounds lovely, my lord. That is, as long as it is not fish."

20

Unfortunate Encounter

The two men wandered the street. Bran considered hailing a cab, but he thought better of the idea. If they walked a bit, some of the fish smell might work its way out of their clothes. Both men continued in silence, each person subconsciously following the other.

Bull broke the silence first. "My lord, I realize it might not be my place to ask, but do you have any idea who those men were or why they were chasing us?"

Bran contemplated how much to disclose from the bank meeting. His trust in Bull was growing daily, or more aptly put, by the minute; but Bran also knew once information hit the servants' floor, you might as well try and hold back the Thames. He chose to err on the side of caution, if only for the time being.

"I am not sure. There was obviously more going on with my uncle than meets the eye. I get the sense there is something running below the surface. How deep? That is what I am not sure about. There are some moments when it seems all I need to do is fully stretch out my hand, and I can grab hold of the truth. At other times it simply feels like a distant shadow, devoid of shape or substance."

Bull was not sure how to respond to the cryptic answer, so he chose to let the matter drop.

They were now on the opposite side of the street from Number Ten. Bran took in the dark brick building. It struck him as an odd sort of place from which to govern the world's most powerful empire. His mind went back to the time he had visited the fledgling United States capital. It had been two years prior, and he had been thoroughly unimpressed. The American seat of government was nothing more than a haphazard collection of government buildings and private residences all connected by muddy roads.

He was about to turn his attention to the task of finding a hackney, when the front door of the famous building opened and out stepped a well attired young man. Upon exiting the building, the man quickly surveyed his surroundings. Catching site of Bran and Bull, the young gentleman crossed the street in a quick but dignified manner, making sure not to get run over in the process.

"Odds fish! Is that you Bull? Of course it is Bull; I would recognize that big wrinkled head anywhere." As the man strode nearer, Bran gave him a once over. He was of average height with curly blonde hair. He had broad shoulders and a strong build. The slightly crooked nose made Bran wonder if the man was a pugilist. That being said, he still retained classic good looks to go along with his obviously aristocratic bearing.

Bull's face broke into a broad grin of recognition. "Lord Wendover! You are the last person I expected to see tonight."

The young nobleman smiled, "I will say; I am the one who should be making that observation. The last I heard, you had left my father to go live in Wales. What in heaven's name are you doing on Downing Street of all places?"

Bull realized he was neglecting the rules of etiquette and he turned to Bran. His voice took on a more formal manner, "Lord Gruffudd, my deepest apologies. Let me introduce the Earl of Wendover. You may have put two and two together, but Lord Wendover is the son of my former employer, the Duke of Denver. Lord Wendover, my new employer, Lord Gruffudd."

Lord Wendover smiled congenially and stuck out his muscled hand. "Extremely pleased to meet you, old chap. My friends call me Tony." Then the man's eyes grew large. "I say, you are the American? I mean, your uncle was the previous Lord Gruffudd." He let out a hearty laugh. "Well, of course he was. I am a prat . . . but I am a little confused, how did the two of you, I mean—"

Bran interrupted, "To sum it up succinctly, my lord, Bull tried his hand at farming, but that did not turn out so well, so he agreed to help prevent me from making a fool of myself every ten seconds. You will have to ask Bull if he has been successful or not."

Lord Wendover heartily slapped him across the back, and Bran staggered a bit, "Good for you! Sounds like there is a bit of a story there. But just so you know, Bull's as good as they come. A little stubborn at times, and not to mention ugly"—he gave the valet a friendly wink—"but a royal chap nonetheless. My father pined for a month when Bull left him. He has fired two valets since then. I guess nobody holds a candle to ol' Bull."

Bran watched the compliment color Bull's face.

"So tell me, what brings you to Downing Street at this time of night?" asked Tony.

Bran gave him a quick summary of recent events, opting to leave out certain details. He specifically omitted the letter and the meeting with the banker. Bran also neglected the part about hitting the man with the tomahawk. He was not sure what a duke's son would think about this American lord if he knew he carried an Indian war weapon under his cloak as he walked the streets of London.

As the story went on, the young peer's eyes grew wider and wider. "Good heavens! I have never heard of such a thing. I cannot imagine what you must think of London right now. I mean seriously, we have been known to make the passing comment about the uncouth nature of the colonies, but apparently England has its own hooligans of which to boast. I am of a mind to go find the authorities right now and have them search out these curs." He paused for a moment; a sudden look of worry beset his face as he rapidly scanned their surroundings. He looked like he thought these unknown assailants might resurface at any moment. When he saw no nearby suspicious rogues his face resumed its jocular grin.

"So tell me, have you all eaten supper yet?"

"We have not," answered Bran, "but I think our first order of business needs to be a change of clothes. That fisherman's cart did not do us any favors."

Tony laughed, "I tell you what, I was just about to head over to my club. It is only a twenty-minute walk. When we get there, you can use one of the private rooms to clean up. I even have some extra things you can wear while your clothes are cleaned. As we wait we can share a meal and a few drinks. I would love to hear more about life in the colonies."

Bran considered gracefully declining, but there was a certain level of finality in the young man's voice. It also occurred to Bran that if their would-be assailants had any mischief planned for the hotel, then delaying their return might not be a bad idea.

He smiled at the young lord. "That is a gracious invitation. I think we will be more than happy to accept."

The three men began to walk as Lord Wendover plied Bran with friendly questions. Soon the trio found themselves entering one of London's most exclusive gentlemen's clubs. Bran quickly deduced the young lord to be a fixture at the establishment. He appeared to know everybody, and to Bran's relief, this did much to deflect any critical stares from the club's other patrons. The closed air of the foyer made Bran and Bull all the more aware of the fish odor they carried with them. To Bran's chagrin, the young earl steered them right into the middle of the main game room. After setting Bran up with a drink at the bar, Lord Wendover and Bull went to make arrangements for a place where Bran and Bull could clean up.

Finding himself without his companions, Bran focused his attention on his drink. He also did his very best to blend in with the carpet. Most club members chose to ignore the aromatic foreigner.

Bran began to fight fatigue. The room was uncomfortably warm, and he continually found himself tugging at his collar with his index finger. His thoughts were racing, flitting from one recent event to another.

Bran was most of the way through his drink and starting to wonder what in the world might be taking the other two men so long, when he heard an insolent voice call his name.

"Can this be Lord Gruffudd?"

Bran turned his head to identify the speaker and stared directly into the face of Lord Gyr. He was standing with three other men of similar appearance. All four wore evening dress and each was holding a drink of choice. From the slight discoloration on their faces, Bran guessed these were not their first drinks of the evening.

Bran hurriedly took the final sip of his whiskey. He was already starting to regret the speed with which he had consumed the drink on an empty stomach.

Lord Gyr flashed him a malicious grin, "Lord Gruffudd, what a surprise to see you here! Why not join us? I have a few friends I would like you to meet."

Bran contemplated walking out the front door but then thought better of it. As the introductions were made he greeted each man with a winning smile. Bran began to hope that perhaps the men's inebriated state would cause them not to notice the pungent fish smell. One of the men was so lit he held onto the chair next to him like a captain holding onto a ship's wheel in a hurricane.

Bran sent one last furtive glance around the room in the hope that Tony and Bull were on their way back, but Lord Gyr brought his attention back to the conversation.

"So, tell me, Gruffudd—"

It was not lost on Bran that the man had dropped the use of his title.

"You never told me you were a fisherman."

"Oh, you know, some men go in for the theater; personally, I prefer a little late-night bass fishing."

"I am glad to hear that," Lord Gyr drawled. "I was trying to remember if you had worn the same interesting scent the other night. It would go a long way to explain how the colonists managed to overcome our forces during that unfortunate incident in the Americas. I would have surrendered too had I been forced to endure that aroma for very long." The comment elicited a few quiet snickers from Lord Gyr's companions.

"I imagine you would not have tarried in your surrender,

regardless of the olfactory situation," retorted an irritated Bran.

The man leaning on the chair snorted into his glass.

Lord Gyr gave Bran a malevolent stare. The marquess turned to his companions, "Did you all know Lord Gruffudd is my cousin's new guardian? I really do feel sorry for you Gruffudd"—then seeing Bran's momentary confusion added—"it is a tough job to keep track of that lady-bird cousin of mine."

Bran stared back at Lord Gyr fixedly.

The marquess put his hand in front of his mouth as if to feign surprise. "My word, do not tell me you did not know." He attempted to suppress a drunken giggle. "I would have assumed . . . but then, I suppose, how could you?" Lord Gyr lowered his voice conspiratorially and leaned forward as if what he was about to share was not for public consumption. "I am referring to the fact that dear Cristyn has enjoyed the company of more men than a prostitute in Devil's Acre. I have even heard she does not bother confining herself to just the upper classes. No wonder your uncle was so willing to take her on."

Bran stiffened. His eyes narrowed and his jaw clenched, but he said nothing in reply. His vision began to cloud at the periphery. He was solely focused on the man in front of him.

Lord Gyr could sense his opponent's rage. He was positively gleeful that he had finally landed an effective salvo. Pressing the advantage, he turned to the group, "It seems my news has our American friend a little distraught. I am wondering if he is disappointed in the young woman's conduct, or if he is simply upset at not having benefited from her attention. I have heard you enjoy a good ride." His comment produced raucous laughter from the others.

Bran began to white-knuckle the glass in his hand. With a

sharp pop the glass suddenly shattered. Lord Gyr's companions both jumped. Little bloody pieces of glass fell through Bran's fingers. Only then did Bran realize Tony had joined the company and was standing at his side. The earl quickly handed him a clean handkerchief so he could bind his wound. The sour look on Tony's face indicated that he had at least caught the tail end of the conversation.

Indifferent to the new arrival, the marquess continued to press the attack. "I am sorry if I have upset you, Gruffudd." The man could barely contain his laughter. "Just look on the bright side. My cousin could not care less if you were a baron or a fisherman, so as near as I can tell, you have twice the odds of scoring." Lord Gyr and his companions chortled, giving up any pretense of containing their mirth.

It was in the middle of the group's high spirits that Bran flung himself forward, grabbing Lord Gyr's collar in a vice-like grip. Bran could feel the artery in the back of his hand pulsing as he twisted the man's cravat like a corkscrew. Slowly but relentlessly he began to apply more and more pressure to his opponent's windpipe.

Lord Gyr was completely caught off guard by Bran's assault. Despite being accustomed to verbal altercations, very seldom, if ever, did he find himself in a physical tussle. Unable to break free from Bran's steel grip, Lord Gyr pulled his head backwards in a futile effort to distance himself from his attacker. Bran could see panic mix with hate in his opponent's eyes.

"Get off of me you filthy Yank, what do—" the man's words were choked off as Bran continued to cut off his oxygen supply.

Tony's broad arms pulled Bran off of the man. Bran fought the urge to knock the creep on his noble ass with a right cross.

He was well aware that the whole room was now staring at their little group.

Bran slowly released his grip, but as he did so he growled under his breath, "This is far from over, your lordship." He did not attempt to hide the derision in his voice.

Free of Bran's grip, Lord Gyr was already preening. His long narrow fingers worked at straightening his cravat. It was stained with blood from Bran's lacerated hand. Now that there was some distance between the two men, Lord Gyr's courage began to find him again.

He sneered at Bran, "I assume that is a formal challenge?"

"A what?" asked a confused Bran.

"A duel, you bloody fool," said an indignant Lord Gyr.

"My lord, I have killed many men, and while you undoubtedly would be an eminent addition to that group, I think I will pass on the opportunity."

"Unfortunate," sneered the marquess.

As Lord Gyr and his friends retreated, he leaned in close and whispered to Bran so only the American could hear. "By the way, tell the little whore that once I am done with you, she is mine." Then with a smirk born of decades of practiced arrogance, he and his friends left the club.

Bran stood rooted to the spot, oblivious to anything around him. It was Lord Wendover who snapped him out of it.

"Hell, Bran! One cannot say you do not have some panache. For a second I thought you were going to kill the sonovabitch right here in the club. Glad you did not though, because my dues probably would have gone up seeing as you are my guest." The twinkle had returned to the young man's eyes. "Still, the whole thing surprises me."

Bran was still raging inside. He felt as though Lord

Wendover was treating the entire matter a little too cavalierly. "What surprises you?" he snapped. Then realizing his response had been a bit severe, he ameliorated his tone, "—that I would try and kill the man?"

Tony waved his hand dismissively, "No, not in the least. You forget, we Brits try and kill each other all the time. The nation's rich and powerful have to find some way to occupy their time. If it is not sleeping with each other's wives, or gambling, then it is trying to shoot each other in duels . . . though I suppose they are all somewhat related," he said reflectively. "No, any self-respecting gentleman with a spine would have done what you did—well, maybe not the try and crush his windpipe part—but, you know what I mean."

Bran was not sure what he meant.

"What surprises me is that Lord Gyr would even hint at the idea of a duel. Lord Gyr is smart, rich, and a pig, but it is you after all—"

Bran cut him off in a voice that sounded a little surlier than he probably intended. "What is that supposed to mean?"

Tony appeared unfazed, "For crying out loud, I would not want to fight you. You are the Hun as far as most of these people are concerned. I am sure a fight with you is a good way to find oneself stretched out on a slab of stone. Do not think that is lost on Lord Gyr."

"Maybe he realized there was no way out and wanted to save face?" replied an unconvinced Bran.

Tony now had a far away, pensive look on his face. "Perhaps, but I tend to think men like Lord Gyr are always of the belief there is a way out . . . no, I get the feeling there is something more to it all. All I can say is watch your step old chap. You may be a bit of a barbarian, but I think I like you. I would hate to see you leave us just yet. I am already looking forward to unleashing you on the West End."

Bran grunted something non-coherent.

Then, with an overly zealous slap on Bran's shoulder, Tony added, "Now how about that bath I promised and a spot of supper? The cook is whipping up some nice plates of fried cod."

21

Crisis of Belief

Bran noisily slammed billiard balls into the ball rack. He was making so much noise he did not hear Roger's subtle tap on the door. A moment later the old butler entered the room.

"Reverend Hughes, my lord." The servant easily perceived his master's ill temper and did not bother to await a response.

The churchman entered the room at the same moment Bran crashed the cue ball into the top of the pyramid. The shot had too much force and not enough accuracy, and one of the balls hopped over the side of the table. Bran let out an expletive as he set down the cue and chased the errant ball. Reverend Hughes made his way to the bar in the corner. A cursory examination of the inventory yielded an already opened bottle of claret. After filling a glass, he turned to ask Bran if he would like anything; only then did he notice a steaming cup of coffee situated on the side of the table.

Making his way over to the table he addressed Bran for the first time. "My lord, am I to assume your little foray into London did not go quite as you might have hoped?"

Bran let out a derisive snort. "Not as hoped? It was more like a bloody disaster!"

Reverend Hughes's demeanor remained placid. He took another sip of his drink and made his way over to an enormous leather chair. After comfortably ensconcing himself, he continued his questioning. "Would you like to talk about it? I am assuming that is why you requested I come over at this late hour." There was no resentment in his voice, just concern laced with curiosity.

Meanwhile, Bran had recovered the stray ball and was back to his table-top tantrum. The priest humorously took note that not a single ball actually achieved its objective.

"I have had enough of this. I am returning to America," blurted out Bran.

Reverend Hughes choked on his drink, but Bran did not notice. After wiping his mouth with the sleeve of his coat, the priest addressed the young man who was obviously in both a stormy and impetuous mood. "That is a significant decision; perhaps you ought to fill me in on how you arrived there."

Bran turned away from his one-man game for the first time since the priest's arrival. Leaning against his makeshift staff he retorted in a mocking tone, "Hmm, where to start? Let me see, first there was the part about the mysterious missing fortune. Then there was the part about the ambush that almost got Bull and me killed. Right after that, there was the late-night boat chase down the Thames, and it was all capped off by me assaulting Lord Gyr in a fancy English gentlemen's club. Yes, it was a dandy of a trip. All that was missing was attending the opera and the running of the bulls. Though now that I think about it, we did have the latter."

Reverend Hughes did his best not to react to the odd bit of news, but his left eyebrow raised nonetheless. "Well, my lord, I have to say you Americans have a way of stirring things up.

Sounds like a thrilling story." Without waiting for an answer, he comfortably settled himself into the chair. "Go ahead, I am ready to be regaled with tales of intrigue and adventure."

Bran frowned, somewhat annoyed by the priest's mocking attitude. He avoided the matter by smashing a few more billiard balls around the table. Like before, all the balls missed their pockets. Reverend Hughes heard the young baron mutter an oath under his breath. Returning the cue to the rack, Bran slammed it into its holder. His overly violent action caused two other sticks to fall onto the ground. Unperturbed, Bran let them remain where they fell. Instead he perched on the edge of the table, mug in hand.

Over the next hour he shared, in detail, the events of the past several days. He started with the bank meeting, moved on to the mysterious countess, recounted the late-night chase, and finished with Lord Gyr's boorish comments. Reverend Hughes sat in silence, only once making his way over to the bar to refill his glass.

It was not until Bran finished his tale and silence filled the room, that Reverend Hughes chose to speak. "So, let me get this straight, my lord. You found out that your uncle did something with a large sum of money before it was even yours. You then responded to a very reasonable letter from a lady, only to barely escape with your life. After that, you were insulted by a drunk swine of an aristocrat, at which point you roughed him up a bit, only after he chose to insult a virtuous young lady who is under your protection. I admit it was not an ideal sightseeing trip, but I am having a hard time seeing why you should be berating yourself."

Bran sat in silence for a moment. "When you put it that way, it does not quite sound as bad."

"Father Hughes smiled, "Sometimes it takes a friend to enable us to view our circumstances objectively."

"But what about Lady Cristyn?" inquired Bran sulkily. "Is there any chance that what Lord Gyr said was true?"

Bran saw the warmth leave Reverend Hughes's eyes. When he spoke again his voice took on a hint of irritation. "My lord, I am disappointed in you."

Bran frowned defiantly, but then shame overtook his countenance. "I know, I apologize. Of course it is not true." He looked at the priest imploringly, as if beseeching the man's forgiveness.

Reverend Hughes' features softened, and warmth crept back into his eyes. "I forgive you for the intimation," reassured the priest. "In truth, it is her ladyship to whom you owe the apology, but considering you did just defend her honor publicly, I think we can let the matter rest."

"Thank you," responded Bran. "It is not that I am trying to make excuses, but I feel like I can no longer tell up from down and right from wrong."

The priest nodded sympathetically. "That is what evil does. It either contains just enough truth to be believable, or it preys on our insecurities. Lord Gyr feeds off the pain and suffering of others. I have known Lady Cristyn since the day she was born. She is good, kind, brave, smart, and everything a lady should be. In fact, you and she share many qualities. Lord Gyr has successfully managed to take most of her money, likely her father, and now he is going after the last thing she has, her honor."

Bran did not interrupt.

"Why Lord Gyr hates her so, I have no idea. It probably has to do with her consistent rebuffs. This is unbearable to a man who views himself as his own god. The only people who have rivaled Cristyn as an object of the man's hatred are you and your uncle. I can only assume it is because both of you positioned yourselves between him and her. I wager there is a civil war going on inside him between two competing desires to both possess and destroy her ladyship."

Bran slammed his fist into his palm in frustration. "Every fiber of my being is telling me I need to do something, that I need to make this whole thing right," but then his shoulders slumped and he let out a sigh, "or perhaps I am simply being capricious."

The priest took the last drink from his glass as he reflected. Finally, the older man spoke, "There is an ancient Welsh tradition that says the king is the land, and the land is the king. I know your spirit is troubled. I sensed traces of your underlying frustration the day I met you. You naturally attribute this unsettledness to specific events and trials you have undergone, as any sane person would. But I would argue it runs deeper than this. The land is sick, and as its lord, a part of you is sick. It is not a conscious recognition, but you feel it in the very fiber of your being."

"But I do not understand. I am no king," said a confused Bran.

"True," agreed the priest, "nor would old George probably want you to be, but you are also not some interloper. The Gruffudds are as deeply connected to this land as any family in Wales. For over a thousand years they have lived, fought, bled, and died here. So do not sell yourself short. Bran the Blessed, after all, was high king of the Island of the Mighty."

Bran was sitting very still. He suddenly felt as though the ghosts of a hundred ancestors were crowding him. "I am sorry, this is a lot to take in. What about Lord Gyr? My holdings are measly compared to his."

There was now a twinkle in the priest's eye. "Nobility is not derived from wealth. As you are well aware, Lord Gyr and his ancestors are English, or more specifically, Norman. The Marcher Lords attempted to legitimize their claim via fiat, nothing more. That can never replace blood lineage, nor will they ever be true Welshmen."

Reverend Hughes smiled kindly, "The important thing to take away from all of this is that there are physical, emotional, spiritual, and even cultural forces at war around us at all times. You commented that you felt like nothing has gone right since you arrived. I do not think this is coincidental. When you arrived at Caer Cigfran, unbeknownst to you, you became a lightning rod. You are one of those people who is compelled to do good, even when your actions put you at great risk. This is not insignificant. A small child can put himself in danger defending a beaten puppy from a gang of bigger youngsters, but when those in authority choose the path less traveled, it reverberates throughout the whole land. How often have we seen nations rise and fall based on nothing more than the character of their leader? In other words, when you arrived the agents of evil were put on notice. When good men choose to do something, evil cannot afford to do nothing."

Bran tugged at his collar uncomfortably. A part of him felt like too many expectations were being heaped on his shoulders unwarranted and unasked. "But if Lord Gyr is truly the abomination we believe he is, what does that mean for me? What does victory truly look like?"

"I cannot answer that," reflected the priest, "but just remember that victory sometimes does not come in a manner we fully expect, and seldom does it come without great cost."

"What does that mean for me?"

"It means something different for everyone. You will know when your moment arrives. What is it Shakespeare says, 'Whether 'tis nobler in the mind to suffer the slings and arrows of outrageous fortune or to take up arms against a sea of troubles, And, by opposing end them.' I cannot chart your course for you, but I also know you represent our greatest opportunity to permanently bring an end to this cancer that fashions himself as a British lord. But whatever you choose to do, it would be foolish to approach the matter with too cavalier an attitude. There was never any linkage between your uncle's suicide and any action on behalf of Lord Gyr, but I have my suspicions, regardless of whether I can prove them or not. The man is clever, devious, and should not be underestimated on any account."

"You have given me a lot to consider," reflected Bran, "not to mention I am a bit of a sucker for lost causes. Besides, sailing back to America probably means another trip to London, which I am not exactly up for right now." He smiled weakly.

Both men returned to thoughtful silence. Bran finally spoke, "You were with my uncle the day he died. What actually happened?"

The priest's face took on a more somber expression. "That is a story you need to hear, but I think we have probably covered enough ground for tonight. We both need our rest. How about we continue the conversation after breakfast if that suits you, my lord?"

"Then tomorrow morning it is."

22

The Death of Uncle Llew

Having just finished his morning meal, Bran stepped through the newly-repaired French windows at the rear of the library. The large stone veranda was built of ancient flagstones. Frequent rains had conspired with thousands of footsteps to create a highly polished surface. Bran remembered his first morning at the estate when he had made the mistake of stepping outside with too much enthusiasm. His leather soles had hit the lingering nighttime dew on the first row of pavers. Only a flailing grab at the doorframe had spared him likely injury and the accompanying loss of dignity.

This morning Bran reflexively probed the first stone with his foot. He chuckled at the thought of a long line of Gruffudds going through a similar morning ritual. On this particular morning the sun had already banished any lingering moisture.

Confidently stepping onto the veranda, Bran's eyes took in the estate's vast gardens. Since Caer Cigfran sat on the crown of a small hill, the estate's gardens took the form of three concentric terraces that radiated down the back slope like a fan. Beyond the gardens was a small lake. Bran could just make out the glass-like surface reflecting the morning sun between the trees.

Lost in the view, he jumped when a person behind him spoke.

"Stunning is it not, my lord?" interrupted Reverend Hughes. The aged priest stepped slowly through the open window. Realizing he had startled his host, he added, "My apologies, I should not have crept up on you like that."

Bran smiled as he turned, "That is alright; now you know why I am no longer an Indian fighter. The enemy was always sneaking up on me while I gazed at the scenery."

The priest smiled in return. "I would not be too hard on yourself. It is difficult not to get lost in the view. Your uncle and I had more than one breakfast out here together. Many times we would not talk. We would simply drink in the Lord's creation."

"Speaking of my uncle," replied Bran. "I have been anticipating this morning's conversation ever since last night. I have been meaning to ask you about my uncle's death, but I have never been able to find the right occasion."

Reverend Hughes looked momentarily lost in thought, but then he spoke, "Yes, but I am the one who is remiss. I should have brought it up long before now. To be honest, the whole affair was a bit peculiar. I was never able to piece the whole thing together to my satisfaction. That being said, in light of your recent adventures, you might be able to place some of the happenings in a context that has eluded me up until now."

"Wonderful, I would enjoy hearing what you have to say. Would you like to go inside and sit down, or do you fancy a turn around the garden?"

"I would prefer to walk. I always find that my thoughts flow freer when my legs are in motion. But if you do not mind, let us go down to the last garden. My joints are old, and they prefer grass walkways to stone, not to mention I find the benches convenient."

Bran nodded his consent, and the two men made their way down one of the two sets of stone steps that sandwiched the three terraces. Once they reached the third terrace, they charted a circular path that would minimize the time they spent looking into the now rapidly ascending sun. Bran left it to the old priest to begin.

"Hmm, where to start?" reflected Reverend Hughes. "I suppose I probably ought to begin by giving you some information regarding your uncle. Am I correct in assuming you did not know your uncle in person?"

"That is right," said Bran. "All I knew was what my father told me, which was not a whole lot. He would make the occasional passing comment like, 'Oh, you are a lot like your Uncle Llew,' but it was always sort of left at that. He never really told me any actual stories. Neither of us ever imagined I would come here, plus, I think we both assumed we had many years ahead of us to discuss such things."

Reverend Hughes smiled kindly. "Oh, it seems like that is always the case. We tend to either have plenty of time or no time at all; seldom is there anything in between. Since you did not really know your uncle, I think it would be good if I told you a little bit about him before I jump to the day of his passing."

Bran listened intently.

"I have known your uncle for a good twenty years. I do not think it would be presumptuous to state that I was closer to your uncle than anyone in these parts, but even as I make that declaration I do not want you to get the wrong impression.

Your uncle was a private man. He was the type of person who kept his thoughts to himself. There was nothing devious about him, but one could say an air of melancholy continually surrounded him."

"Did he ever marry?" asked Bran.

"It is interesting you should ask. In short, no, he never married. But as to why, I am not sure. It always puzzled me and he never spoke of it. One would think he would have presented quite the catch. He was handsome, titled, and wealthy."

The priest continued his story with a question. "How much do you know about your uncle's death?"

"I know he took his own life. I picked that up from the solicitor when I stopped over in London immediately following my arrival in Britain. I am ashamed to say my knowledge stops there. Like I said previously, I had considered asking Lady Cristyn for a few details, but she seemed particularly reticent regarding the matter."

"Yes, it appeared your uncle did take his own life, but I would also be remiss if I did not say the whole series of events smelled a bit. But I am jumping ahead of myself."

He paused momentarily, as one does when attempting to mentally organize a long series of events. "As I mentioned before, your uncle tended to be a solitary man. Besides myself, he really had only one other friend of consequence. I am referring to the previous Lord Gyr—Lady Cristyn's father. The two men knew each other from childhood and even attended university together; yet despite their longtime friendship, I would not go so far as to describe them as intimate. It was a friendship bred by the length of acquaintance more than by close personal ties. When the marquess died, your uncle was deeply troubled. I will also tell you everyone was a bit surprised to learn that Lady Cristyn's guardianship passed to your uncle. However, everything was legally in order, and when the local community became better acquainted with the new marquess, most people attributed it to wise foresight on the part of her father."

Reverend Hughes momentarily stopped to examine a white solitary flower growing on a hedge that was otherwise covered in brambles. "It is fascinating to see such delicate beauty alone amongst so many thorns and thistles . . . but I digress. I can tell you, the period following Lady Cristyn's arrival at Caer Cigfran was the happiest I ever saw your uncle. He was not fully free of the melancholy, but there was a marked improvement in his demeanor. I dined frequently at the estate during that period. Lady Cristyn likes to entertain, and I think it was your uncle's attempt to satiate that desire." He chuckled to himself, "Not that two old men, one of which was a clergyman, were exciting company for an attractive young lady, but to her credit she never complained, at least in public; and she was always a most charming hostess."

Bran quietly walked beside Reverend Hughes, his fingers laced behind his back. A small part of his brain made a mental note to invite guests over to the estate in the very near future.

"A few months prior to his death, your uncle began to slip deeper into his famed melancholy. The difference this time was that his moods became even darker than before, and how might I describe it . . . more severe."

"And you had no indication of what triggered this?" asked Bran.

"No idea, though I suspected the current Lord Gyr—Caradoc—was somehow involved. On at least two occasions I witnessed the two men sharing heated arguments.

Consequently, I was not particularly surprised when I learned your uncle had challenged Caradoc to a duel."

"Lady Cristyn indicated she had no knowledge of what instigated the affair."

Reverend Hughes nodded in agreement. "None of us knew what prompted the supposed breach in honor. I was simply commenting that there was no love lost between the two men, nor did they go to great lengths to hide their mutual animus."

Bran paused to flick a bee away from his collar as he turned to face the priest. "Why do you think my uncle committed suicide, especially if he was reputed to be such a fine marksman? That does not make sense to me."

Reverend Hughes smiled grimly. "You are not the only one who has been bothered by that irregularity. That is the main reason—but not only reason—why I desired to speak to you."

"So you have additional causes to be suspicious?"

"Yes, and no," answered the priest. "There were many things amiss about your uncle's death. Some were more public than others. You already hit on probably the most public discrepancy which is, your uncle's proficiency with a pistol. Why would a person of his skill take his life in the minutes prior to a pistol duel? But there are others, less publicly known. Being that I am the resident doctor, I am also the defacto medical examiner. There were a few irregularities that came out of my post mortem examination, but our doddering old magistrate was less than interested in discussing them. I think he simply wanted the matter to go away quickly. Not that I blame him."

The priest now had Bran's full attention. "What irregularities?"

"Yes, my lord, I would like your opinion. But before I get there I think it would be good if I gave you some context."

Sensing the old priest was starting to weary a little from their walk, Bran gestured to a nearby stone bench. Reverend Hughes assented, and the two men sat down.

"Hmm, where to continue? I have already told you nothing is known about the disagreement in question. The first I heard of it was two days prior to the actual event. Your uncle came to me and told me the news. He offered no explanation other than it was a matter of honor." Reverend Hughes paused for a moment to rub his stiff knee, but then he fixed his eyes on Bran. "Do you know much about duels, my lord, that is duels here in Britain?"

Bran's face screwed up in visible confusion, "I am not sure I am understanding you."

"Procedurally speaking," clarified the priest.

"Oh . . . not a whole lot, I suppose."

"Then let me explain a few things, but also bear in mind there are no hard and fast rules for duels. Typically, when a duel occurs there are six people involved. The aggrieved party, the party being challenged, the master of arms, two seconds, and a medical man, if available. The first two are pretty straight forward. They are the combatants. Next is the master of arms. He is essentially the officiant who oversees the affair. Each combatant also often has a second, a person who can be called upon to fight the duel if the primary party becomes incapacitated. Seconds may also serve as liaisons between the two aggrieved parties. Last, you have a doctor who is ready to tend to the wounded."

"Who was the master of arms for my uncle's duel?" asked Bran.

"Had the duel happened, it would have been me. But as I will share in a moment, events never progressed that far."

"And what about the seconds?"

"There were not any."

Bran was a little taken aback by the priest's answer. "How come? That seems a bit irregular."

"Yes, and no," reflected the priest. "Typically, seconds must be of similar social station as the individuals fighting the duel. When a couple of aristocratic gentlemen decide to take shots at each other in a London suburb they can take their pick from any number of other peers, but it becomes a bit more problematic when you live in a more isolated place like we do. Also, the nature of the duel was very private. To this day I do not even know what it was about. I think both men sought to keep the circle small. That is an old man's long-winded way of saying neither your uncle nor Lord Gyr had a second."

Bran slowly stroked his chin. "I did not know they were such highly ritualized affairs."

"Yes, aside from being a means to settle matters of honor, duels are also a way for young men to proclaim their bravery to their peers. There is nothing like a scar earned in a duel to set you apart from the weaker masses."

"I would rather keep all my physical extremities intact," said Bran, "but we are also digressing from your tale. Please continue."

"The duel was to take place at eight in the morning on a Tuesday, in the old stone quarry. I am guessing the location was settled on because it was midway between the two estates. I was supposed to travel to the site with your uncle, but instead I happened to find myself at Lord Gyr's estate about an hour before the encounter. One of his stable hands was suffering from severe stomach cramps, and I was called out to attend to the lad. About twenty minutes before the appointed hour, the marquess sought me out. He suggested I accompany him to the quarry since I was already at the estate. I agreed.

"We walked in silence for about fifteen minutes through a steady rain. I remember it was raining because I was annoyed that I had forgotten to bring my waterproof cover for my great coat. We finally reached the point where only two small ridges separated us from the quarry. That is when we heard the shot."

"But you could not see my uncle?"

"No, we were still separated by some high ground. As soon as the blast resounded across the landscape, Lord Gyr and I momentarily shared a look. Then in a flash, the marquess took off over that last rise at a dead sprint. I followed, but at a much slower pace. A couple minutes later I crested the second ridge. As I surveyed what lay below, I saw Lord Gyr stooping over your uncle. When I came closer I saw your uncle with a pistol in his hand and lying on his back. The middle of his chest was a bloody mess, and blood was oozing everywhere. I walked up just in time to see a final haunting—almost pleading—look in your uncle's eyes. Lord Gyr's face had also taken on quite a pallor, and he was in a fretful state."

"Did my uncle say anything?" asked Bran.

"No. He died before a single word passed his lips."

"And when you say the wound sat in the middle of his chest, do you mean just that, in the very center?"

"It is funny you should ask that particular question," answered the priest. "That is actually the first irregularity I wanted to discuss with you. The entry wound was right through the metasternum."

"The what?" asked Bran.

"Oh, I am sorry, I am slipping into medical speak. I am referring to that fleshy piece of cartilage that lives right below the sternum."

"That is odd, is it not?" asked Bran.

"If by odd you are wondering why a man would shoot himself right below the sternum, then I tend to agree. I have not done many post-mortems on self-inflicted gunshot wounds, but the few I have done have all been head shots."

"I agree," said Bran, "or at least a clean shot through the heart. Getting shot in the gut is a notoriously painful way to die. I am guessing my uncle would have known that."

Both men sat quietly for a moment. Bran broke the silence. "What kind of pistol did my uncle have in his hand?"

Reverend Hughes paused as if searching the deep recesses of his memory. "It was a medium sized weapon as far as pistols go, standard flintlock design made of some type of dark wood. I also remember that the barrel bore ornate engravings, almost to the point of being gaudy. At the time it struck me as being a strange weapon for your uncle to own."

Bran stroked his chin pensively. "Do you happen to remember if the wooden receiver extended out to the end of the barrel, or was it a short receiver?"

The priest did not hesitate, "Oh, that is easy. The barrel extended a good five or six inches beyond the receiver. I remember because those engravings I mentioned went all the way around the barrel. Why? Is that important?"

"Oh, I do not know. I was just curious. My uncle owned a very nice brace of Durs Egg dueling pistols. They are currently sitting in a box on the side table in my study. I examined them at length one rainy afternoon. They are made of a light-colored wood, and the receivers extend to within half an inch of the end of the barrels. They are also in pristine condition. I would be surprised if they have ever been used. I wonder why he would have brought a different pistol with him. It seems unusual."

Both men sat quietly in thought for a good minute. Bran's brain was still mulling over the issue of the pistol. Reverend Hughes began fishing in his pocket for his pipe and tobacco.

"Would not Lord Gyr have been expected to supply the pistols, being that he received the challenge?" asked Bran.

Reverend Hughes was already puffing on his pipe, but he nodded in the affirmative. Bran allowed him another minute to get the pipe fully lit.

"Sorry," said the priest, "the old girl has been a devil to light as of late. But to better answer your question, the answer is yes. Lord Gyr had a pistol case under his arm as we walked to the quarry together. I distinctly remember him complaining that the rain was going to ruin the finish on the old box."

"Hmm," said Bran, "that implies my uncle brought the other pistol for the sole purpose of shooting himself."

Reverend Hughes removed his pipe and added, "Yes, but then why buy a completely different weapon when you have two excellent pistols at home? One does not just go buy a pistol on a whim around here. It implies this is something he had been thinking about for some time. But then again, there were only thirty-six hours from the time the men settled on the duel and when your uncle shot himself."

Bran stood and began to pace. "This is infuriating. I feel I am overlooking something obvious. Tell me, reverend, do you recall finding a cartridge box or powder horn on my uncle's body? Basically, anything that could be used to load a pistol."

Reverend Hughes did not hesitate in his answer, "No, nothing of the sort. The reason I can tell you with certainty is that I helped put together an inventory of the items found on the deceased. To be honest there was not much, a pocket watch and a handkerchief, but that was about it."

"So, he had no rags or strips of cloth on his person?"

"No, not that I can remember," said the priest.

"And the handkerchief, was is dirty or clean?" asked Bran.

"It was clean, neatly folded in his pocket. I remember thinking it ironic that it was the only clean thing on him."

Bran felt like he was approaching the edge of the fog.

"Well, reverend, you yourself said it was raining considerably. If my uncle arrived at the quarry with the intension of using the mysterious pistol, but without powder or cartridges, then the logical conclusion would be that he loaded it before departing Caer Cigfran. But if it was raining hard, that would be impossible. A heavy rain would quickly remove the priming powder from the flash pan. The only away around this would be to wrap the pan in a rag to protect it, but in a heavy rain even that preventative measure will not last you for long. I was thinking maybe he would use a handkerchief for that purpose, but you adequately dispelled that suspicion. It is also possible to use bee's wax to seal the pan, but why he would have bothered with that, I am not sure. It would have been easier to simply bring extra powder.

"One more question, do you happen to remember what my uncle's wound looked like?"

"What do you mean? Other than being a bloody mess?" asked the priest. His face registered complete confusion.

"I mean, was there anything else inside the wound other than the musket ball?"

Reverend Hughes thought for just a moment and then answered, "No, it was just the ball, and it was not even particularly deep. I barely needed forceps to remove it."

Bran replied with a simple, "Hmm."

The next several minutes passed in silence. Bran paced back and forth like a restless tiger in his cage. The priest sat and smoked his pipe, never taking his eyes off of the younger man. Finally, Bran turned to look at the priest. Reverend Hughes could see a fire in his eyes.

"My dear reverend, I think I know what happened."

"What do you mean, my lord?"

A scowl had slowly begun to spread across Bran's face. "Uncle Llew did not commit suicide. He was murdered."

23

Murder Anyone?

Reverend Hughes did not say anything, but his left eyebrow rose slightly higher than its counterpart.

Bran resumed his explanation. "This is what I think happened. My uncle must have arrived early for the duel. I am also guessing you and the marquess might have been delayed, am I not correct?"

The priest nodded, "Quite true. The rain and my old legs slowed us down a little. We were probably five minutes late."

Bran nodded as he continued his pacing. "Unfortunately, unbeknownst to my uncle, he probably was not alone. If my theory holds true, there would have been two other men hiding somewhere in the rocks. From what I have seen of the old quarry, it forms a natural bowl with a flat grassy area at the bottom. Surrounding the flat area is a vast array of boulders and jagged stony outcroppings."

"That is correct," said Reverend Hughes. "We found your uncle in the bottom of the bowl. That would have been the natural place to fight the duel. It would have also limited the chance of an errant shot bringing an innocent bystander to harm. Not that it would have been particularly likely."

Bran continued, "I am guessing one of the concealed men was equipped with a rifled musket. A skilled marksman with such a weapon can deliver a killing shot at over two hundred yards. I was never that good, but I had more than a few men who served under me that were capable of such a feat. However, due to the weather and the nature of the terrain, he could have been much closer and still remained concealed. This would have especially been the case if he had situated himself ahead of time, which it sounds like he did. A gray blanket dropped over a shooter in a prone position could make a man virtually indistinguishable from the surrounding landscape."

Reverend Hughes nodded his understanding, then asked, "And the other hidden man?"

"The timing of the shot was critical. If my uncle was killed prior to your arrival, they would not have gained the crucial witness in the affair."

Dawning recognition hit the priest's face, "Me!"

Bran smiled slightly, "That is correct. It was the role of the second man to keep a lookout at the top of the ridge. Once he saw the two of you approaching, he could give the signal to the shooter. It would only take the shooter a few more seconds to set up and take the shot."

Reverend Hughes had the look of someone who was only partially fitting the pieces in their places. "But how can you be so sure there was a shooter in the rocks?"

"For all the reasons we have already discussed," said Bran. "First, there is the powder, or lack of. Why would a man set on killing himself not bring any? I have never attempted to kill myself, but it seems if anything, you would be extra prepared. Second, there is the location of the wound. Maybe one in a thousand men trying to commit suicide is going to shoot himself right below the rib cage. I am guessing the shooter did not adequately factor in the impact of the rain on the ballistic trajectory of the shot, or he simply was not a skilled enough shooter to hit his target dead on; not to mention the added difficulty if my uncle was moving in any way. Lastly, there is the issue of just the ball being found in the wound. Had he placed the barrel of the gun against his chest, as he would have undoubtedly been forced to do, the weapon would have fired the wadding along with the bullet into the wound. A wound clean of any wadding implies the gun was fired at some distance other than at point blank."

Bran stood silently, eyes fixed on the priest, awaiting feedback on his theory.

Reverend Hughes sat silently for a moment, teeth clamped on the pipe, thinking over what he had just heard. His eyes carried a far-away look. In truth, he was trying to reconcile this theory with the real-world impact it would have had on the death of his friend. He finally came out of his reflective stupor and turned his attention to Bran. "I am sorry, my lord. This is a lot to process. I cannot deny that I am pleased to think your uncle did not kill himself, but murder is just as ugly an end-state, and what is worse, the malignant entity who brought it about is more than likely still walking the earth." He took another puff on his pipe, "Am I correct in assuming that is not the end of your postulations?"

"Yes, you are correct," responded Bran grimly. "You probably would not be surprised if I told you I thought Lord Gyr was behind this entire affair. For a while now, following my uncle's death, it has been apparent that a third party has been seeking to possess something that was in my uncle's possession. What that is we cannot know; but based on the continuous attempts to rob the estate, we can only assume they have been unable to realize their objective. We may not know what they are looking for, but we can only assume it is either of great intrinsic value, or it is of particular personal value to the person who is seeking it."

"—and," Reverend Hughes interjected, "we can also assume they have been unsuccessful up until this point since you and her ladyship were able to interrupt their most recent attempt, and there have been none since."

Bran's hand instinctively massaged the side of his head, as if to see if his souvenir from the fight was still present. "That being said," Bran continued, "I believe Lord Gyr is the one behind this. It is the only answer that makes sense, and believe me when I say I am trying really hard to separate my personal loathing of the man from the facts of the situation. But regardless, there was something going on between Lord Gyr and my uncle, to the extent it deteriorated into a duel. While there may be many thoughts regarding what angered my uncle enough to demand satisfaction, one likely theory is that Lord Gyr was upset over Lady Cristyn's continual rebuffs, and my uncle unequivocally told him to move on. Unfortunately, that theory fails to explain the frequent break-ins; plus, in some ways, you might expect Lord Gyr to do the challenging if the circumstances were such. So, we will leave his motive unsettled for now."

Reverend Hughes slapped his knee, "I have it! What if your uncle had some type of evidence that young Lord Gyr had murdered her ladyship's father, the previous marquess?"

Bran stood still, stroking his chin with his hand. "You know, I had not thought of that, but I suppose it is a possibility. But to play devil's advocate, if Uncle Llew had some type of evidence that Caradoc killed his uncle, why sit on it? Would it not make sense to take it before the House of Lords?"

"Maybe his evidence was only circumstantial," countered the priest.

"—or my uncle was blackmailing Lord Gyr." Bran said this with a degree of reservation. "I do not like the thought, but perhaps it is a possibility, is it not?"

"Not in a thousand years," said Reverend Hughes. "Your uncle was not the type. Besides, we are forgetting about the missing money. If he was blackmailing Lord Gyr, he would have had mysterious funds flowing into his bank account, not out. But what about the actual events of the day your uncle died, aside from the sharpshooter that is?"

Bran started to slowly pace again in front of the sitting priest. "Bear in mind this is all still conjecture, and if you feel I am too far afield with any of it, please feel free to interrupt."

"Will do, but please continue."

"When Lord Gyr was unable to obtain what he sought from my uncle, whatever it may be, I think he figured the next best solution was to have my uncle killed. So, when the prospect of the duel arose, it was the perfect opportunity to achieve his ends. Unfortunately for Lord Gyr, there was one problem. My uncle was an outstanding pistol marksman, as many have attested. That being said, Lord Gyr had to find a way to tilt the odds in his favor without risking himself. Therefore, he hatched a scheme. On the morning of the duel he had one of his more trusted servants feign a stomach ailment shortly before the appointed hour. You were called for, which in turn assured your coincidental presence at the estate. Meanwhile, my uncle showed up at the meeting place, but with no pistol since Lord Gyr was going to supply the proverbial tools of the trade. Before my uncle arrived, I am guessing the shooter and the lookout were already in place. Meanwhile, Lord Gyr's request for you to accompany him not only assured the presence of a second witness, but the fact that he was the one who asked you to accompany him gave him a degree of immunity in the affair. When the lookout saw the two of you were within earshot, he gave the signal to the shooter. A moment later the two of you heard the crack of the shot, and then—"

The old priest spoke with a dawning realization in his eyes. "—Lord Gyr took off over the ridge to where your uncle lay."

"Exactly," said Bran, "and what probably seemed like a very natural act to you at the time, in truth bought him a crucial minute unobserved with the dead or dying man. Upon reaching my uncle, I am guessing Lord Gyr extracted a third pistol from within his coat and pressed it into my uncle's hand. The pistol may have even been recently fired, and of the same caliber as the musket. He could not risk such matters in case there had ended up being a more in-depth inquiry. Fortunately for him, no such inquiry occurred. He also might have repositioned the body to make the affair look more natural. Lastly, this precious minute alone with my uncle's dead or dying body probably also had a third, very grisly, but vital aim associated with it. Lord Gyr had to ensure my uncle was dead. The fact that Uncle Llew did not expire until moments after your arrival helps explain why Lord Gyr was in such a nervous state."

"—And that look in his eyes. At the time I took it to be a dying man's petition for forgiveness, but if what you postulated is indeed true, then your uncle perhaps sought to communicate the truth of what befell him."

Both men stared at each other in silence as if to fully take in the magnitude of what had just been said.

The priest knit his eyebrows in concern. "Would I be right in assuming, my lord, that you are not going to just let this lie?"

"Absolutely not," responded a resolute Bran. "I am going to make sure the sonofabitch hangs for his crime."

Reverend Hughes could not help but smirk at the younger man's intensity. "Hmm, that sounds like a plan I can get behind, but if I am not mistaken, are we not a little short in the evidence department?"

"True," said Bran, "but I think there might be a way to get the evidence we need."

"You have managed to pique my curiosity. What is your plan?" The priest took a big puff on his pipe as the younger man collected his thoughts.

"I thought I might employ a gambit. I think we can also assume the person behind the various robbery attempts is none other than Lord Gyr, and I will go so far as to say that he is desperate to recover said item. I am thinking this unknown item is either what the duel was about, or it somehow incriminates the marquess. I am going to use this piece of information against him."

"I am following," said the priest.

"I will write a letter to his lordship. In that letter I will tell him I have the item he seeks, and I would like to meet him at the stone quarry tomorrow morning to discuss the matter. Nothing more, nothing less."

The priest puffed thoughtfully for a moment before questioning Bran. "To be honest, I am not quite sure what you are seeking to gain through this ploy."

"A couple of things," said Bran. "First, I am hoping my bluff causes him to either say something that gives some indication of what the missing item is, or where it might be found. My desire is that the item will help us link the ugly affair back to Lord Gyr."

"And the second thing you hope to achieve?" queried the priest. He saw something reckless in the younger man's eyes that he did not fully like.

"I plan on tempting Lord Gyr's sharp shooter with the chance for an encore performance."

The priest's eyes widened until they matched the size of his round spectacles. "You are going to use yourself as bait? That is ridiculous. You will end up like your uncle."

Bran grinned. "Perhaps, but there is an old war proverb that says, 'The opportunity of defeating the enemy is provided by the enemy himself.'"

Reverend Hughes sat stony-faced, but then dawning realization began to creep across his face. "You are going to employ the use of your own sharpshooter?"

Bran nodded.

"To shoot his lordship?"

"If it comes down to it," said Bran, "but I was mainly thinking of the other shooter. I am hoping it will be someone who has close ties with Lord Gyr. That in itself could be the evidence I am seeking."

"But who did you have in mind to watch your back from the rocks?"

"I thought Mr. Stanton might oblige. He has already saved my skin once—"

"—and he is more than big enough to handle trouble." The old priest finished his sentence for him.

"Exactly."

"And the reason you are wanting to meet him in the quarry is to bait him into using his shooter for a second time?"

"Correct again," said Bran.

"You do realize you are still taking a terrible risk?"

"Of course, but this really is the only way to come up with the needed evidence. Now if you will excuse me, reverend, I have a letter to write to Lord Gyr."

As Reverend Hughes watched the younger man ascend the garden steps back up to the house, the cold feeling of dread began to pluck at his heart strings. He felt like they were missing some crucial element.

24

Convergence

Bran paused in a sally port at the side of the house and gazed into the calm, steady drizzle soaking the green countryside. The morning held a deceptive calm, and he suddenly wished he was in another time and place. The confidence that came so freely the previous day had slowly evaporated during the night as he lay awake contemplating the different potential outcomes of his plan. But Bran also knew events were carrying him along quickly, and the only viable course was forward. In the crook of his left arm he held his Pennsylvania rifle. In an oil skin bag he carried ammunition.

It took him only a few moments to wind his way through puddles of standing water on his way to the stables. A minute later he located Stanton in one of the horse boxes. The man had his hip pushed up against the hock of a large, white stallion as he cradled the horse's foot in his left hand. With his other hand he was using a hoof knife to clean some debris from the horse's foot. The groom heard Bran's approach and was able to tilt his head just enough to identify his visitor. The giant man dropped the hoof with a thump, and the horse ambled to the other side of the box in search of some oats.

"Good morning, my lord, I did not expect you this morning. Were you wanting to go for a ride? If so, give me ten minutes and I can have Jackie ready for you."

"Thank you, Stanton, but I require your assistance with a different matter, if you would be willing."

"Course, my lord."

Over the next few minutes Bran explained his suspicions regarding the existence of a sharpshooter at his forthcoming rendezvous with Lord Gyr. Bran left out his misgivings regarding the death of his uncle; neither did he mention why he anticipated the presence of a shooter.

When Stanton heard the news that Bran wanted him to come along as a lookout, his face blanched, but the color soon returned. "Sounds like a bad job if I have ever heard one, my lord."

"I agree," said Bran.

"Let me get this straight. You want me to take a musket and head out to the old quarry separate from you?"

"That is correct," said Bran.

"And you want me to keep an eye on things while you talk to the marquess?"

"Precisely." Bran was pleased to see Stanton's face devoid of tension. The man simply took on the look of a soldier who was wanting to ensure that he accomplished his piece of the mission without mishap.

"And what do you want me to do, my lord, if things begin to look suspicious or if I run across somebody hiding in the rocks?"

Bran spelled out his plan of attack. When he was finished he looked Stanton directly in the eye. "Tell me, Stanton, are you up for it? Do you think you can pull it off? My life will be in your hands."

"Yes, my lord, I would be honored to help. This is not my first scrap, but mind you be careful, my lord. I did not save you last time just to see you get all shot up." He gave Bran a toothy, lopsided grin.

Bran returned the gesture with a slap to the man's beefy shoulder. "Good chap. You ought to head out in about fifteen minutes. That should give you plenty of time. You will want to approach the location in as secretive a manner as possible so as to not give your presence away. I would recommend going without a horse. I am going to depart just a little after you. That will allow me to also keep an eye on things in case someone else decides to show up early too."

Stanton merely nodded his understanding.

Bran smiled at the man. His simple rural ways gave him a certain likability. "Oh, and I almost forgot," said Bran, "here is my old rifled musket. Probably a little different from what you are used to, but I am sure you will figure it out. Cartridges are in the bag. I would probably wait to load it unless you come across anything suspicious."

The burly man took the bag from the young noble. "No worries, my lord. I will have your back covered."

After his discussion with the groom, Bran returned to the house to get his own things. Thirty minutes later he began his journey to the quarry. A worn leather pouch loosely hung over his shoulder. The small bag contained an assortment of his own pre-packaged cartridges. Deep inside his coat he had stashed both his tomahawk and one of his uncle's dueling pistols. The weapon was primed and loaded, but not charged.

Bran had considered riding Jackie to the site, but then opted to walk. He figured a brisk hike would be good to get his blood flowing. He also hoped it would aid in settling the queasiness he was beginning to feel in his stomach. Bran had been in combat more times than he could recall, but each and every time he harbored the same feelings of trepidation in the hours leading up to a confrontation.

When Bran was about halfway to the quarry, he came upon a patch of low ground that was extremely spongy due to the falling rain. With the practiced skill of an infantryman Bran artfully maneuvered around the north side of the bog. Even with his careful maneuvering, his boots were beginning to soak through. He began to regret his decision not to bring a mount. Also, what if he became wounded? Without his horse, he would have to walk injured all the way back to the estate.

Once clear of the low ground, Bran started up a steady incline. Five hundred feet to his front he saw a copse of trees. From previous rides around the estate he knew the copse meant he was heading directly towards the quarry.

In another ten minutes he arrived. The quarry was essentially a giant limestone bowl. In addition to being the halfway point between his and Lord Gyr's estates, the quarry was once the primary limestone repository for the whole region. Bran guessed his own little castle was fashioned using stone from this very quarry. However, the open mine now sat derelict. It was as if a giant claw had scraped a jagged gash in the lush countryside.

Once Bran had found his way to a flat area in the middle of the quarry, he searched his surroundings for a place to temporarily retreat from the rain. It became quickly apparent that he was going to have no such luck. Bran took a moment to check the priming on his pistol. Satisfied it was still dry, he sat down against a large boulder and adjusted his angle slightly to keep the tomahawk and pistol from digging into his sides. Then he waited.

The gnarled wood door let loose a creaking slam as Bran departed the box. Roger Stanton stood completely motionless for a good three minutes. His ape-like arms were slack, and his left hand still gripped the oil skin bag and musket from his master. The man's face was expressionless as he slowly contemplated everything the young lord had just shared with him. Then deciding he had been standing long enough, he made his way to a bale of hay. With an audible sigh he plopped down his sizable frame, depositing Bran's musket on a nearby pile. His thick fingers instinctively found their way into his pocket. He fished out a cotton bag and small stack of rectangular pieces of paper, and with practiced dexterity skillfully rolled a small cigarette. A moment later he was inhaling the sweet smoke.

The groom took a moment to marvel at the trust some people automatically bestowed upon their fellow human beings. He typically found it was the blasted aristocracy that suffered most from this shortcoming. Spend your whole life having people fawn over your every move, and of course you were going to assume the whole world was there to serve you.

He had witnessed this trait in the junior officers who had commanded him in India and more recently in Ceylon. But why would they think otherwise? Most of the men who served under them had sufficient street smarts to render the appropriate, "Yes, my lord," when the situation called for it. He sometimes wondered how many of these gentlemen knew all that separated them from a private's bayonet was an NCO's sword or the lash. Not that any man with brains would expect anything otherwise. The men who filled the ranks were either tricked, desperate, or forced to take the king's shilling in lieu of a prison sentence. But how could you expect a smarmy duke's son to know any of that?

His thoughts went back to a particular young ensign who had joined their company right before the invasion of Ceylon. Stanton had known from day one that the little prick had to go. The young viscount treated all enlisted soldiers like they were members of his household staff back in Kent. "Williams, be a good chap and fill my canteen," or, "Sharpe, please go water my horse while I read this dispatch."

Stanton chuckled to himself. He would never forget that evening when the captain assigned Clayton and him to go with the young officer on a short reconnaissance mission. It had been so easy. They had departed just after dark. The two privates were on foot, but the ensign decided to bring his great black charger. They were barely gone an hour when he and Clayton concocted a scheme. As they approached a sharp precipice overlooking the valley, Clayton asked the ensign to come give his opinion on the enemy's position in the valley. Stanton could still picture the young viscount climbing off his horse. He was arrayed like a little peacock, complete with accompanying plumage. The kid paused to dust off his uniform before he sauntered over to the edge of the cliff. He barely had a chance to raise his mama's forty guinea telescope to his eye before Stanton gave him a shove worthy of royalty. It was glorious, even though it turned out peacocks do not fly that well. The little fool flailed his arms and legs through the air as he screamed, that is until he impaled himself on the remnants of an old stump two hundred feet below. There he stuck, and probably remained stuck to this day, at least the parts the animals did not eat.

Stanton and Clayton had laughed until their sides could take no more. But the best part of the whole escapade was the story they fed their captain. They simply told him the horse had lost its footing, and the young officer had been thrown over a cliff. There were no subsequent questions. That was simply the end of it. Yep, they were all too damn trusting.

But Stanton knew he could not live in the past. The past neither put bread on the table nor ale into one's hand. So with a great heave he propelled himself back to his feet. Grinding the remnants of the cigarette under his heel, he headed to the door of the stable box, scooping up the oil skin bag and musket as he went. After all, what was one more killing or two?

Twenty minutes later Stanton began cursing. What had started as a gentle rain deteriorated into an all-out downpour. The burly groom hated the rain. It reminded him of cold nights in Yorkshire as a child. The flimsy roof on the family's little hovel frequently failed to keep rain out. Rainy nights meant sleepless nights in the Stanton household. Not that he had much to complain about. When your father was a drunk and your mother a whore, you were lucky to have food in your belly, let alone a roof over your head. Fortunately, he and his younger brother, Quentin, had been first rate thieves from the time they started walking. Of course, if you are going to live in a small village and steal, then you had better be good, because there is nowhere to hide.

Little brother Quentin possessed a knack for anticipating things. This made him good at pilfering. He always seemed to know the very moment a farmer or shop keeper would look the other way. But he did not stop there. In the close confines of the market he was able to watch four or five people at once and anticipate the exact moment they all would have their eyes turned. In the literal blink of an eye the small urchin in their midst would claim his prize and vanish.

Even the best are eventually caught though, as was the case with Quentin. He received a blistering beating at the hands of the local baker. Quentin then and there forever lost his nerve. Not that Stanton blamed him. Quentin never had had his older brother's strength.

Instead, Quentin turned his skills to service. His ability to anticipate his master's every need allowed him to quickly rise to the station of gentleman's gentleman.

Stanton, on the other hand, did not go in for subtlety. If he was going to steal something, he preferred to simply bludgeon the person into unconsciousness. This allowed him to rob the person at his leisure. But like Quentin, his methods eventually caught up with him. By the time young Quentin was ironing shirts for some lord, Stanton was forced to take the king's shilling. The next week he boarded a troop transport to India. His younger brother died of consumption a year later.

The rain now started to ease. Stanton pulled an old, gold pocket watch from inside his coat. The timepiece was the most valuable thing he owned. He had looted it off of the body of a dead sergeant following an especially bloody battle with the Maratha. The watch revealed that he was plenty early. After making an initial reconnaissance of the quarry and coming across nothing suspicious, Stanton turned his attention to his weapon.

Like any good soldier Stanton had his musket loaded in less than a minute. He would have been much faster if he had been standing with a smooth bore musket in his hand like he had used in the army. However, the riflings made it three times as hard to push the ramrod down the barrel. He also did not want to stand lest he give away his location, so he was forced to do the loading hunched up against a boulder. But it did not much matter, time was his ally. Lying in the prone position, Stanton placed the oil skin bag atop his musket where it could serve as an effective barrier between the rain and powder. He then nestled his big frame up under the shallow outcropping of a large rock and waited for the curtain to go up on Lord Gruffudd's little show.

Cristyn precariously snaked her way along the narrow ledge. To make matters worse, incessant moisture gave each stone a slick mossy coating. If navigating her way along the two-inch-wide ledge was not difficult enough under normal circumstances, she had the added difficulty of holding two well-used quilts over her head. She had little choice; other than her bonnet, the well-loved patchwork hand-me-downs were her only shelter from the rapidly increasing downpour. She was confident she would make it unscathed, but then it happened. As her left foot came down on one of the scalloped edge stones, the hundred-year-old mortar gave way. Not all the way, but just enough for her to lose her already precarious footing. Her attempt to adjust her center of balance resulted in a fatal act of overcompensation. With a terrific splash both feet unceremoniously landed in the three-inch-deep water that filled the rectory's walkway. She let out a small scream as her ears filled simultaneously with laughter. She looked up from her sodden feet to see Reverend Hughes leaning both arms against the stone doorway, clearly unable to contain his mirth. She flashed him her best imitation of wounded aristocratic pride. Then with as reproachful a tone as she could muster, she took the offensive. "Reverend Hughes, has my family not given this parish enough money over the years to enable you to fix this ridiculous nuisance of a walkway? I thought the idea of a path was to keep your feet dry when it rained, not wash them."

By now the priest's laughter had subsided to a mere chuckle. "I suppose you are right, my lady, but then I would lose what I have enjoyed for the past fifteen years."

"And what is that, may I ask?" She was working to keep her face straight, especially considering she was pretty confident she already knew the answer to her own question.

"Why, your lovely balancing tricks. Every rainy Sunday since you were five I have been watching you navigate those edge stones. I would think you would be better at it by now."

She gave a soft "Humph," but her expression softened. "But never mind that, it just means you owe me a cup of tea; and I barely had time for breakfast, so if you have anything to go with it, I would not say no." She knew she was being less than ladylike, but every once in a while the little girl in her strained to burst forth, especially with Reverend Hughes.

"Of course, of course," the old priest smiled. "I even have a fire going, so you will be able to dry out a bit. But tell me, what brought the prettiest young lady in the district to my humble doorstep at such an early hour?"

Cristyn already had her shoes in her hand and was sliding over to the priest's well-tended fire. "Oh, it was my own forgetfulness. I promised Mrs. Simmons I would bring her these two old quilts yesterday, but I forgot. I knew rain was imminent, so I thought if I went out early I might be able to get ahead of it." She then pointed her soggy, stocking-clad toes toward the fire and gave a theatrical sigh, "But alas not."

The priest chuckled again, "No, alas not, but it is just as well. I suppose we could both benefit from the other's company while his lordship is thus engaged."

Cristyn furrowed her brow at the comment.

Reverend Hughes knew instantly he had erred.

"My dear reverend, pray tell, what are you referring to?" The whimsical tone that had filled her voice seconds earlier was now gone.

Reverend Hughes frantically searched for a way to minimize the damage. "Oh, nothing of importance, my lady. It was simply my understanding that Lord Gruffudd went to discuss something with your cousin this morning. Nothing more."

Cristyn sat stony-faced. "Just a discussion, reverend? Was he meeting Caradoc at Foxglove, or Caer Cigfran per chance?"

The priest knew he was cornered. "I do not believe either, my lady."

"What do you mean? Where else would they meet?"

Reverend Hughes felt a lone bead of sweat make a painstakingly slow journey from his temple to his chin. In search of a diversion, he rose to his feet to tend the fire. As the flames began to reclaim their former life, he returned his attention to his guest.

Cristyn was still staring at him, expression unchanged. "Come now, reverend, it would be easier if you just told me. I will undoubtedly discover the answer one way or another."

The priest's face took on a sallow complexion, and his voice communicated defeat.

"My lady, I believe they are meeting at the quarry." He braced for what he knew was coming.

"Bloody hell!" she exploded. Her outburst overwhelmed the room.

Reverend Hughes winced, pinching the bridge of his nose.

"Forgive me, reverend, but are you telling me the moron went off to get himself killed in a duel just like his—"

"—No, my lady, you misunderstand me," the priest interjected. "The purpose of their meeting was to simply talk through some things."

"Talk through some things? What things?" Her eyebrows knit together in a look of perplexity.

"Lord Gruffudd believes his uncle did not commit suicide, but instead was caught up in a murder plot orchestrated by your cousin. In the absence of hard evidence, he wanted to see if he could goad Lord Gyr into betraying himself."

"Are you sure he was not going just to pick a fight? Because I can see him picking a fight."

"That I cannot be completely sure of, my lady. You know how Lord Gruffudd is. Action never seems to be too far in the offing, but I am pretty sure the intent of the rendezvous was simply to talk through some things." Reverend Hughes cringed slightly inside. He knew he was perilously close to being less than truthful concerning the matter.

"Did he take a weapon, reverend?"

"That I cannot be sure of either, though I am assuming he at least took that tomahawk of his."

Cristyn sat back in her chair. She was regaining control of her emotions as she wrestled with this new collection of information. "Do you have any idea what prompted this foolery?"

"I do, and while I was not sure if it was my place to share this information with you at first, I think it is best to tell you now. However, it is a story that will take a few minutes. Do you mind if I finish making the tea first?"

She dumbly nodded her head, not quite sure what to expect next. He slowly shuffled around the kitchen, and the familiar clinking of pewter and china filled the room. A minute later he brought her a cup of tea. A single sip told her he had prepared it just the way she preferred it—a dash of cream with two lumps. Somewhere deep inside she smiled.

The old man had barely touched his backside to his armchair when she again plied him with questions. "So, what is this all about? I mean, what is it you are willing to tell me?" There was nothing accusatory in her voice, only a longing desire to know something, anything.

He sat for a brief moment organizing his thoughts, but to Cristyn it might have been an eternity. Then over the next twenty minutes he did his best to convey the finer points of the previous day's discussion. Fortunately, the young lady's quick wit allowed her to fill gaps he may have otherwise left unattended, and she impassively drank in every detail. It was not until the revelation about the sharpshooter in the rocks that her aspect began to change.

"Excuse me, reverend—" her voice began to take on an air of desperation "—but you are telling me there might be a shooter lurking in those rocks even as we speak?"

"Yes, my lady, but do not worry, Lord Gruffudd was well aware of the risk. That is why he took help with him."

"Took help? Who? Surely not Thornbush or Joseph?"

"He took Roger Stanton, my lady. If you recall, he used to be a soldier himself, and I dare say he can handle—"

The sound of breaking china reverberated around the room. Cristyn's shattered cup lay on the floor, hot tea rapidly spreading across the flagstones.

"What time was this meeting to take place?" Her voice was raspy and broken.

Frightened by the sudden change in her aspect, the priest blurted out, "Nine this morning."

Cristyn glanced at the old clock on the wall and, observing the hour, catapulted to her feet. "I think there is still time."

Reverend Hughes was now growing more and more alarmed. "My lady, what is it? What have I said?"

She responded sharply, but the terror in her voice had been replaced with a steely resignation, "Reverend, do you own a pistol?"

"Yes," he responded reflexively, "over on the mantle."

Her eyes fell upon the old navy service weapon. "And cartridges?"

"In the box next to it."

Then to Reverend Hughes' utter astonishment, she rapidly moved to the mantle and, with a proficiency he never would have imagined, she loaded the pistol. Before he could think of what to say, Cristyn had her wet shoes back on her feet, loaded pistol and spare cartridges wrapped in her bonnet, and then she was gone.

25

Tables Turned

Water dripped from every inch of Bran's body, and even in the open air his nostrils filled with the stench of wet wool. Without a hat for cover, he wiped his hand across his face, temporarily freeing his eyes from the endless deluge of water. The heavy rain brought his thoughts back to the pistol, and he took a moment to check the state of the priming one more time. He had just completed the task when he caught sight of a figure approaching from across the quarry. Bran reached inside his coat, cocked the hammer to the rear, and rose to his feet. He had spent the last half hour trying to anticipate the many ways the conversation might unfold. As the marquess drew near, Bran stood immobile but ready for any eventuality. The newcomer stopped once he was within eight paces of the American. Bran spoke first.

"Lord Gyr, how kind of you to meet me on this lovely day. Granted, we could have shared tea back at my estate, but I always took you for an outdoorsman, so I thought this might be preferable."

"What is it you want, Gruffudd?" Lord Gyr's tone was devoid of pleasantries.

"I think I have something you might want."

The marquess could not hide a flinch. "And what would that be might I ask?"

"What you and your cronies have been looking for."

Lord Gyr paused, measuring his next words. "I am not exactly sure what you are referring to. Perhaps you would take a moment to enlighten me."

Bran knew his bluff would become flimsier with every word he spoke, but he still had some distance to go before he learned anything of consequence. "We are both gentlemen, my lord, so let us not insult each other. I have what you want, and I want to now negotiate the terms of an exchange."

Lord Gyr's countenance clouded, but Bran could also tell his mind was nibbling at the hook. "And what is it you want to exchange for this *thing*?"

Bran had anticipated this line of questioning, and without knowing what the item in question was, he knew any answer he gave would be fraught with risk. He chose the only answer that made sense. "I want money." The marquess smiled, and Bran knew immediately he had played the wrong card.

"Money?" said an incredulous Lord Gyr, his eyes wide in dawning realization. He now knew he was being played.

Bran saw the man's hand dive for the inside of his coat, and Bran did the same. The next thing he knew, both he and Lord Gyr were each looking down the barrel of the other man's pistol. "Lord Gyr, does this mean we have moved on to negotiating a price?"

"I do not know what you are playing at Gruffudd, but this is going to end badly for you."

"Like it did for my uncle?"

"Your uncle was a fool, but apparently that is a family trait," sneered the marquess. "The whole lot of you would have been better off going to the colonies."

"Is that why you had someone shoot him?"

Lord Gyr smiled and his eyes were full of malice. "My dear Lord Gruffudd, I do not think you have quite the handle on the situation that you think you do."

At one hundred yards Stanton had a clear field of view to most of the flat area below. He wiped the beading rain from his eyes and strained to see through the downpour. His slow scan of the terrain yielded nothing at first; however, on the second pass he caught site of a solitary figure sitting against a large boulder. Stanton tensed but then relaxed. It was only Lord Gruffudd. He was not sure how he had missed the man's arrival. The man was good, there was no doubt about it. Leaning the back of his broad shoulder against the boulder, he remained a horizontal statue. He could tell Bran was searching the rocks, wondering if the ex-soldier was already out there, but Stanton did nothing to betray his position.

Fifteen minutes later things became decidedly more interesting. A second figure slowly began to approach from the far side of the quarry. The person was still some distance away, but Stanton assumed the newcomer was Lord Gyr. Having identified both key players in the little affair, Stanton began to scan the surrounding rocks, searching for anyone else who might have joined their little soiree.

His eyes remained on a swivel for the next few minutes, at which point he thought he detected the slightest sign of movement in the rocks far off to his left. Without lifting the barrel of his musket, he slowly repositioned his body on his right arm to afford a better look. He barely breathed lest he give his own position away. There was definitely someone else, or something else, out there. He could feel it in his bones. Experience had taught him that much. The question was, who and where? He considered repositioning to get a better look but knew he would risk exposing himself. After all, he was fully confident he would be able to spot the stranger before he came too close.

Stanton shifted his attention back to the drama unfolding below. Seeing his approaching counterpart, Lord Gruffudd had risen from his meager retreat. He stood in the largest open area, waiting for Lord Gyr to come to him. When the two men were within about twenty feet of each other, the marquess stopped. Stanton could tell the two lords were discussing something, but with the rain and distance they may as well have been two mimes as far as Stanton was concerned.

Stanton turned his focus back to the area of the movement he had seen earlier, but all was calm amongst the surrounding rocky outcroppings. Resettling himself in the prone position, he removed the oil skin bag off of the musket's firing mechanism. He gave the pan one quick check to make sure the powder was still present and dry. Only then did he notice beaded water in the musket's iron sights. He flicked it clear with his thumb. Weight resting on his elbows, chest off of the ground, he pulled the stock tight into his shoulder.

Stanton was again watching the two lords having their silent discussion, when the unexpected happened. Both men extracted pistols from their great coats at the exact same moment. The next thing he knew, each man had the other locked in his sights. Stanton knew it was time to do his job. Prior experience taught him that rain could cause long musket shots to miss low, so he fixed the sights on his target's head. He began the process of slowing his breathing, lest his inflating lungs jar his shot.

It was then that he heard the clatter of sliding pebbles behind him. In that instant he knew he had underestimated his opponent.

The light shower was now a steady downpour. Cristyn made good progress for the first fifteen minutes after leaving the rectory, but things now slowed substantially. Water-sodden fields full of muddy depressions meant she was forced to continually backtrack. More than once the sticky mud removed one of her shoes. In frustration she now carried both shoes in her hand. Finally she approached her destination, and even though she did not have a pocket watch to mark her progress, her gut told her she still had time. Straight ahead was the north edge of the quarry. Countless summer strolls taken as a child allowed her to hit her mark unerringly. Scrambling up the outside of the rocky bowl, she glanced down at her attire. What had been a beautiful white muslin dress an hour earlier was now a mud-spattered, dirt-colored mess. On any other day she would have grimaced, but today it brought a small smile to her lips. The dirty dress with its uneven discoloration of brown hues, would now give her the perfect camouflage to move undetected among the rocks. In a moment of inspiration she ran her hand against one of the juicier, more persistent globs of mud attached to her hem. She used her fingers to rub it over her usually fair face. Had she not been so worried about Bran's welfare, she would have laughed at the idea of her friends seeing her now.

With her facial camouflage complete, she continued to the top of the small rise, only slowing after she reached the crest.

Using a large boulder to obscure her position, she took in the surrounding situation.

Down below, she could see the two lords approaching each other. They were still separated by a short distance. She turned her attention back to the rocks to her front. She knew there was a shooter out there, and unbeknownst to Bran, there was only one. It was the man Bran had asked to accompany him.

As Cristyn's keen eyes swept from rock to rock, she considered what the next few minutes might ask of her.

The truth had made itself known to her the moment Reverend Hughes presented the idea of a sharp shooter in the rocks. When Roger Stanton had first arrived at Caer Cigfran, like everyone, she had been blinded by the man's timely rescue of his lordship. She never considered a connection between him and Lord Gyr's deceased valet who shared the same surname. In retrospect, she wondered how she could have been so foolish. The man was obviously a plant. What Lord Gyr could not acquire by thievery he sought to gain by treachery, and Stanton had been sent by Lord Gyr to play the hero that night.

She glimpsed a subtle movement next to a large rock approximately two hundred feet away. Her eyes slowly traveled along the belly of the rock, where she was almost sure she could make out the indistinct outline of a large person lying prostrate on the ground. But how to be sure? It did not matter. Certainty was not a luxury she could afford right now. If she did not act fast she might as well do nothing at all.

Crouching down low, she began to move in a large arc with the suspected shooter's position at its center. Cristyn hoped to move undetected until she could take possession of the high ground behind the shooter. One by one, she sprinted from boulder to bolder. Each time she would pause, taking a moment to assess whether she had been sighted. Second by second, boulder by boulder, she closed the distance.

She was within fifty feet of her goal and was in the process of sprinting hunchbacked to her next position of concealment when she lost her footing and stumbled. She reflexively extended both hands to break her fall, but she involuntarily dropped the pistol in the process. Even as sharp rocks lacerated her hands and knees, her only thought was to keep from calling out. To her relief, the pistol slid behind the rock she had been moving towards. Using every piece of remaining momentum from her fall, she scurried next to it. She heaved a great sigh and clutched the pistol to her breast. Thank goodness she had not charged the weapon before now. An accidental discharge would have proved disastrous.

Cristyn waited for what seemed like an eternity before she considered moving again. Had her adversary seen her? God willing, the man would dismiss her movements as that of a fox or some other small animal. When she felt like she could afford to wait no longer, she pulled herself back to her feet. She continued her strange dance through the rocks, but this time more slowly. Desperation overtook her as she saw the two lords in the field below pull their weapons on each other. With a last burst of adrenaline she closed the remaining twenty feet to the shooter. Her haste almost proved to be her undoing as her bloody feet refused to stop on the loose gravel. She grabbed a large boulder with her right hand to arrest her momentum, and she simultaneously cocked the hammer on the pistol with her left. It took all the strength in her hand to lock the mechanism in place. The mechanical clicking sound caused her adversary to start, but before she could say a word, the shooter squeezed his own trigger.

No sooner had Lord Gyr finished his declaration of Bran's naiveté than the crack of a musket rent the air. Bran's eyes caught a powder flash among the rocks, and something snapped past his right ear. Instinctively, he threw himself into the course grass and out of the line of fire. As he fell into a prone position, his eyes surveyed where the shot had originated. Bran hoped to spot his assailant, but the rain made a kaleidescope of the rocky outcroppings, making it extremely difficult to see. *Come on Stanton, I could use a little help right now.* Barely lifting his head above the tall wet grass, he thought he could discern the faint silhouette of the mystery shooter in the rocks. Bran took aim and applied steady pressure to the trigger, and his own piece of lead screamed through the air. The odds of scoring a hit were astronomical, but it was the diversion that mattered. Bran was instantly on his feet sprinting to the nearest man-sized boulder between himself and the shooter. Three seconds later he half dove, half slid behind the rocky outcropping. Small bits of stone bit into his knees, but he was oblivious to the pain. Confident that he now had full concealment from the sniper, he reached for the small box of extra ammunition hanging from his shoulder. Finding nothing, he frantically searched his person. The futile effort yielded the same result. Then he saw it, the small red cartridge box lay clearly visible on the green grass where he had lain twenty seconds prior. He berated himself as he stared down at the spent pistol.

Bran's thoughts suddenly returned to Lord Gyr. He turned his crouched frame to get eyes on the marquess. The imbecile had not moved. He just stood there, pistol in hand, with a slightly bemused look on his face, as if he were observing a mildly interesting cricket match. Bran considered making a rush at the man in order to commandeer his pistol, but he quickly dismissed the suicidal act. Instead Bran crouched and waited. *Your move gentlemen.* His only hope now was that a long enough delay might give Stanton time to get himself into the fight; that is, unless the shooter had already dealt with the giant groom.

Cristyn held her breath as a musket ball roared towards Bran. An instant later his body fell to the ground.

Rage supplanted fear. She was about to empty her pistol into the shooter when Bran's dead body disgorged a yellow flame. The musket ball impacted the rocks eight feet short of Stanton. Gravel and rock fragments hammered the man's exposed face like a hail storm.

Cristyn found herself unable to process what was happening as Stanton yelled an oath and jumped to his feet to escape further harm. Like the would-be assassin, Cristyn was momentarily caught off guard, but she quickly reclaimed her wits. "Leave the gun where it is!" she screamed. "Otherwise I will shoot you where you stand!"

The man hesitated, then slowly turned. His calculating eyes took in his unlikely captor. His face was bleeding from the stone shrapnel. She knew Stanton was assessing his chances if he rushed her. But seeing the resolute determination in her eyes and the steady aim of the pistol in her hands, he raised his hands in a gesture of mocking surrender.

"You have bested me, your ladyship. The next move is yours." Disdainful sarcasm fell from every word.

Cristyn's brain rapidly ran through various scenarios, none

more attractive than the last. She finally settled on a course that would allow her to check on Bran's condition, but as her eyes swept back to Bran's fallen body, she was stunned to see that it was gone.

She fought to maintain control. "D-down the hill, now!"

The pair ponderously navigated their way down the embankment. Bran's army musket remained nestled against the rock where Stanton had dropped it.

They were halfway down the hill when Lord Gyr first caught sight of Stanton. The initial angle of the descent prohibited him from observing Cristyn.

The marquess bellowed in rage, "Stanton, what the hell do you think you are doing? And where is your weapon? He is right behind the rock to your left you bloody fool!"

It was then Lord Gyr caught sight of Cristyn. She was barefoot, her filthy dress was torn, and matted clumps of blonde hair stuck to her mud-streaked face. Realization slowly set in. "Cousin, is that you? What in the world is going on?"

The pistol trembled in her hand and her voice cracked. "Caradoc, shut up!"

As her voice echoed across the dell, Bran emerged from behind the rock.

Catching sight of the young American both alive and well, all self-control disintegrated for Cristyn. Forgetting about Stanton and her cousin, she ran to Bran. Throwing her arms around his neck, she began to emit great sobs. Her pistol lay forgotten in the wet grass. It was as if all the emotions of the past hour had been dammed up and then allowed to break free in an instant. Bran held her tight, all the while keeping both men under his steady gaze.

Lord Gyr stood immobile. His eyes fitfully darted from

Bran to the pistol in the grass and back again as if to say, *what to do now?* The marquess nervously wiped the rain from his face over and over again. He was a trapped animal, and desperation gnawed away at reason. Rage gave birth to hate. He knew in his heart there was only one way out.

Bran clutched Cristyn, but his attention remained fixed on Lord Gyr. Not only was the marquess the only person holding a weapon, but there was something in the man's eyes Bran did not like. For the first time in ages, Bran became aware of his tomahawk. Still holding Cristyn tightly in his left arm, he slowly eased the weapon from his belt using his right hand. When Lord Gyr raised his pistol to fire, Bran was ready. With a single motion he shoved a surprised Cristyn into the grass and sent the small bladed weapon flying.

Six rotations later the weapon buried itself in the base of the marquess's throat. The instantaneous severance of the man's spine caused his dueling pistol to tremble. A split second later it discharged.

Bran's grisly satisfaction gave way to horror as the errant musket shot caused Cristyn's body to jerk backwards into the grass. He tried to call her name, but all he could muster was a garbled choke. He fell to his knees beside his ward. The entire left side of her face was soaked in blood.

"God, please no!" Bran frantically ran his hand through the sticky substance, searching to find the source of the blood. More and more of the life giving fluid seemed to fill the side of her face. In desperation, he tore his jacket off, using the clean lining to wipe the blood clear. Then he saw it—a deep grazing wound on the left side of her head just above the hair line. He was almost sure the musket ball had only skimmed the outer edge of her skull, but he knew head wounds bled copiously.

Blood loss was Cristyn's biggest danger at the moment. The sickly-sweet smell was already filling his nostrils. He quickly tore off the left sleeve of his linen shirt. Ripping the sleeve into two strips, he took the cleaner strip and folded it into wadding. This he placed over the injury while using the other strip to tie it tightly in place.

"Stay with me girl," he muttered to himself. The final tying of the knot proved to be difficult because her whole body was beginning to shake from shock. After he was sure the bandage was affixed securely, he recovered his coat and covered her torso. The added warmth of the thick garment slowed her body's convulsions.

Bran leaned back to examine his handiwork. The bandage darkened from cream to crimson as the blood worked its way through the loose weave of the fabric. He was on the verge of thinking he would have to attempt something more when slowly the blood halted its relentless advance. He waited a few more moments and then heaved a great sigh of relief. Setting her head softly on a flat smooth rock, he fell backwards onto his elbows. He could feel his strength leaving him as the fear of the moment slowly gave way to an adrenaline hangover.

He looked up and gazed upon the lifeless frame of Lord Gyr now lying crumpled where he had formerly stood. It was only then that his thoughts returned to Roger Stanton, but when Bran looked around to locate the hulking Yorkshireman, he was gone.

26

Watching from Afar

Two men stood near the top of the hill. Wearing identical gray overcoats and matching beaver hats they were nearly indiscernible from the surrounding rocky landscape. Aside from a gap of twenty-five years, the two men were virtually identical. The older of the two held a small, collapsible telescope up to his right eye. Without removing the spyglass, he spoke to the younger man in the crisp, clear diction indicative of the upper classes.

"Well, Tony, an interesting series of events; but the final outcome is not particularly surprising. Any thoughts?" When the younger man did not answer he turned to look at him. The younger man's face was decidedly wan. "What the devil is your problem?"

"My lord, do you think we—I—should go down there and assist? Cristyn seems to be in a bad way."

The older man let out a soft snort. "Do not be daft—and let Lord Gruffudd know we have been spying on him the whole time—I am sorry, but they are on their own."

"But, my lord—"

"I know you still love her, but do you not think it is time to move on? Do not forget that she rejected you. From what we have seen, I think Lord Gruffudd can more than take care of matters." He said the last comment with such finality that the younger man held his tongue.

Indifferent to his son's pain, the older man continued his line of questioning. "Tell me, what did you think of the fight, aside from her ladyship getting hurt, that is?"

The younger man refrained from answering as long as he could, but in the end he knew it was useless to resist his father.

"My lord, I cannot say I am sorry to have the pig gone. You know I would be the last to wish ill on a fellow aristocrat, but the man was refuse. I will never forget what he did to poor Perkins in school, not that I even liked Perkins, but no chap deserved that. No, Lord Gruffudd has just done the British peerage a service."

The older man fished inside his coat and extracted an ornate, embroidered handkerchief. He used the delicate cloth to wipe beads of rain water off both lenses of the telescope. "I do agree Gyr was a pig, but what a way to go. That bloody hatchet hit him so hard it took him off his feet."

"I believe the term is tomahawk, my lord, and I agree it was a hell of a throw. He hit the man at a good thirty yards, and dead center at that."

"The marquess's uncle was a fine man. I always hoped, perhaps unjustifiably, that the current Lord Gyr's shortcomings would fix themselves over time. I honestly believed the responsibilities of his marquisate would have eventually made him more like the old man, but I guess we will never know."

Tony chose to keep his silence.

"What do you know about young Lord Gruffudd other than the fact he is a bloody Yankee, not to mention he stole my valet?"

The younger man bought himself a moment by removing his hat. He then gently beat it against the side of his leg to remove the excess build-up of water. "I only had the chance to spend a little time with him the other night. He is not the overly loquacious type, but has a fiery temper. He is also reputed to possess certain talents, but that information now seems a bit superfluous in light of what we just witnessed."

The older man grunted before responding. "We already know he did away with that disagreeable chap on the streets of Cardiff shortly following his arrival. He has only been here a few months and his body count is already two. Not hard to tell the man is a beast in a fight, not to mention resourceful, but it does make you wonder what kind of a man he is."

"I am not sure, my lord. Based on the brief time I spent with him he seems like a decent enough chap. He definitely did not stand down when Lord Gyr said some pretty abominable things about Cristyn. He also comes from an extremely ancient Welsh family, and we know the kind of man his uncle was. I would be willing to guess the apple does not fall far from the tree."

"And what about he and the lady?—and please do not give me that sick puppy look—what I want to know is . . . well, you know . . . is there anything between them?"

The young earl stiffened. He knew his father was trying to irritate him. "I was not able to perceive anything of the sort, but I also have never seen them together. Regardless, I suppose the match would make sense from a certain point of view." His gut twisted in his stomach as he made the statement.

"I dare say he has grit," observed his father, "but the real question that must be asked is, can we trust him, and more importantly, would he be willing to help us? He may come from a prominent Welsh family, but he is also an American. That place does strange things to people, not to mention the colonies' historical relationship with the frogs has been friendly."

"I know they both espouse their own versions of Jacobinism," said the younger man, "but what is the American attitude towards Bonaparte?"

"I have no idea. I am having my agents in the colonies try to ascertain Washington's stance. Not much luck so far."

"I suppose it would never hurt to ask, my lord. To your point, the man would be a powerful ally. We do not have to tell him too much up front. We can always feel him out a little and see where things go from there."

The older man gave the slightest nod, which the younger man could only take as agreement. He then added, "Perhaps, though I might give him a little time to see how he shakes out. You cannot rush these things. In the meantime, make sure Lord Gruffudd does not run into any unpleasantries with the authorities, but also make sure he does not get wind of our involvement; it should be similar to what you did following the Cardiff incident. We were both witnesses to what occurred, but of course we cannot exactly testify in court, can we?"

"My lord, it will be taken care of discreetly."

Shoving the now collapsed telescope back inside his overcoat pocket, the duke turned around to limp back over the next rise to his waiting carriage.

27

The Long Journey Home

Steady rain mixed with Cristyn's blood to create rose colored puddles under her body. The mud coating her face slowly gave way under the downpour, revealing an increasingly pale complexion. Bran sat on his haunches, resting his head in his blood-coated hands. He had managed to stem the bleeding for now, but there was a much bigger problem in front of him. How was he going to get Cristyn back to the estate? Despite his field expedient first aid efforts, time was of the essence. The decision to leave Jackie behind moved from a matter of inconvenience to possible calamity. What should have been a relatively easy journey home was now going to be a slow, perilous journey for Cristyn.

Fortunately, Bran's self-reproach was just what he needed to rescue him from his lethargy. With a vigorous push from both knees he propelled himself to his feet.

He gazed at Cristyn's limp, dirty, blood-soaked body, and then he glanced over at his tomahawk. It was fifty feet away and stuck in Lord Gyr, so he would have to leave it, but that was not important right now. Every second was precious.

Bran knew traveling back the way he had come was no

longer an option. The sustained rain and uneven terrain made the route increasingly treacherous in light of his fragile burden. Fortunately, he had a second option. They were about five hundred yards from the road, and although probably covered in puddles, the road would allow him to travel much faster. It also raised the possibility of running into a farmer with his cart.

In a single fluid motion he squatted, extended his arms, and scooped Cristyn up in front of him, not much different than a mother might carry a hurt child.

Bran turned his full attention to the task in front of him. As he walked he craned his neck to wipe his eyes on his shoulder, and little by little they made their way to the road. He soon discovered that what should have been a relatively short walk was mind numbingly slow. On several occasions he almost lost his footing in the undulating terrain, and in each instance a few fearful lurching steps were just enough to salvage his balance. To compound matters, rain, mud, and blood all worked together to make his grip on Cristyn tenuous at best. He could not keep his mind from racing back to the night when he had been bound and shoved down a dark forest path by Maneto's braves.

Finally, their faltering trek came to an end, and Bran's feet found the security of the compressed dirt and rock of the road. He was almost ecstatic. Bran paused for a moment, to lean against a tree so the burning sensation in his back could abate. He considered setting his fragile cargo down so he could truly rest, but there was not time. As soon as he regained his wind, he pushed off from the tree and began the next leg of the journey. Once he had eaten up about a hundred feet of road he started to find his stride. He softly spoke words of encouragement to Cristyn, but they were more to motivate himself than to encourage his unconscious cargo.

He had been on this road two different times, both on horseback, and he had a pretty good sense of the circuitous course it took back to the estate. Bran knew the first third of the journey would find them slowly winding their way up a gradual hill. Once it reached the top, it would begin a rapid decline that would ride the edge of a small cliff for two hundred yards. While not the White Cliffs of Dover, the hundred foot drop-off was enough to bring about a similar outcome to any person unfortunate enough to plummet over the edge.

Bran felt the burn in his back and shoulders as his legs ground away at the hill. His breathing was labored but rhythmical. His confidence began to grow as he inched his way closer to the top.

A few minutes later they reached the summit. Despite the overcast skies and lingering rain, Bran could see Caer Cigfran in the distance. The dirt road snaked up to it like a brown thread. It was the most beautiful thing he had seen all day.

Bran's mind was busy charting the last leg of their journey when a splash in a nearby puddle caught his attention. Snapping his head to the left, he was just in time to see the massive form of Roger Stanton barreling down on him. Despite his awkward position, Bran managed to shift his body enough to only receive a glancing blow. The gorilla of a man bounced off his left side, and a Cristyn-laden Bran staggered sideways. Off balance and desperate, he dropped Cristyn in a small patch of tall grass. He cringed as her jostling head slowly came to a rest.

As he deposited Cristyn in the grass, the crunch of gravel signaled that the Yorkshireman was coming around for a second pass. Before he turned his body, Bran bent his knees low. When he sensed his enemy was close, he pivoted his hips. Like a coiled spring, he channeled the full force of the rotation into a single uppercut. His right fist tightened on impact, delivering a blistering blow to Stanton's jaw. It felt as if his fist had splintered on the man's iron facade. "Bloody hell!" Bran exclaimed under his breath.

Despite the pain, his well-orchestrated maneuver accomplished part of its intended effect. Stanton staggered back a few steps, surprised by the fury of the strike. His hand reflexively reached up to massage his jaw, and he spit a gob of blood into a nearby puddle. His face stretched into a malicious grin. "I always took you for a fighter, Yank, but that is quite a punch you pack. If you were at the fair fightin' someone else, I might even put money on you. Guessin' this will be more fun than I anticipated."

Bran's right fist tingled. He massaged his hands together in an attempt to regain feeling. "Stanton, why in the world did you come back? Lord Gyr is dead. You could just leave the district and no one would ever care."

The sneer had not left the big man's face. "Oh, I will. But I have some unfinished business. Cannot leave no witnesses, see. Otherwise you and the lady will send the authorities after me, and they will hunt me like some filthy fox. I cannot have that. I deserve better. No loose ends this way."

Bran turned his eyes to Cristyn. The bandage on her head looked like a splattered tomato and it was growing in size by the second. Fresh rivulets of blood were already working their way down her cheek. As much as he did not relish a fight with this hulking opponent, he knew he needed to speed things up. Otherwise she was going to die while he brawled in the mud.

"Okay, Stanton, have it your way. But let us move this thing along. I am tired of standing in the rain." Bran knew his voice was full of false bravado.

The two mud-spattered, water-logged combatants slowly

began to circle each other like hippos engaging in a strange ritualistic dance. In truth, each man was trying to decide if he should take the offensive or simply wait for the other to make a move. Bran periodically wiped the rain and mud from his eyes.

Time was not Bran's ally, and with every rotation of the circle Bran became more and more restless. He slowly began to move closer, hoping the collapsing distance would provoke the bigger man to rash action, but it became apparent that the giant Yorkshireman was content to let Bran make the first move.

Bran continued to circle while keeping his hands in a tight, defensive posture. Stanton mimicked his every move. *The oaf is enjoying this*, thought Bran.

When Bran was about five feet from his opponent, he casually brought his left leg slightly forward. Then with lightning speed, he rotated his front plant leg. Bringing his rear leg up, knee bent and parallel to the ground, Bran snapped his leg straight as he drove his heel at his opponent. Unfortunately for Bran, his front leg lost its footing in the mud. The power behind this otherwise devastating side kick evaporated long before it reached Stanton. With frightening speed Stanton violently slammed his forearm into Bran's knee at the same moment that Bran's leg feebly made contact with Stanton's mid-section. The Yorkshireman let out a mild grunt, but it was Bran who suffered. He gave a painful cry as his back slammed into the mud and rocks.

Attempting to seize the advantage, Stanton took two hard steps forward. He lifted his right leg to deliver a bone shattering heel strike against an exposed, decumbent Bran. This time Bran used the slick mud to his advantage. By the time the giant's heel began its descent, the smaller man had spun himself like a top ninety degrees. Now it was Stanton who was exposed. Bran used the momentum of the spin to bring a powerful leg sweep against the larger man's plant leg. With a groan and a crash the giant Yorkshireman slammed into the mud next to Bran. It was as if a great oak had been felled in the forest; mud sailed in all directions. As his opponent completed his fall, Bran leapt to his feet. Foregoing all sense of fair play, Bran drove his right boot into the big man's head. The hard leather caught enough flesh to elicit an angry scream of pain from Stanton.

Stanton staggered to his feet and both men faced off for a second time, each dripping with mud. Their clothing was indistinguishable from flesh, and each looked like a creature of the pit. The young baron was contemplating his next offensive when he suddenly realized how close their last encounter had taken them to the cliff's edge. In fact, Stanton even now stood only eight feet from the ledge.

Bran instinctively glanced over at Cristyn, as he did so he also glimpsed a solitary rider down in the valley, headed in their direction. Bran could not identify the individual, but relief washed over him nonetheless. Help was on the way.

Stanton was eyeing Bran, and the malevolent smirk remained solidly plastered across his face. Stanton lifted one of his large, muddy hands to wipe blood away from the side of his mouth. "Had enough, your lordship, or is there still a little more fight in you?"

Bran wanted to say he thought he was doing quite well, all things considered, but he held his tongue. He paused for a moment as if to indicate he was considering his response to the question. In reality, he knew there was only one way to bring the fight to a quick and decisive end. In that snapshot of time Bran was struck with the thought that sometimes life's biggest decisions are made in the briefest moments.

Without a second thought, he charged. With both arms outstretched, his goal was to wrap Stanton up and send them both careening over the cliff to whatever fate God chose to bestow upon them.

As a lifelong brawler, Stanton was sure he knew what might be coming next. However, when Bran sallied, ready to deliver a tackle that would make a member of the Eton rugby team proud fifty years hence, the big Yorkshireman was not prepared. Bran's chest slammed into his opponent, and the two conjoined combatants staggered backward towards the edge of the cliff. Bran used his own body as a fulcrum to send them both teetering on the brink of catastrophe. In that instant, Stanton panicked and slammed his fist against the side of Bran's face. Why the big man did it, Bran would never be sure. Perhaps he thought that in breaking Bran's grip he might have been able to arrest his own momentum, yet as the massive sledgehammer of a fist met the smaller man's left eye socket, Bran could do nothing but let go. This last-ditch assault on Bran's face may have succeeded in breaking the American's grip, but the blow drove Stanton further backwards and became his undoing. As he disappeared over the edge, he let loose a final rebellious roar and fell to meet his fate.

Bran sank to his knees with dizziness. His brain could not comprehend what had just happened. Nausea overtook him, and he retched. Now covered in blood, mud, and bile he crawled on all fours to the still-unconscious Cristyn. Her body was again trembling from a combination of wet, cold, and residual shock. Lying down next to her, he placed his arm around her in an attempt to warm her. Then he closed his only eye that would still open. It was like this that Bull found them.

28

Looking Down the Barrel

Bran stood over Cristyn. She was alive, barely, but alive. What had been a dirty, bloody gash a few hours earlier was now carefully wrapped in clean linen. Her face was still as white as a sheet, but Bran assumed this would improve over time. He was amazed that her small frame had been able to sustain the loss of so much blood. Bran also knew that Reverend Hughes had gone to extraordinary efforts to debride the wound. The priest commented that, aside from it being a head wound, Cristyn was fortunate because the injury remained free of the dirty clothing fragments that normally accompanied gunshot wounds to the torso. As a result, she had a much better chance of avoiding severe infection in the hours and days to come.

Squeamish over the treatment process, Bran had stayed outside the room as Reverend Hughes and Mrs. Clarke had attended to the then conscious Cristyn. By the time the wound was cleaned and wrapped, she had returned to the realm of unconsciousness, but her breathing was returning to a normal, steady rhythm.

Bran delivered a gentle kiss to her hand. She continued her slumbers, completely oblivious to his presence.

Bran turned towards the door and saw Reverend Hughes leaning against the doorframe. The priest had just returned from washing his hands, and he had a contemplative look on his face.

"She will be fine, my lord, do not worry. She is young and strong, a true fighter; and although deeper than I would have liked, the wound is now clean. By the way, you did an excellent job applying that pressure bandage. Where did you get the clean linen?"

"I tore off the sleeves of my undershirt," said Bran somewhat absentmindedly.

"Well, that saved her. She owes you her life. The greatest risk of this type of injury is bleeding out. Why in the world many of my peers engage in the practice of bloodletting beats me."

"I am the reason she was put at risk in the first place. If anyone owes anyone anything, I owe her."

Bran glanced around the room. "What happened to Mrs. Clarke? She was here a minute ago."

"My apologies," said the doctor, "while you were preoccupied with her ladyship, I took the liberty of sending her downstairs to collect some fresh bandages for later. I hope that was all right?"

"Of course, of course," said Bran. He drew near to Reverend Hughes and leaned his sore back and still-aching head against the opposite side of the doorframe. Both men gazed across the room at the convalescing young lady for some time.

Reverend Hughes finally spoke. "You know, she loves you deeply." His voice was matter of fact, stating the objective observations of both physician and priest.

Bran did not answer. He had the look of a man deep in thought, and his face took on a melancholy countenance.

Reverend Hughes continued, "I would expect today's events to further solidify those feelings. Shared traumatic experiences tend to have that effect."

The corner of Bran's mouth curled downward into the slightest of frowns. "And why would you say that? She has never given me any indication of a particular attachment."

"Yes, the recipients of such affections are typically the last to notice," said the priest with a gentle smile, "I have no doubt. In fact, I have had my suspicions for quite a while. But when I was with her this morning, the moment she realized you were in peril, both fear and love filled her eyes. There was no possibility of misinterpreting her feelings in that moment."

To his surprise, Reverend Hughes observed that his statements regarding the lady's affections only served to agitate the young lord.

Bran responded in a hollow voice. "It grieves me to hear you say that."

"Why, my lord? Surely you do not think you could do better? She is strong, kind, beautiful, and devoted to you. Not to mention she is now rich beyond measure."

For a brief second Bran's thoughts shifted. It had not occurred to him that upon Lord Gyr's death—in the absence of any other male heir—the Gyr family estate reverted back to Cristyn. But that thought only lasted for an instant. His attention went back to the priest, and he looked into the old man's face with eyes overflowing with sorrow.

"Please forgive me, my dear reverend. I think you misunderstand my meaning. It is not that I do not value this young lady's admiration of me. No, in fact it is the opposite. Having been the recipient of such love one other time in my life, I treat it with the greatest reverence. My concern is that I would not be able to return to her a love that matches the deep affections of which I know she is capable."

Like a beam of sunlight piercing a bank of thunderclouds, the priest felt he could now discern the heart of the matter. "You loved your first wife and daughter deeply, but when they died you felt that a part of you died as well; and to offer your love to anyone else would be to offer only remnants, am I correct?"

Bran nodded. He began to speak again, and his voice cracked at the edges, "It is not that I feel incapable of loving again, but rather that my soul contains an open gash which has not been able to heal. Therefore, any future love will be tarnished by that wound."

Reverend Hughes solemnly nodded in understanding. Bran's pain was almost palpable. The clergyman weighed his next words carefully. "My lord, I am not sure if it will help, but know that what you are feeling is common unto man. Your life for the past two years has been beset with trauma and grief, and the pain is still raw and untended. Hearts require careful treatment and time to heal, no different than flesh. If we do not treat a wounded heart, if we do not remove the splinters, it will never fully mend. Any healing that does occur will be in the form of a hard scab or callus, no better than stone. The great paradox of the human heart is that God designed it to work best when soft and supple, and because of that, full of life. This is in sharp contrast with a world that tells us strength must be imbued by that which is hard and unbending. Please do not think me out of place when I say that you have not allowed . . . no, let me correct that . . . your heart has not been able to heal just yet. It will happen if you allow it, but it will take time. Whatever you do, though, please do not exchange a heart of soft, supple flesh for a heart of stone."

Bran took in the words. His inner eye seemed to be flashing back and forth between his wife's empty bed in Philadelphia and Cristyn's bleeding body in the here and now. He felt bombarded by a sense of sorrow and guilt.

Fortunately, he was rescued by the return of Mrs. Clarke and Cristyn's maid. After some detailed instructions from Reverend Hughes to the ladies, the two men made their way down to Bran's library. On the way, they ran into a twitchy Rogers. After allaying the butler's fears regarding the young lady's recovery, Bran requested some sandwiches be brought to them in the study. Rogers hurried off to fulfill the request. A few minutes later the two men situated themselves in opposing leather arm chairs, each with a drink in his hand.

As they settled in, Reverend Hughes let out an exclamation. "My lord, forgive me. In all the chaos of attending to the needs of her ladyship, I have forgotten to attend to your injuries."

"It is nothing," said Bran crossly. "I am perfectly fine." Even while saying the words his fingers gingerly began to probe his left eye socket. While doing so, he noticed for the first time that his knuckles were swollen beyond recognition.

The priest gave him a disbelieving smirk, "Come now, my lord, you look like you are wearing some sort of grisly eye patch." Bran acquiesced and the old man made his way over to the patient. His practiced fingers began to tenderly probe the area around Bran's eye. Bran tried to hide a wince but was unable.

"Tender, is it?" observed the priest. "Hmm, it is my fault. I should have had you put something cold on it when you first returned to the house." He applied slight pressure to a particularly inflamed area. Bran all but let out a yowl. Reverend

Hughes chided the younger man, "Come now, my lord, her ladyship showed more pluck than this."

Bran frowned, "You get hit in the face by a gorilla and let us see how you feel."

Reverend Hughes was now chuckling, "Well, my lord, it appears that you fought the man with just your face. Probably the result of American bravado."

Bran let out a sarcastic, "Ha, ha."

But the priest was not about to let him off the hook so easily. "Your lordship has only himself to blame. After all, you did agree to hire the man."

"Yes, to be one of my grooms, not to try and shoot me and then pummel me with his fists." He knew the old man was just teasing him, but he was not feeling particularly playful.

The priest concluded his examination. "Your face will be fine, you just will not be quite so pretty from now on. Now is there anything else? Any cuts under your clothes, numbness anywhere?"

Bran ran his hands over his arms, legs, and chest. In reality, everything hurt to some extent, but in light of Cristyn's fragile state upstairs, he did not think it was the time to start complaining about small aches and pains. "No, I think I am fine. A few small abrasions, but they are of the sort that should heal quickly. I am actually shocked I made it out in as good a shape as I did."

Reverend Hughes was settling back into his chair. "You Gruffudds have always had a certain resilience to you. It is another way you are similar to your uncle. I can only guess your father was the same. Even Lady Cristyn, though not a Gruffudd, shares many of those same qualities. I guess it goes back to the days when your ancestors spent their time repelling marauding invaders and killing Englishmen."

Bran laughed for the first time, "See, my discolored eye is just an attempt to color my face blue like some ancient Cymri war chieftain."

"Yes, except you are confusing the Cymri with the Scottish Picts" said Reverend Hughes with a chuckle. "I think Bull would be happy to have you claim his ancestors, but I am simply glad you had a fine shield maiden to watch your back."

"Agreed."

"So, any more thoughts surrounding what may have precipitated this peculiar confluence of events?"

"It is funny you should ask me that. The other day in the garden it seemed like the events of the strange affair were starting to unwind, but I still had not been able to pry loose the underlying motivations propelling things forward. However, as I was getting ready to literally tumble over that cliff I had a strange thought. Why my brain chose that particular moment, I have no idea."

"Not that it is relevant," reflected the priest, "but I sometimes think it is in moments of great stress or turmoil that our brain is able to cast off some of the inhibitions that keep it from operating at its fullest capacity. But I digress, what was your thought?"

Instead of responding, Bran gingerly rose to his feet with a barely audible groan. He wound around the great oak desk until he stood in front of the stone wall full of weapons. There was an ancient broad sword with a leather wrapped hilt. Next to it was a massive two-sided battle axe that looked as if it had been plucked straight off the body of some barbarian invader. There were a few newer muskets that Bran guessed were for hunting game. But in the center, slightly out of reach, hung an old blunderbuss. Bran pointed to the stubby firearm. "Do you know anything about that weapon or where it came from?"

"It is funny you should ask. That is an old French blunderbuss called an Espingole."

"Do you know where it came from?"

"I do as a matter of fact. It was a gift from your father to your uncle."

"From my father?" asked Bran. His face conveyed a sudden look of surprise.

"Yes, he sent it to your uncle as a gift following the conclusion of the Seven Years War. He knew your uncle liked firearms and figured he would be amused by it. If I remember the story correctly, your father plucked it off of a French captain shortly after he ran his sword through him. Your uncle was always proud of the story. He liked to use it as an example of Alun's grit. It has hung there in a place of honor ever since. But why do you ask?"

"Oh, it is just a guess, but if I am right it might help answer a lot of our lingering questions." He then took hold of the stout wooden chair behind the desk and wrestled it over to the wall. The scraping of the wood across the floor let loose a woeful whine. Reverend Hughes winced, but Bran was unperturbed, and a second later he was on top of the chair, lifting the old firearm off of its mounting bracket.

The old priest had a bemused look on his face, "It is a good thing you Gruffudds are all tall, but I still do not understand what you are getting at. What does all this have to do with recent events, my lord?"

Bran now had his hand firmly around the stock of the old weapon. It was shorter than a rifle. The receiver, if you would call it that, was stained a light brown. For whatever reason, it made Bran think of a beaver's coat. The barrel started out silver but then slowly transitioned to brass by the time it reached the muzzle. Ornate engravings covered almost every metal surface. The end of the barrel flared out in the defining characteristic of the blunderbuss family of weapons.

Bran slowly walked back around the desk. He was doing his best to orient the barrel in the direction of the window. To Bran's chagrin, the bright rays of morning had long since passed.

"What are you doing?" asked a mystified Reverend Hughes.

"I am trying to get a look inside the barrel. I was pretty sure of my theory before you told me about the weapon, but now that I know it was from my father, I am absolutely certain."

Thinking he could just make out something in the barrel, Bran swept his index finger across the interior. For the briefest moment, the priest saw disappointment in the young man's eyes, but in the next instant it transformed into triumph. After a short struggle, Bran extracted what appeared to be a narrow tube. As he flopped back down in his seat he leaned the blunderbuss up against the side of the chair. Reverend Hughes could now see that it was not a tube, but a handful of tightly rolled papers secured by a small piece of twine. Bran struggled with the twine for a moment until the priest tossed him a small knife, and then he made short work of the restraint. Free of their bonds, four pieces of paper uncoiled in Bran's lap. At a cursory glance, three of them appeared to be a lengthy handwritten letter. The last had the look of a legal document, complete with a series of signatures and a seal at the bottom.

Reverend Hughes's jaw hung slack in disbelief. "My lord, how in the world did you ever think to look there? I do not think in a hundred years the thought would have ever occurred to me."

Bran's face colored slightly. "Honestly, I was daft not to think of it sooner. In fact, I do not know why I did not, other than the fact that my mind has been occupied by so many other things since I arrived. Before my arrival someone sought to acquire something my uncle possessed, but it was during the fight that I finally remembered."

"Remembered what?"

"That my father's favorite place to hide important documents was in the barrels of old firearms. My grandfather used to do the same thing. I figured it was more than likely that my uncle adhered to this family tradition, especially if it was something he wanted to keep hidden but wanted my father to be able to find should it prove necessary. But enough of that, let us see what the man had to say."

Choosing the letter first, Bran prepared to read aloud.

29

Uncle Llew's Secret

It took Bran a moment to get the paper to lie flat enough to read. He also had to adjust his eyes to his uncle's tight, but fairly tidy, script.

Dear Brother,

Much like a will, this is one of those strange letters some are forced to write in their lives, but at the same time, hope are never read. If you are reading this, I can only assume I have passed on and you have inherited our family's title. First, let me say there is no one who I would rather take over our ancient family responsibilities, and between you and me, you may have been worthier from the beginning, as will become evident from the information outlined below; and while I have my share of regrets, perhaps one of the greatest is the past thirty years which I have not been able to spend with you. You were always a man of great honor and strength, and even as a child I learned much from you, despite you being the younger brother.

But alas, time is short, and I dare not fall prey to an old man's proclivity to ramble. If you have arrived here at Caer Cigfran, it is because I have passed away in a duel against a truly despicable man; that is, Caradoc, who recently became Lord Gyr. In some way, it only makes sense that my life should end with a failing . . . that is, failing to rid the world of a human parasite. But for this to make sense, I must go back a number of years.

Shortly after you left for America I spent considerable time in London. I think with you gone, I feared that spending too much time at the estate would make me all too aware of the companionship of which I was now deprived. So instead, I flitted from social function to social function. Amongst my companions was the former Lord Gyr, Caradoc's uncle. There were also a few other old school mates. It was during that time I met a young lady. She was the third daughter of an Irish Earl, and her name was Maoliosa. She was enchanting, and for the first time in my life I was truly in love. However, I was not the only person taken with the young lady. My friend—Lord Gyr—had also fallen under her spell. We both competed for her attentions for some time, and while I think I may have had the advantage all things being equal, it was my friend's title and holdings that won out. I know this, because the young lady later told me so. The pressure put upon her by her family had been great. Having loved, but then lost, I was never the same again, and over time I found myself slipping into a deeper and deeper melancholy.

Now we must transition to the very recent past. It was just a few years ago that Lord Gyr came to me with two somewhat strange requests. Before I go any further it is probably important to clarify that I never held any animosity towards my friend. He was a wonderful husband to Maoliosa up until the day she died, and for that I was grateful. That aside, his two requests were as follows:

The first was a matter of finances. Despite his wealth, my friend had made a series of poor investment decisions. These decisions brought him precipitously close to ruin. However, he did have a means of recovering his position at very low risk, but it required a temporary infusion of a large amount of capital. It was from me that he requested the loan.

The second matter was of a much more intimate nature. Lord Gyr's heir was a young man named Caradoc; yes, the same man I fought against. He was my friend's nephew and only remaining male heir. Of course, this meant my friend's title and estate would go to the young man in the event of his death. According to Lord Gyr at the time, and despite his best ministrations, the young man had grown up to become one of the basest of human beings, so much so that my friend feared for both his welfare and the welfare of his only daughter, Cristyn. He requested permission to put a provision in his will that would allow Lady Cristyn's guardianship to pass to me in the event of my friend's untimely demise. He said he could not allow his sweet flower to pass into the control of such a vile human being.

It may or may not surprise you that I immediately agreed to both requests. In fact, I responded in the affirmative so quickly that it took my friend somewhat aback. But this is where I must come clean and share the great stain that has blemished my soul for almost twenty years. And while I ask you not to judge me too harshly, there is a part of me that feels my soul deserves it.

What my friend did not realize is that when he won Maoliosa's hand so many years prior, he had not won her heart. Her affections had remained with me. But to make matters worse, I did nothing to discourage the young lady, and in that I forsook my honor and became yet one more miserable wretch that takes advantage of a devoted woman.

Yes brother, if you have not guessed by now, sweet Cristyn is my child, and not Lord Gyr's. Now you may ask, 'Did he know?" and the answer is not in the slightest. Shortly after their marriage, Maoliosa confided in me that she was pregnant, and that she knew it was my child. I then resolved never to speak to her again, not in a desire to punish her but to protect her from any further stain that might come from a liaison with one who had forfeited his honor. It also means that despite her true identity as my daughter, Cristyn is one hundred percent Lord Gyr's progeny as far as the law is concerned.

So now you see why I so quickly agreed to both of my friend's requests. In the matter of the money, I felt like it was the least I could do for the man I had wronged so greatly, even if he had been unaware. I will admit there was even a part of me that wished the investment would run aground. Not so that my friend would be ruined, but so as to perpetuate my own ruin, and in such, perhaps atone for my sins.

As for the second request, what man would not agree to take over the protection of his own daughter? I will even admit I was shamefully somewhat thrilled at the prospect of getting to know the daughter I had, up until then, only known at a distance.

Bran paused there and looked up; he had to take a moment to process what he had just read. His hand numbly reached for his drink. He looked across at Reverend Hughes who had been listening intently. However, the priest's face was completely non-communicative. "So, reverend, any thoughts, or should I continue the letter?" Subconsciously, Bran was hoping the priest would help him process the wide array of emotions that were flowing through him at this moment.

The priest slowly stroked his beard. Inside he was going through his own collection of intellectual and emotional gyrations. Finally, he spoke, "It is interesting, I will give you that.

I fancy myself at being a pretty perceptive individual, but I never guessed any of this. Though now in retrospect it does answer a great deal. It solves the riddle of why your uncle never married. It also shines a light on his deep fits of melancholy. It must have been a great burden for a man who held honor so dear. I am sure he felt he had not only failed himself and her, but hundreds of years of Gruffudds as well. I am even somewhat surprised he was able to communicate this to your father. Though the Gospel of John does say, 'Then you will know the truth, and the truth will set you free.' Confession is good for the soul after all. What about you? Any thoughts?"

Bran paused before answering. "I am just struck by the irony. All this time Cristyn thought she was Caradoc's cousin when in fact she is my cousin."

Reverend Hughes smiled for the first time, "It does explain a lot, especially the young lady's pluck and inner fire. The mixing of that ancient Cymri and Irish blood is quite the combination."

"Do you think we should tell her?" Bran asked hesitantly.

The priest answered, "That is easily answered. Were you in her place, would you want to know?"

"Absolutely," exclaimed Bran.

"Then there, you have your answer. Though you probably should wait until she is a little stronger. Besides, I suspect deep down inside, she probably already knows. Women have a way of discerning such things. They have the ability to pick up on nuances that most men would miss if it were staring them in the face. But please, finish reading the letter, my lord. I want to see if this whole thing ends as I now suspect."

Bran resumed where he had left off.

At an age younger than I would have ever expected, my friend became ill. It was a strange wasting disease, and I suspected from the beginning that young Caradoc had something to do with it . . . perhaps some slow acting poison the young deviant picked up on his foreign wanderings. However, I never spoke of this to my friend, nor did he ever feel it necessary to discuss the matter with me. A short while later, he died.

This in turn brings me to the last piece of my tale. My friend died before he was able to pay me back the loan, though I became aware that the investment had yielded its promised reward almost immediately following his death. After allowing the family the appropriate amount of time to grieve, I approached young Caradoc about the matter. The conversation did not go as planned, and he rapidly became belligerent, though I know he was fully aware of the loan. Many times in the following months I appealed to his honor to pay the debt, especially since my own holdings were starting to suffer considerably because of the loan. I even threatened to take legal action, but the young man was unmoved. We finally had a discussion that became so heated it resulted in me questioning his honor as a gentleman. And there we are left. In the end, it is probably just as well. The man is vile, and perhaps through this one action I can regain what is due to me, win Cristyn back her home and fortune, and allow the man she called father to fully rest in peace. Though if you are reading this it probably means I failed and that I am not leaving much of an inheritance for you. I can only hope we both died as a result. Thank you, brother, and God bless.

Your humble servant and affectionate brother,
Llew.

Bran sagged in his seat. He felt like he had just been beaten up again. Now that it was all laid out it made perfect sense. But he had also been so far from guessing the truth.

His hands deftly moved to the last document. As he expected, it was a promissory note guaranteeing the repayment of the loaned money. The bottom bore the signatures and seals of not only Llew, but also two other noblemen with whom Bran was unfamiliar. His eyes scanned the document for the amount of money owed. There it was, in the middle of the second paragraph. His eyes grew large as they took in the exceedingly large sum.

He turned to Reverend Hughes. "Here is the guarantee for the loan. It looks to be in order. I am assuming this must have been the object of those repeated break-ins. Take a look at the amount."

The priest received the piece of paper in his aged hands. Bran could tell he had found the amount when he let out a soft whistle. "Now that is a king's ransom if I have ever seen one. No wonder that conniving Caradoc was bent on ensuring the money was never repaid. I suppose if both you and your uncle died, there was a good chance the debt died too. You still have a problem though."

"What is that?" Sudden concern crept into Bran's face.

"Her ladyship," said the priest. Bran noticed a mischievous grin was beginning to make its way across the man's face. "She can be a pretty hard nut at times. Perhaps she will not pay you back either. I am pretty sure she could whip you in a duel if it came down to it."

"Well then," responded Bran dryly, "perhaps I will marry her, but I will do it before I tell her about the money. That way it will be all mine."

"True, and when she finds out maybe she will murder you in your bed and take all your money instead. You should know better than to try and cross even a half-Irish woman."

Bran went to open his mouth, but could not think of anything else to say.

Epilogue

The small group of four riders meandered their way down the road. The landau trailed them at an easy distance. The otherwise rocky terrain looked like it was draped in a large, green, bear rug. It was late spring and the meadow was in full bloom. Bran could see a mob of lambs trailing behind their mothers. Their legs were free of the tremors of lambing, and they leaped back and forth as if to publicly declare their independence from their elders. Thousands of snowdrops invaded a pasture to their left, and the view reminded Bran of a more delicate version of the cotton fields back in America. The breeze was mild but cool and carried a salty hint of the ocean. Bull's horse came up alongside Bran and Jackie.

"My lord, are you alright? You seem a bit pre-occupied," drawled the Scot.

Bran looked at Bull. "Yes, I am fine. I am just feeling a little melancholy. It is definitely not the weather, that is for sure. This is the prettiest day we have had since I arrived."

"That it is. I wish there were more like it, but I suppose we should be grateful for what we have."

"Amen to that," exclaimed Bran.

Both men turned their attention to the couple riding twenty yards ahead.

"It was nice of Lord Wendover to come pay you a visit, my lord; especially since her ladyship is returning to Foxglove this weekend."

"I suppose it was," said a pensive Bran, "though it is not my attentions he seems to care about at this moment." There was no resentment in Bran's voice, but simply resignation. Ever since he had read his uncle's letter, he had known it was only a matter of time until she returned to reclaim her family's estate. He felt a little like a schoolboy who had enjoyed a lovely summer holiday, but who was now returning to the world of lessons and chill weather.

Bull glanced concernedly at his master. "I know it is not my place, my lord, but have you considered asking her to stay?"

Bran leaned back in his saddle as he felt Jackie's strong muscles ease along in a rhythmical stroll. "Perhaps, but it would not be the best thing for either of us." He did not want to explain further.

They rode in silence for a while longer.

It was Bull who resumed the conversation. "The loss of a spouse is not something one easily gets past, my lord, no matter how far you travel."

Bran gave a self-deprecating chuckle. "Am I really that open of a book, or have you been talking to Reverend Hughes?"

The valet gave him an embarrassed grin. "No, my lord, but you forget I too recently lost a wife. Sometimes it takes living something to be able to see something."

"Hmm, well put. See, reading all that Milton is starting to turn you into a philosopher after all."

"Oh, I do not know about that, my lord," but Bran could tell Bull was pleased by the compliment nonetheless.

"So, what do you think, Bull? Is Lord Wendover Lady Cristyn's type? After all, he will be a duke someday. It is hard to pass on that."

"Well, she already passed once."

Bran's eyebrow went up slightly, "Did she really?"

"Yes, it was two years ago. I was still serving his father at the time. It was quite the to-do in the house. I remember thinking the duke would be angry with her ladyship."

"But he was not?"

"No."

"That seems a bit surprising," said Bran.

"No, the duke said something about 'The bigger the prize, the more difficult to get it on the line.'"

Bran chuckled, "We had better not tell her ladyship her potential father-in-law thinks she resembles a tuna."

Both men laughed.

"Besides, my lord, I suspect he might have a better chance this time around."

"Why do you say that?"

"He has changed a lot in the past couple of years. He was a lot more boy than man back then. I would say the man has now fully asserted himself."

Bran gazed at the broad-shouldered man on the horse in front of him. The man leaned sideways in the saddle, as if to share a private joke with Cristyn. Both young people let out a laugh.

"Yes, the man has definitely asserted himself," observed Bran. "If you are indeed right, I hope they will make one another happy."

"As do I, my lord," and then in a voice Bran could not hear he added, "I just hope you can find a way to be happy too."

Made in the USA
Columbia, SC
20 February 2018